SPELLCRAFTER — DELTA

BOOK ONE IN THE SPELLCRAFTER SAGA

CHRISTOPHER J. KIRKLAND

CONTENTS

This book is dedicated to my love, Madison, my very own lucky Penny. She pushed me to continue writing even when I wasn't sure if I would be successful. If it weren't for her, this book would not even be in your hands. Because of her, these characters have come alive, and the universe has been born.

TORI

There was nothing but a quiet forest. Pure white snowflakes fell all around, the wind blew, and animals scattered, desperately trying to find a spot to keep warm. The white sheets continued to pile up. The only human for miles trudged along the gentle slope of the snowbanks. They finally stopped and looked around wearily. There was nothing but snow and trees in every direction. Surely this was not the only thing here, there had to be a cabin or some sort of civilization that resided somewhere near. The stranger removed the scarf from their mouth, reaching down to take a sip from their water canister. They lifted it above their mouth and upturned it, lips parted. Nothing. Empty. They threw the container down in frustration. The hood drew back: it was a boy with emerald green hair, blue eyes, and a melancholy expression. Would he die out here?

He folded his arms, feeling colder than cold. A small chirping sound came from somewhere in front of the direction he was facing. He began to head in that direction, following the sound. A small fruit bat struggled before him, fighting against the wind and snow to stay airborne.

"Are you cold too? What are you doing out here?" he asked the creature.

It flew away from him toward the large snowy mounds. He followed, his feet dragging in the snow. Numb, aching, and exhausted tears were frozen to his face. The creature had disappeared. He began to search around the nearby trees, and what he believed to be bushes, behind one of the many trees to his right. He spotted the creature's remains.

"It died so quickly?" he wondered aloud to himself. The bat slowly vanished and became snow through his fingers, and as the wind blew, it took to the air. He was alone yet again.

Suddenly, he heard the calls of an owl and it scared him. He looked around to find the source. After a while, the owl's calls became a voice speaking clear English. *"Mr. Spellcrafter!"*

The cold world around him faded into darkness. He died, and that was the end.

Chris lifted his head to find all of his classmates were laughing and snickering. The teacher wore a grey sweater, dark grey pants, had a clean all-around fade haircut, green eyes, and a less than pleased look. The other students in class had turned to watch, only a few remained working.

"You fell asleep during your assignment yet again. I'll have to tell your parents--" he paused. Chris made a face. "...Just see me after class, alright?" the teacher asked politely.

"Yes, sir..." he replied quietly. A few kids began to laugh. Chris shook his head, irritated, and tried to ignore them. Who cared if they laughed? He had a good reason for staying up late. The students always laughed if you did something wrong. It was something he had grown used to. It died down after a while and his classmates returned to work. He lowered his head and took a deep breath before letting it out and relaxing himself. He looked up from his desk, nodded at the teacher, and faced the front.

As the teacher left, time seemed to slow down as Chris noticed the girl in the very front row, third seat to the window, watching him. Her brown eyes focused solely on him and *only* him. She slowly turned around and went back to her work. He found this behavior to be quite weird; why would Victoria, one of the prettiest, nicest, smartest, and most popular girls in school be looking at him? She was still fairly new to the school. She had only been at this particular school for a month, yet she took it by storm. She obviously knew he existed if she was staring at him, but it wasn't common for her to notice anyone. People thought she had ADHD because she barely paid much attention to *anyone*. She would always glance over them, including Chris.

He sat in the middle of the classroom, third row; the desks had a grey, shiny color with a red interior. The floor was a clean and shiny white color; the janitors did an amazing job on upkeep. The bell chimed; it was time to go to lunch. The class stood up to leave. Mr. McCormack waited patiently at his desk for Chris. Two others remained in the room, obviously having some significance to him.

"I'm sorry I called you out like that, Christopher. But you must try to stay up in my class and stop staying up so late. I know you can do the work, I've seen you do it. You're smart, and when you understand something, I see you leading other kids and teaching them what to do. You have to stop searching for your sister and rest. She wouldn't be too happy if she came back and found out you got no sleep," he instructed.

"I know," Chris replied plainly. "I can't focus," he said dully, walking past the teacher and out into the white hallway. The teacher did not make a move to stop him. The girl and the boy who were still in the room looked at each other and then at the teacher.

"Go on after your friend, enjoy your lunch, keep being good friends," he told them. They immediately took off after Chris. After they caught up, they began to walk at his pace.

"Hey, Sleeping Beauty, are you alright?" asked the girl to his left, bumping him with her hip.

"I'll be fine, Jackie."

"I'm noticing a pattern here," Jackie mused with a tilt of her head and a sly smirk. "You always say that *after* people get worried," she elbowed him in his chest.

"I don't always say 'Jackie' with it," he replied with a smirk.

"You're right, this is the first time I've seen Jackie display any form of concern for anyone, I think we should celebrate!" Ty suggested jokingly.

"Pretty sure you could arrange that, Ty. Ever since you got elected as our homeroom leader, you've earned Mrs. Johanna's trust. I'm sure she wouldn't mind." Chris said as he began to laugh.

"I'm always nice! Ask anyone!" Jackie insisted.

"Well, I think you can be if you really want to be, but--" Ty began. Chris began to drown them out. They were his only friends here, and they really did care about him, he smiled to himself. *At least I have a reason to come to school. I don't have any other reasons,* he thought to himself.

Chris felt himself tripping over something and bumping into a person taller than him. Tim was one of the best players on the football team. He was also on the wrestling team, and all of his friends resided behind him.

"For the last time! Watch. Where. You're. Going." he snarled, yanking Chris' collar.

"You're too big to miss," Chris muttered.

"What was that?!"

Jackie quickly stepped forward and attempted to shove Tim off, only to be knocked onto the floor. "Get away from him, I'm sick of you beating him up! I could take--"

"Jackie, please think." Ty pleaded as he helped her to her feet. A girl with black hair made her way through the crowd.

"Ty, he needs help." Jackie hissed as she prepared to try again. Jackie noticed a girl moving through the sea of people. "That girl, that's-"

"Victoria! Hey," Tim chuckled as he tightened his grip on Chris. "Do you want to watch me teach this kid a few things?" Victoria made her way out of the crowd and quickly observed the situation. Tim callously smiled as he turned his gaze to the girl now standing beside him. She walked over and stood by Chris. Then she folded her arms and stamped her foot on the ground.

"No, Tim," Victoria scoffed. "I don't want to watch you beat up my boyfriend!" she spat, pouting. "Now put him down and go."

"Boyfriend?!" Ty and Jackie cried in unison. Victoria turned slightly and held up her finger to hush them as she continued to cause a scene.

"Put him down and let him go," she commanded.

Tim stared at her in disbelief, dropping Chris who fell and made a slight 'oof'! "You and him? Hold on, when did you and moss hair get together? I thought we were going to be a thing," he began.

"Well you thought wrong," Victoria sneered. "Now leave us alone. Don't bother him again. Go away." Filled with embarrassment and contempt, Tim shoved his hands in his pockets and sent a hateful glare Chris's way.

"This isn't over, Spellcrafter," he growled. Chris sent a smug look back as he trudged off in defeat.

Victoria turned to Chris and smiled. "Before you say anything, there's no twist. I honestly did want to help you."

"Why? And why did you call me your boyfriend?" Chris asked, baffled by her actions.

"I wanted to help. The way you were being treated wasn't right. You did nothing wrong and so...here we are." Victoria shrugged.

"Um hello?" Jackie yelled from behind Chris. "We can't trust you! You've been with that group of jerks for a month, and now you help him?!" Jackie had always been a very protective friend and full of energy. "Let me at her!" she snarled. Ty was currently restraining her and trying to hold her back by holding her arm and covering her mouth.

"Jackie, just calm down, give her a moment to explain!" he advised her in exasperation. He let out a sigh of relief as Jackie finally ceased her writhing and turned to him with a disapproving glower.

"She's never helped him before, Ty. We can't trust her if she's one of those kids."

As the students stood alone in the empty hallway, Chris finally spoke up.

"Wanna...come to lunch with us?" he hesitantly offered.

Before she could answer, a watch on her wrist began to flash and ring. Hastily, she hid it behind her rear and out of sight.

"I will, but not right now. I forgot I have something to take care of, I swear I'll catch up. What table?" she asked as she trotted backwards.

"The one closest to the windows," Ty replied as she took off. "And thank you!"

The three of them disappeared as they turned left toward the lunchroom and out of earshot. Victoria went into the first empty classroom she could find and brought up her watch. An interface projected from the device in a brilliant blue light. She pressed the green button. After a moment of silence, a girl's voice spoke, and a volume bar appeared on screen.

"Toriiiiiii, how much longer until you come home? I miss my sister. I'm so bored and I only have Morgan to keep me company!" The girl whined.

"Hey now, I thought you liked Morgan and she was a 'good friend?'" Victoria cracked a smile. "And hello to you too." As Victoria and the girl continued their talk, it was clear that Victoria had been gone for some time.

"I guess I should let the bookworm get back to work." The voice said as it hung up. Her sister had always called her a bookworm, so this was nothing new. Still, Victoria did feel bad for leaving her sister alone for so long. She took a deep breath and lowered her arm, then she walked out of the classroom. She turned left, continued down the hall, then turned left again. There she saw the lunchroom, the same dull color as the rest of the school. She sat beside Ty and across from Chris and Jackie.

"Aren't you hungry?" Chris asked.

"No, I ate earlier actually." she answered. "I was wondering maybe we could walk together to P.E since we have the same class. I don't want to go alone. It gets boring and I don't really know many people in that class."

Chris agreed. After lunch, they began to walk through the many halls until they were outside. They continued to a large white and brown gym with a white roof. Victoria explained that when she came to this school, she did not expect to meet so many different "personalities." Chris guessed Victoria was just trying to be friendly, however, he continued to wonder why. Victoria had gone from never speaking to him, to immediately wanting to help him. He found it weird, but maybe she just felt like it. He wondered what was going through her mind as they made their way into the gym.

2

DYNAMIC DUO

When they got to the gym, they quickly proceeded down a small ramp and into the main area. There were about thirty kids heading to the locker rooms. After changing, everyone came back into the main area. They were all wearing white shirts with a blue patriot on the back, and blue shorts with a red "E" on the right leg. Victoria placed herself beside Chris at the back wall. There was an excited atmosphere about the entire room and rubber balls lined the white line at the center of the court. Today they would play dodgeball.

Victoria commented that she had never played dodgeball, so Chris explained the rules. Despite Chris saying how likely it was to get hit with a ball in all of the chaos, Victoria just smiled and said "Yeah, yeah. We'll be fine," every time he tried to warn her. The coach stepped out of "no man's land" and stood on the right side from where they were standing. There were no less than fifteen students per side.

"I want a clean game. If you catch a ball, the person who threw it is out. If you are hit, you are out. In this game, if you are hit in the face, you are out. Remember that you cannot cross the white line. The last team standing wins. If the game takes too long, I will say that every ball caught allows back one team member." The coach announced.

He had big muscles, wore a blue shirt, and shorts. Even though he had a megaphone beside him, he did not need it. He was loud enough for the whole gym to have heard what he said; even the health classrooms could hear him.

The whistle blew. Both armies charged, soldiers grabbing ammunition. Chris was unable to grab one of these. Instead, he stayed more toward the middle, dodging shots and handing off the balls he picked up to the other members of his team. One down on the opposing team. Two down on theirs. Victoria caught a ball a few inches from her face and tossed it back, knocking the other boy, who was running to avoid fire, onto the floor.

The shots kept flying through the air. Many of the less enthusiastic players on both sides stayed more toward the back and eventually got out anyway. Chris saw a red ball coming straight for him. He reacted instinctively, tucking and rolling forward, then dodging it completely.

"Nice play, Spellcrafter!" the coach roared with a hefty laugh. Victoria took note of this.

She tossed Chris a yellow ball and told him to hit the one farthest to the right who was now moving left, for he was one of their heavy hitters. He threw the ball and hit him square in the stomach, and despite some protest, he did walk out and off the court. After some time, only five remained on their team and ten on the other side. The other three were taken out easily, leaving only Chris and Victoria. She grabbed two of the balls and tossed one to Chris.

Victoria dashed forward and hit two people closely grouped together. Eight remained. Chris threw another ball and missed.

"It's okay, we can do this!" Victoria called over the cheers from their team. Victoria quickly caught another ball and tossed it to Chris. "I'll get another. You worry about covering me, okay? I can't do this by myself."

"You got it!" Chris replied. He tossed out another ball, this time in such a way that it was like a homing-missile angrily seeking its target: the brown-haired boy. It struck him on his leg, and as if he had been hit elsewhere, he fell. Seven remained.

"Team two is making a comeback, and team one is getting obliterated by just two."

Victoria jumped up, caught another in the air, and hit a kid about to throw a ball at Chris from across the court. Five remained. Victoria cartwheeled out of the way of another ball. Chris watched her, astounded. She was good; she said she had never played this game before, but with the way she moved, he had to assume that she had. As their shots flew and littered the opposing side of the line, fewer of team one remained in play. It was now even. Two against two.

"Alright, time to make things interesting. From now on, catching a ball does not make the other player out. It now brings in one of your teammates in the order that they got out! One catch equals one teammate! This should be a blessing team one...believe me...it is for you..."

"*Hey!*" called one of their team members. "Don't worry about catching. If they catch some just drop them again! You two can do it!" He was the third to last boy to get hit.

"Alright. Tori?" Chris asked.

"Oh yeah, I'm up for it," she smirked.

"Hey, let that rule only apply to us! They don't even care!" cried the girl with red hair on team one. "They don't need it anyway. We're getting destroyed!"

"Fair enough I suppose," the coach smiled, he seemed excited to see how this progressed. "They do need a handicap," he agreed. "Still, I've never seen two people take on ten and win."

As the dodgeball battle continued, more of team one's members returned to the field. There were now six in total. While the remaining members of team one were panting and sweating, Chris and Victoria still seemed full of energy and ready to go.

"We should let them throw at us until they run out, that way we have all of the balls." Chris decided.

"No," Victoria said, shooting him down. "If they stay distracted with attacking they are open-" she stopped mid-sentence then quickly dropped on all fours to dodge a ball.

As she pulled herself up with her left hand, she threw the ball in her possession with her right, once again hitting two people too close together. Chris hit one person with a ball and quickly caught another, then he hit one to his far left who was too focused on Victoria. Three remained once again. Chris managed to hit two more by faking his throws and then letting it leave his hand a second later. The final boy was rather skinny. He stood with his feet apart, ready to catch a ball.

Victoria smiled and told Chris to step back. "Let me get this one, okay?"

Chris seemed surprised. "He'll probably catch it."

"Oh Chris, I'd love to see that happen," she smirked. "He'll have to watch this carefully then."

Victoria took one step back toward her right, turned herself slightly, then winded up the throw. The boy prepared himself for her attack. She threw the second "homing-missile" of the game. As it left her hand, the boy realized he could not catch a ball going so fast coming straight for him. He decided to duck the ball instead. He had a smug look on his face.

"Tori?" Chris raised his eyebrow. "You missed..."

Victoria simply smiled. "Nah," The ball ricocheted off of the back wall and into the back of the unsuspecting boy's head. Once again, the whistle blew. He turned toward the coach, seeking confirmation that he was out.

"It did not touch the floor; the ball was still legal. You're out.

Team two wins. Now everyone, I want you to get some water. You're going to climb that wall before you leave here today." There was a shared moment of groans and sighs. "I know, I know. But it's still part of the curriculum, so you have to. Stop being lazy before you have health issues."

"Climbing, huh?" Victoria said to herself. "Now that'll be easy. You just gotta have good hand-eye coordination."

Eventually, everyone in class was in a crowd in front of the wall. The coach was taking volunteers, and while no one else made a move, Victoria was the first to step forward. There was no climbing gear, but this area of the gym was in fact lined with blue soft mats and pillows at the very end (in case anyone fell). Climbing the wall was not an easy task. The goal was to climb the wall with specifically colored areas of where to put your feet and place your hands. Then you had to transfer yourself to the roof where you had to essentially do monkey bars across. Finally, you land onto the area, where most of the pillows were, to cushion your fall.

Victoria had already started climbing (if you could call it that). She would occasionally climb, but then she would jump up and pull herself up with both hands to skip a few areas entirely. She jumped to the monkey bars with ease, and she would swing across them instead of grabbing them and moving one by one. She then swung off of the final bar and landed perfectly at the very edge of the pillows. Her feet were firmly planted onto the floor. She made contact with her feet together, and her arms out, as if she had just done a circus act. The coach announced that she had made a time of seven seconds; so far, the fastest time anyone had ever done.

"Alright, volunteer or get volun-told," he commanded to the class.

Everyone else stepped back as Chris stepped forward. He looked back at Victoria who simply waved and smiled her extremely friendly smile. Chris began to scale the wall, occasionally jumping like Victoria did; he simply felt he could do it too. He continued to climb until he reached the top. He felt his foot slip on top of one of the many-colored areas. The coach made a move to catch him in case he fell; although, there were many areas to land safely. However, it wasn't needed. Chris had, in his panic, leapt from the wall and onto the third monkey bar he would have needed to land on. Victoria smirked. The group below watched as he swung across to the next few, before landing and falling on his butt at the very end.

"Eleven seconds," the coach breathed in bewilderment. "That's the second fastest time I've seen in my time here...they're getting faster!"

Chris sat there in disbelief once again. He thought about how he had done that, if he was always able to, and why he could not do this earlier in the year. His thoughts were interrupted as Victoria walked in front of him. She held out her hand, and as he took it, she helped him up.

"Good job, I don't think anyone can even beat your time." She whispered as she gestured her head in the direction of the students either going too slow or slipping like Chris, but falling instead, or attempting to jump and failing.

The third fastest time was twenty-six seconds. It was about time to leave school and so most of the students in the gym class went to go get changed back into their normal attires (some did not bother). Victoria headed into the locker room and went for her locker. After putting in the code, she removed her purple and white string bag. She pulled out her normal clothes once again, and as a precaution, she also packed a spare outfit in case of an emergency (or if she felt like changing).

She closed her locker. The other girls in the room were leaving now that they were changed. Victoria stripped down and began to change but before she got her skirt fully on, she noticed a name three lockers down on a sticky note for a new student: *Gatchi*. Victoria stopped what she was doing and stared at it for a moment, feeling her heart drop slightly, but unsure why. All in one motion, she put her shirt on and put her watch back on her arm. Then after pulling up the interface, she hid behind one of the many walls of lockers, ensuring no one would hear her.

Chris waited outside for Victoria for about seven minutes before she finally came out. She explained that she was having trouble and that was what took her so long. There was a thunderstorm going on outside. Victoria explained that she, like Chris, lived alone. Victoria requested to stay at his house for the night since it was raining so hard and she had not lived close. At first Chris refused entirely, but because it was pouring down so hard, he decided to allow her to stay the night, especially since she had a change of clothes. He wasn't sure how he felt about the idea. However, it was too late, he had agreed now.

The sky cried down upon them as they left down the steps of the school that day. They walked together through the town to a quiet neighborhood somewhere nearby the school. Victoria asked him about his past and his family, but Chris would only reply to other questions not related to that subject. Even so, Victoria pressed on and she didn't seem to want to give up. Chris asked himself why she was so interested, but he assumed she was just nosey.

They arrived at a tan house with a brown roof and a fairly large lawn between two other similar houses. As they entered, Victoria shut the door behind them and scanned the area. A black leather sofa, a black leather reclining chair, a clear coffee table, widescreen T.V, and a kitchen were visible from the living room. A comfy place to live and very quiet; and since it was just him, he had the place to himself. Victoria smiled.

"Hey, can I take a shower?" she asked. "I'll be quick!"

"Upstairs to your right," he replied. "I'll make us something to eat. Maybe watch some T.V or something."

Chris began to make turkey sandwiches with lettuce, tomato,

cheese, and of course, mayonnaise with the tiniest bit of mustard. He set them on the coffee table and sat on the sofa for about ten minutes before quietly going up to check on her.

"Hey, Tori, are you alright?" he asked aloud. "Tori?" She was not in the bathroom.

He checked each room before finally checking his sister's room down the hall. Victoria was on the other side of the room holding a picture frame. He paused a moment to gather himself before speaking.

"Emily isn't coming back, but I try to keep this room clean just in case," he said as she replaced the picture on the brown desk and turned to face him.

"I'm sorry, I couldn't help myself...You two look so happy in that picture...but now it's just you, and it's sad to me..." She waited a moment, seeing him look away to break eye contact, now looking at the picture. "I'm sure she misses you too."

"Honestly, if she is alive, she should have come back."

"Maybe she just can't though, you know?" Victoria hastily replied to this, attempting to raise his spirits. "Maybe she wants to, but literally can't."

"You should take your shower..." he advised. She nodded, realizing she had possibly made him upset.

"I'm sorry...I just wanted to give you some hope."

"No, it's alright. I guess...I wish she was here now telling me what I'm doing stuck here for...and if she's been sending me money, where she is." He walked past her as she made her way to the door. She took one last glance before closing the door and continuing on her way to her original destination.

Chris took a small breath as he looked at the picture: a six-year-old boy with green hair sitting on the shoulders of a twenty-eight-year-old man wearing a red bowling shirt and shorts. He had a brown mustache, a smile that said he was a people person, and he was holding up his right hand, pointing at a young Chris. A woman with beautiful, healthy green hair, blue eyes, and an amused look on her face looking at the son and father. She wore a red shirt tied at the stomach with a white tank top underneath. She also wore pants with a white jacket wrapped around her waist, and had her hands on the shoulders of an eleven-year-old girl. The girl had green hair, brown eyes, and a shy look as if she was hiding from the camera by trying not to notice it. She wore an orange top, shorts, and black headphones around her neck.

Chris stared at it for a long time before taking the picture and placing it face down. He then shook his head. He felt sick and he did not wish to see the memory any longer. He looked back in the direction in which Victoria had gone and wondered why she had been so interested. He then began to think to himself: could she know something?

3

THE PROMISE

The next morning, Chris and Victoria had arrived at school. Victoria wore a black and white top with a black skirt. Chris wore a white shirt, with a red hooded jacket, and jeans. Victoria had tried several times to apologize for snooping and bringing up his family with no response in return. It was an ominous day, as if it was going to rain again. It would be a while before the bell rang, so they sat together on the steps. Jackie was late and Ty had gone on inside to the science hall to put away his project so he would not have to carry it. His project was titled, "Terror Strikes Japan" after that attack on Japan a little over two years ago. The island was now uninhabited, according to the news. Because of that, Ty thought he should study how the land was affected and gathered his research. However, Chris thought this topic was far too dark.

A girl with red hair, blue eyes, and a yellow cat hoodie approached them. She was slightly shorter than Chris. Her hair was short and her bangs came near her right eye, almost covering it. She also wore brown shorts and yellow high-top shoes. Her hood was drawn over her head. She had no bookbag to speak of. When Chris first saw her, he figured she was new; she seemed scared.

"I- um...hi," she hid behind her books for a moment before looking him in the eye, she was slightly shorter than him. "I'm a transfer. I was told to find Christopher Spellcrafter...he said look for green hair..." she said in a gentle tone.

The girl lowered her hands and placed them just in front of her, holding her books against her thighs. She seemed shy and even a little bit nervous.

Victoria raised her eyebrow and answered before Chris could. "He's not here." she shook her head. "I'm sorry, but maybe someone else knows where he is."

"B-but I was told to find him, is he near here? This boy has green hair and-"

"Sorry, no. Wrong guy."

Chris looked at Victoria with a disapproving glance before turning his attention to the girl. "I'm Christopher. I'm sorry, what is your name?"

"It's Gatchi Mitchell," she repeated. "I'm a transfer, like I said."

"*Really?*" Victoria asked. "I don't believe it. I've heard your name before."

"Yes. We used to go to the same school before you moved, and you left our group of friends." Gatchi told her. "They wished you hadn't left though...we miss you and your sister." her tone gave off something passive-aggressive.

"Oh yeah, I do remember you now," Victoria said through her teeth. "Sure, *we* can show you to your class."

"Actually, since I have all of my classes with Chris, I'd rather go with him." she said, stepping to his side.

Victoria opened her mouth to say something further, but the look Chris gave her encouraged her not to mess with the new girl any further. Thus, Victoria stayed behind, watching Chris disappear with Gatchi into the school with the flood of students.

Gatchi commented on how Chris had stood up for her, and that she could tell they would be good friends. Chris explained that he did not like how Victoria was treating her on her first day, and that he was never a fan of being treated horribly physically or verbally.

"Is she your girlfriend?" Gatchi asked.

"No."

"I figured...not your type?"

"No, not at all." he answered with a gesture of his hand and a sigh.

Victoria had a class with both of them during Social Studies, and she was none too happy to see Gatchi. Chris sat in the front near the board, Gatchi sat behind him. They were talking about something Victoria could not hear, but she did notice Gatchi going through Chris' things when he left to go to the bathroom. She checked his folders, his bag, his binder, everything. Later, when they went to their lockers to put everything away, Victoria kept a close eye on her. Gatchi was up to something and she intended to find out.

Throughout the day, Chris and Gatchi spent their time together. Chris took note that Gatchi was a rather strange girl, much like Victoria, but he still found her to be nice and so they quickly became friends. Not much happened that day. Gatchi suggested that Chris come with her to get some candy after school. It wasn't raining yet, so he agreed.

"I'll bring my friends too." he told her.

"Oh...Really? Because I figured you'd- who's coming?" she paused.

"Just Victoria and my two best friends, is that okay?"

"Err. Sure..." she replied with uncertainty. "I know a shortcut to a candy shop."

Chris agreed, informing his other friends, and they headed to the candy shop together after school. The five of them proceeded away from the school and toward the town. It had begun to rain and Jackie seemed to love it. Ty disliked the idea of getting hyper on sugar, but he went along because Jackie was going. Chris just wanted to spend time with his new friend, despite Victoria's constant warnings and bickering throughout the day. The streets were somewhat deserted because of the rain, and lights flashed yellow, swinging in the wind.

They crossed through an alleyway close to where Chris' house was. Gatchi stopped walking in the center of the alleyway. She did not say a word, she stayed stationary.

"Okay no. Um no. I'm cold, I'm wet, and I don't have a jacket," Victoria said. "Can you please keep walking?!" Victoria yelled. Gatchi turned toward them, her lip curled slightly under the darkness of her hood.

"Can we please go home?" Victoria begged, looking at Chris and his friends. She was shivering.

"You can go home, Victoria, and so can these two, but he's staying," Gatchi declared as she pointed a finger at Chris. "You can all leave now if you'd like."

"What are you talking about? Weren't you going to eat junk or something? I thought that was what you wanted to do." Ty was as confused as everyone else.

"I-I don't like where this is going..." Jackie whispered to Ty.

"Gatchi?" Chris stepped forward. "Is there something wrong?"

"No, everything is just right, actually," she began to laugh. "You're exactly where I need you to be, and it only took me a day...funny, Victoria, I always figured I was better than you."

Jackie stepped forward slightly to protect her friend once again, but Victoria held out her left arm to stop her.

"No, stay back." she warned. Victoria returned her attention to Gatchi. Two people stepped out from the darkness of the alley. One female and one male. Victoria stepped back, keeping everyone else behind her.

"Aww, Tori, don't look so spooked!" Gatchi said with a sinister smile. "I thought you remembered our friends."

"You are not friends of mine." Victoria corrected. She seemed very aware and ready for anything that may come next.

The male assailant peered out from his black cloak and drew a dagger. The female wore a gothic hoodie jacket, leather boots, blonde hair, from what they could see, a pouch on her side.

"Gatchi, quit screwing around and kill her." said the male.

"We just need the boy. If you all leave now, we don't have to fight," advised the girl. "I don't want to fight you," she said as Gatchi held up her hand to silence her.

"Laura, Robert...enough. We take him either way."

"We can't have witnesses," Robert reminded her. "They have to die now."

Jackie once again moved forward, so did Ty. "If you think I'm gonna let you take him-" Jackie paused. Victoria had once again stopped both of them and pushed them back. Chris moved in front of Victoria and looked Gatchi dead in the eyes.

"So, let me get this straight...you lied about everything..." he began, in complete disbelief.

"We can still be friends if you come with us. Otherwise I'll have to kill your friends. I don't want to hurt you...You honestly do seem really nice."

Gatchi reached out her hand to take Chris's and pull him to their side of the alley, but before her hand could touch Chris, a purple orb of solid energy flew down and collided with her hand, almost breaking it. Gatchi held her wrist and winced. The orb was now orbiting Chris as if he was a planet.

Gatchi and her friends focused their attention on Victoria, who stepped in front of Chris once again.

"I won't let you hurt her brother," Victoria declared. "If I have to take all three of you down, I will. I won't even hesitate."

"Now can we kill her?" Robert asked.

"Yes. Definitely kill her." Gatchi replied.

Robert charged at Victoria, who quickly jumped back into the air, her orb flying away from Chris and colliding with Robert's dagger. Sparks flew. Robert retreated as the orb returned to Victoria and into her hand. The orb was large, about the size of a head, but to her it seemed light as a feather as it resided in her single hand. Laura held out her hand and fired a bolt of lightning. Victoria absorbed it into her orb and fired it up into the sky.

When Laura saw this, she was taken aback for a moment. She regained herself soon after. Robert once again charged; Victoria did too. She extended her leg to trip him, his legs removed out from under him. He quickly used his left hand to spring back to his feet, using his right to swipe at her all in one motion. Victoria took the advantage and began to beat him down with rapid punches, then a few hits from her orb. Right. Left. Then she flipped him over her head and left him to lay on the cold ground. Finally, she turned her focused gaze back to the remaining two.

"Whoa...I didn't like you before, but you kick butt!" Jackie cheered.

"Jackie, this is a serious situation..." Ty reminded her, giving her a side glance.

"Well she's winnin', ain't she??"

Laura approached Robert and knelt down near his head. He wasn't injured very much, but he definitely was somewhat dazed.

"You didn't kill him..." Laura whispered. "Not even close..."

"Of course not."

"Why?"

"I don't need to have a reason other than the fact that Wizards don't kill if we can help it. If you leave, you can take him and get out of here," Laura thought for a moment, looking back at Gatchi, who was too focused on Victoria. She nodded, gave Robert her arm, and began to leave. Gatchi gave Laura a disapproving glare as she began to pass her.

"She's too powerful, we can't beat her...You should come with us." Laura advised.

"Come on, she isn't playing around and-" she tried to explain.

"If you want to go back empty handed, fine. But I won't look like a fool coming back without anything. I'm going to take him even if I have to kill her," She hissed. "I don't need you."

Laura didn't seem surprised. She shook her head and continued to walk, muttering something along the lines of "Whatever, Gatchi..."

Victoria turned to the others. "Start running, now!"

Gatchi made a move to run at them. Victoria ran on the brick wall and used her orb to hit Gatchi in the gut, knocking her back a few feet. The crushing force caused her to land on her back. They all began to run.

"I want an explanation, now!" Chris demanded. "What's going on?"

"Later!" Victoria cried out from in front of him. "I will tell you, we need to get to your house before it's too late or she might cause us some serious problems!"

"Don't lead her to my house!" Chris yelled hysterically. "You're crazy!"

"She won't be able to attack us there. I made sure of it!" Victoria assured.

They took a right and headed down the street, pushing past the few people remaining on the streets (which were mostly empty by now due to the storm).

"Faster!" Victoria cried.

"We can't take her?!" Jackie questioned.

"I can, but I'm not taking the risk of any of you getting hurt!"

Victoria paused, a haunted expression on her face. There, at the end of the street, was Gatchi. She smiled at them a few feet away, her sword drawn. It was a sword with a golden yellow hilt and a grey blade.

"How...how is she here already?" Chris asked. Victoria said nothing.

"You saw my friend shoot lightning. Are you really still confused?" Gatchi casted Chris a brief glance before focusing her eyes on Victoria.

"She has a point..." Ty muttered to Chris.

"Thanks for the input, buddy..." Chris sighed.

Gatchi began to cast something. Yellow particles began to appear around her. Then she smiled.

"I'm afraid this is where it ends for you. I'm sorry we couldn't play longer, but Victoria isn't the most powerful person here." She held her hand to her chest, a prideful look upon her face. "That would be me!"

"Dammit, no no!" Victoria ran full speed at Gatchi. "Tackle her! Stop her!"

Jackie and Ty ran with her in an attempt to stop her. Then suddenly, everything vanished in a flash as the world around them was devoured by white and nothingness.

4

THE INTERNAL WAR

C hris awoke on the concrete road. He felt as if his body was new to him, as if he had just been born. He looked at his hands. These were his hands, right? So why did they feel foreign? He looked around, and there was nothing. It was a clear night and there were no ongoing cars or pedestrians. He lifted himself up and entered his house, turning back to confirm that no one was there. His friends were just with him and now they were gone like a dream. It was just him now. He closed the door, locked it, and sat on the sofa, covering his face. He asked himself if he was crazy and if he had seen what he thought he saw, or if it was all just a dream.

Chris took a few minutes to slow his breath, control his thoughts, and convince himself none of it was real. The silence was broken by the sound of a guitar playing upstairs. He froze and looked up from his hands. He listened for the sound again. The tuning of a guitar could be heard. He got up and moved to investigate. He crept upstairs and checked each room once again as he did before. The sound could still be heard, but this time he knew where it came from. As he moved in that direction, he felt his heart drop. He wanted to stop his advance, but his legs wouldn't listen to his mind. He pushed open the slightly cracked open door the rest of the way. His eyes were closed, afraid to believe anything after today. The room was somewhat clean, there was sheet music on the floor, the bed wasn't made, and there was a person sitting there playing the guitar.

She had green hair that was currently in a bob cut with bangs in the front, sea blue eyes, a blue tank top, blue jeans, and red tennis shoes. She didn't seem to care how she looked.

"Hey, little bro, wanna help me work on this song I'm writing? It's a work in progress." Emily offered kindly. She laid her guitar on her bed and stared at him. "You look spooked..."

Chris forced back tears that came anyway. As the stinging in his eyes worsened, his eyes flooded, and he began to cry, unsure of what to say or even do.

"You're even crying...what's wrong?"

Chris stopped hesitating, ran into Emily's arms, and hugged her around her torso.

She slowly wrapped her arms around him in slight confusion. "Chris?"

"I would love to." He answered. And so they did.

They began to work on Emily's song. It was a song about colors, people, and love: finding that one right person for you. Emily sang as she played the guitar, but Chris was only half listening; he was relieved. He loved the way she acted, the familiar smell of her perfume, her guitar skills, and the way her hair tickled her face when he was younger was a familiar feeling.

"You seem like you've been through a lot in Dreamland, huh?" She asked him as she wiped his tears. Chris was now smaller. He was a six-year-old having to look up to see his sister, swinging his feet that now dangled off the red bed sheets.

She smiled. "For a moment there, you seemed older."

"Emily?"

"Yes?" she replied softly, brushing his hair back with her fingers.

"Would you ever lie to me?" he asked her in a quiet voice.

"Never." she answered.

"Are you real?" he asked, following up his last question. Emily said nothing. She stared off for a moment to ponder her answer.

"Sis?" She said nothing, staring straight ahead.

"Answer me, sis!" he cried out as tears streamed down his face, he shook her arm frantically. She stopped him, with a soft expression.

"I'm...afraid not...but...I *can* tell you, you need to get out of here and find your friends." she answered. This was not the answer he wanted to hear.

"I don't care, let me stay here with you!" she shook her head. "Please..." she once again shook her head. "I don't care if you're not real, please!" She held him tightly and squeezed him like she did when they were little. He relaxed.

"If you don't leave, you'll be taken to the Sorcerers, away from me and against your will. I am with the Wizards on our home planet of Terminus. If you don't leave, you will never see me again...the real me." She told him. "The Sorcerers are the ones who committed that horrible attack on Japan a year ago...you are being held captive by one too."

"Gatchi?" Chris asked, Emily nodded.

"Chris, this is a place called the imagination realm. An Imagination magic user can send you here and hold you captive. Your body isn't even in the real world right now," she explained.

"Here, anything can happen. Think it, and it'll happen. I must have been what you thought of to calm yourself down." She explained. "And I can protect you, but you need to find Tori and get yourself out after you find your friends. I can't protect you with my magic...only the way you remember me. I also cannot technically imagine anything."

Chris looked down at his feet, feeling himself wanting to ask to stay with her again. He would see the real Emily if he only made it out. He nodded. She stood and smiled.

"Good, now come on." She took his little hand and led them out of the house. There were now people on the streets, but they all seemed almost zombie-like, and they were missing faces. Chris hugged Emily's leg.

"I'll protect you if you only stay with me, alright? I've never let anything happen to you."

She took his hand and led him across the street toward the town. They walked for a few seconds before she stopped him. She pulled him into a pizza parlor and quickly ran out the back with him. Victoria was hiding in the alleyway.

"No... not her," Chris pleaded as he hid behind Emily. "She lies too."

"No... I never lied to you once, but I couldn't tell you everything either or I would scare you. I was planning on doing it today, but I just had to show you, I guess."

Victoria and Emily looked at each other for a moment, but did not say anything. His sister was the one to break the silence.

"Tori, I need you to take him and get him safely to-" she started.

"I know...I'm going to keep my promise to you." Victoria replied. Chris was confused.

Emily was now displaying Victoria's memories as well. She did in fact know his sister.

"Go with her...please?" Emily urged.

"You have to come with me just a little while...then you can never speak to me again ,hate me, whatever...but I'm trying to help." She extended her hand with a smile.

Chris hesitated a moment, unsure, but he still took her hand. Emily vanished from behind him and he returned to his normal age. The ground began to shake as the sky turned red and a storm began over the town.

"Now come on, hurry!" Victoria took Chris' arm and began to run as fast as she could with him.

"Okay, quick! Where is the first place you imagine Jackie being?"

"She would probably be...on the baseball field of the school practicing her swings." Chris answered.

"Then she's close...and Ty?"

"Ty..." Chris sighed slightly. "He'd probably be somewhere in the school honestly..."

"Would he be anywhere specific?" She asked. Chris shook his head and continued to run with her.

Sure enough, they found Ty on the steps of the school, as if he was waiting for them. Ty had not gotten caught up in his dreams or desires, instead, he realized it was all a trap to get him killed and simply waited for whatever was to come.

He stood, obviously having seen them coming. He held a small pistol and had a bewildered expression on his face.

He spoke, "You know...This place is weird, but interesting in an... eerie kind of way."

"I wouldn't know...This is my first time in here, but I did learn about this in my classes." Victoria commented.

"Classes?" Chris questioned.

"That's off topic- Jackie, have you seen her?" Victoria asked, turning to Ty and making her orb reappear at her side and float there.

Ty explained that he had an idea of where and what she might be doing, and that she had probably fallen for the illusions. He also told them that the reason he had a gun is because he had to fight his way out of the school. Victoria seemed impressed that he had done this himself and without being told none of this was real.

There was a sound like glass cracking in the distance, but it grew closer. A long, spine-tingling sound followed, like an explosion or a ripple. Ty anxiously pointed his gun back in the direction they came from.

"That sounds like one of the things that attacked me..." he whispered.

A large creature towered over them, it was two stories tall, carried a large stone axe, and wore a knight's armor. It also had glowing red eyes, and rock like skin. Chris looked at Victoria, who gave him a slightly scared look, letting him know that she could not take on this behemoth easily. All three of them began to quickly run into the school before they were spotted, and shut the door, quickly barricading it with a chair in case anything small showed up and tried to follow.

They quickly cut through the gym, where there were more of the zombie-like people with no faces, and ran out of the back entrance. There they could see in the distance, the track and field area. Jackie was down in the batter's box practicing her swings for a faceless pitcher. They approached her, but she did not seem to notice them.

"I'll get a homerun and I ain't scared of your weak and slow pitches. Give me something real!" She cried as she swung again. Victoria caught the baseball bat as she swung it and took it from her.

"What are you guys doin' here? I have a game goin' on right now." She sounded irritated now. The umpire disappeared as Jackie stared at them angry and confused.

"Jackie, this isn't a game...we need to get out of here." Chris told her.

"But my game! No way. This is the championship game for the Yankees and I ain't abandoning them." She said, taking her bat away from Victoria. "And there's nothing left to be said about it."

The faceless people in the crowd and on the field began to have faces and they could now see people taking pictures, hear them cheering, and see the runners who were currently on second and third base.

"I promise you, this is not real. If you step away from the plate, you'll see, otherwise, we'll never get you to listen." Chris reasoned with her as best he could. Jackie took a step back and loosened her grip on the bat before dropping it.

"I ain't gonna play anymore. Sorry, guys...find a new player...." She said, taking off the baseball cap that was never there and tossing it to the ground. She apparently saw it, but they didn't. The faceless people all around them began to come toward them.

"Oh okay, that's messed up, okay. I don't like it..." Chris began to wonder if he could also imagine whatever he wanted...something to protect them. Nothing happened.

Victoria quickly imagined a barrier between the swarm and them. She turned and began to walk away. Chris and his friends exchanged glances before following behind her.

"Time to go find Gatchi," Victoria declared.

"Where would she be?" Jackie asked. "And can I imagine something?"

"I have an idea," Victoria twisted a strand of her hair around her finger for a moment. "And yes, you can." she answered without looking back. Jackie imagined herself carrying a bow and arrow.

"*Oh, cool!*" Jackie laughed excitedly.

Chris began to wonder if he would be able to imagine anything; he was too focused on the current situation to think about anything but escaping and finding Emily. They walked for a while until they came to the edge of town where there was nothing but mist and white everywhere, as if someone had forgotten to color it in. There were no buildings or people anywhere.

"Chris, I need you to think of something right this second, before she attacks us." Victoria commanded.

"I've been trying." he admitted. Chris closed his eyes and began to imagine the first thing that came to mind. Nothing but the darkness of his eyelids to be found here.

He kept trying while Victoria was waiting. She knew Gatchi

would realize Chris was missing and start searching. She only had to wait, and by then hopefully Chris would be armed.

Chris saw something: a glimpse of a girl. She had somewhat long, slightly wavy, black hair that dropped to shoulder length, side bangs, and brown eyes. She wore a black, V-Neck style shirt with a subtle yellow outline, a black undershirt, a black skirt that dropped just to her knees, and black ankle boots. She turned to look at Chris, but before she could, she vanished. He reopened his eyes to find a sword in his hand. The hilt was golden with a red ribbon on the end. He was surprised to find it there, and it felt strange, as if he was holding it all this time. He gave it a swing and felt it move like it was a part of his arm.

Victoria smiled at him and clapped. "Just in time, we have trouble coming. She has red hair and blue eyes, and she's coming angrily this way." she said with a smile as she placed her hand on her hip and pointed behind Chris at Gatchi, who was approaching quickly.

She vanished into the mist suddenly and Victoria took up a fighting stance. Chris pointed his sword and stayed at her back. Ty and Jackie stayed together, aiming in different directions.

Suddenly, from the mist, Gatchi appeared with red demon-like wings as she grabbed Chris by his shoulders and flew away into the mist. The last thing Chris saw before he couldn't see anymore was Victoria running after them. Chris attempted to raise his sword.

"I wouldn't do that if you value your life." she said simply.

Chris rapidly began to think of options to save himself from this situation. To Chris' left he could hear a soft whizzing that grew louder and louder. From out of the mist came Victoria's orb of energy once again, striking Gatchi, causing her to drop Chris and fall out of sight. Chris began to fall. The weapon flew underneath him, so he landed on it. It was soft and fuzzy now. Even though it had not changed visually, it was pleasant to the touch for him. He wondered to himself if she could change its feeling based on friend or foe. He was slowly levitated to the ground to see Victoria dodging Gatchi's sword attacks and avoiding everything she could. She would occasionally counter with a kick or a swipe from her hand.

"Hey!" Ty's voice sounded. "Don't forget about us!" He began to fire his pistol.

Gatchi quickly ran at Ty, blocking the shots with her sword and swinging at him. His gun exploded in his hand and knocked him back into Jackie. They were both knocked to the ground.

She turned to see Victoria's orb coming at her once again; blocked it. Sparks flew. Gatchi parried and charged again at Victoria, who dodged out of the way by moving right. She was slightly cut on her shoulder as she passed.

Chris surprised Gatchi by attacking her from behind. She ducked under Chris' first swing and hit him in the stomach with the hilt of her sword, being careful not to use the blade on him. Victoria moved to attack Gatchi, but she caused hands to come up from the ground and grab her would-be attacker. Victoria could no longer move, but because Gatchi was trying not to hurt Chris, she wasn't trying to fight as much. Chris began swinging somewhat randomly in her chest region, and then surprising her by cutting her leg.

Victoria watched, she was impressed. An untrained fighter was sometimes more dangerous than a skilled and trained one. Gatchi couldn't predict his moves, she didn't know what to do, and Chris didn't need help. Even so, she had to help him, she couldn't take the chance. She attempted to move her hands, but she couldn't. She could just move her wrists enough to control her orb. Gatchi and Chris were still battling near her. Gatchi was now on the defensive, blocking any attack coming her way; she had given up on offense. Victoria's orb came from nowhere, striking Gatchi in the ribs and leaving her exposed. It came back around to hit her again in the head, knocking her to the ground. Chris came over her and held his sword to her neck.

"You actually beat me and you aren't even trained...You don't know a thing! I don't care if you had help! I was beaten by a traitor and a weakling..." Gatchi spoke furiously through gritted teeth. Ty and Jackie came over a while after both looking confused as to what had happened in their absence.

"We came over to help, but you don't seem to need it." Ty observed.

"Whoa! He's like a superhero now!" Jackie cheered, slapping Chris on the back who winced. Gatchi glared at them all together at once.

"Finish her so we can get out of here." Victoria told him. Chris did not move, he merely stared at her.

"I don't need your pity, end it. I'm not scared of any of you. At least I'm not getting killed by the traitor!" She spat at Tori.

Chris moved his sword to the side and released his grip, and it vanished from existence. He knelt down beside Gatchi.

"What are you doing, Chris?" Victoria asked as she watched him. She didn't seem as surprised as the other two.

Chris extended his hand without a word to anyone but Gatchi, "If you let us out, you can go."

"Why?"

"Because I still think of you as a friend despite trying to kill me. I mean you seem nice and I don't get what the heck this whole thing was about, but honestly, I don't care. I don't want to kill you, because all of us are alive and I don't like the idea of it. So, let us out and you can go," he offered. "Plain and simple. I really don't want to kill anyone. I just want to find my sister. So, I say you let us out, you get to leave, and that's that."

"I don't get it...he's letting the crazy girl who tried to *kill* us go?" Jackie asked Ty.

"You're making a mistake. Anyone would kill you the second they had the chance." Gatchi told him, curiously looking for any signs that he might kill her anyway.

"Your guard is down. I could try to kill you in an instant."

"That's your decision, but I don't think you'd do that."

"The heart of a Wizard won't help you, the moral high ground gets you killed every time. One day you'll see that." She looked him directly in the eye, he shook his head calmly.

"Then I guess that's my problem to deal with, unfortunately. I don't think I have it in me to kill, and I don't think I want to try. If I have to kill someone, I want it to be a last resort."

Gatchi thought silently for a moment. She looked at Chris and then at everyone around her before nodding. The white mist disappeared, they were back in the street, the rain had stopped, their weapons were gone (minus Victoria's). It was a cold night, the moon was full, and the stars shined brightly in the night sky.

Gatchi looked at Chris and then slowly got to her feet, curiously looking at him the whole time. She seemed very confused; not because she was being allowed to live, but because of how after everything she did, he still called her a friend.

"...I don't understand you. You must have something wrong with you. If you continue to be like the Wizards, you will only get yourself, and other people you care about killed. You'll see." Gatchi ran off, disappearing down the road and going somewhere out of sight.

"You let her go," Victoria said. "Good."

"Wait. Wait. You wanted me to kill her." Chris reminded her.

"Wizard's don't kill. Most people kill at least once, but you didn't, so I don't have to lecture you. Now, we need to go. I need you to say goodbye to your friends." Victoria explained.

"What?! Just like that? No way are you gonna just do all this voodoo crap and then abduct our friend!" Jackie said, slightly outraged.

"Jackie..." Chris began. "She knows where my sister is. I have to go." Jackie paused and looked at him, slightly peeved.

"Fine, but if you don't come back, I'll come find you and take you down a few." Chris looked at Ty, who just nodded and took Jackie by the arm.

"Hey, Chris! Wait!" Jackie called to Chris. "You...stay alive okay? I don't want to find out someone like that got the better of you...kick butt! And save lives! Be good!" Ty began to pull Jackie again. "Don't do drugs and don't abuse your power!" They too disappeared after a while.

Chris looked at Victoria who just smirked and commented on how strange Jackie is compared to Ty. Chris agreed, but explained that she was the first one there for him when no one else was.

Victoria looked at Chris and took his arm. She explained that she would need to teleport them, because that is the fastest way to get back to Terminus. She left a teleport code, and thus she can use her magic to teleport if she remembered it. She only needed to get them into the sky and out of sight so no one would see them vanish and panic. Chris agreed. Victoria waved her hand in front of the sky and a broom flew from the school's direction. Victoria must have stashed it somewhere. The broom hovered in front of him. Victoria mounted her magic broom and looked at Chris.

"Aren't you getting on?" She asked kindly.

"Is it safe?" he questioned anxiously.

"I forgot you're an Earthling and you're new to this...I'm sorry," she laughed slightly. "Yes, it is definitely safe, but if you're scared, hold onto me. You'll love what you see."

Chris got on behind Victoria and sat down carefully. It felt awkward for him and he could not imagine flying like this for long periods of time. He wrapped his arms around Victoria and they began to ascend. It only took a few moments for her to begin flying full speed at the sky. He held on tighter, deeply afraid to fall; he hated heights. He could feel his stomach turning and his heart dropping the faster and higher they went. His eyes were shut tight throughout the entire process.

"Hey...Are your eyes closed? Open them." She told him over the wind. She slowed the broom to a gentle flight.

Chris opened his eyes and sat himself up slightly. They were just below the cloud cover, and down below he could see the lights filling the night. Buildings, cars, signs, everything, all from a skyward view. He felt his jaw drop, he had never been on a plane and rarely got to leave his hometown. To Chris, this was indeed the most breathtaking view he had ever seen.

"When I first came to this planet," Victoria began over the wind. "I had to take in the view...although, the pollution and violence is ridiculous...I can't deny that view," she smiled. "You have a nice planet."

"Yeah...yeah, I guess I do." Chris agreed as she flew them up into the clouds.

Chris caught his final glimpses of his home, his school, and the hospital where he was born. It all vanished as they passed through the clouds. Victoria reached out and let her hand scrape the clouds, and so naturally, Chris did too. It was cold, and although it was somewhat wet, it felt good to him, and then he remembered a dream from his childhood that had followed him for years.

"You've never flown before?" She asked him.

Chris was not listening anymore, this had always been his dream. To take to the sky, but he had never imagined that when he did, he would be leaving everything behind to find something new. He had never imagined that he, of all people, was special. Why did the thought of leaving make him slightly...sad?

"Have you said your goodbyes to this place?" Victoria's voice came again over the whistle and howl of the wind.

"I'm...not sure if I'll be able to let it go despite how much I hated being alone. Mom, dad, Emily, Jackie, and Ty...we all shared memories here and I'm unsure if I'll come back...If I'll ever *want* to. It's strange," he admitted. "I feel relieved and-"

"Scared." she concluded. "I get it...You remind me of my sister that way, but I'll tell you this...Terminus is so worth it, *and* to me, the view is more beautiful. You'll see."

They flew a while longer before they were now out of the clouds. He saw nothing but the moon saying farewell, the stars shining as bright as before, and the city limits below them. Behind him, he could see his home. His old home. Victoria's words echoed in the back of his mind...that Terminus is worth it and seeing his sister again...and he thought to himself...reminded himself, that being a family was worth it too.

Victoria looked back at Chris, "Time to see your new home. Ready?"

"I... honestly don't know if I am," he held onto her tighter. "It's been a crazy day already." he hesitated as he said this.

Victoria smiled and laughed softly, "By the way...that password...You'll never believe what I decided it to be because of your sister. It might put you at ease."

"What?" Chris inquired.

"Trust me." She said, focusing her attention forward as they teleported, vanishing into thin air and ripples of reality.

5

THE GIRL FROM THE DREAM

As they appeared over the green forests and plains, there was the occasional lake or body of water. Chris thought he saw animals from up above, but he wasn't sure. Here, it was day, and even though it was a different sun, it felt so welcoming and warm. Despite flying for what seemed like forever, there was no city yet. Chris began to wonder if they were off course, but Victoria told him that she made sure they were farther so they would not fly directly into a building. He did not mind the view, though it was undeniable that most of this planet had clearly not been touched by anything but nature, and at most, had been explored. It was so... tranquil.

It appeared to be almost sunset in the city since the horizon was slowly becoming an orange color. In the distance, Chris could see a city with somewhat tall buildings. One of the many buildings was a clocktower. From a distance, the city was large. There was a village to the right of the city, it was not as close, but there appeared to be a lake between them. There were no structures beyond the city or the village, the rest were plains, and beyond the plains were forests.

Victoria flew lower to the ground and toward an area filled with shops and people. As she lowered them, she took care not to land on anyone, but it was easy since they stayed out of her way. They both dismounted and she took a moment before she took his arm and began to take him along the street. The ground appeared to be cobblestone. The buildings on this part of town were not as high, but shops littered the area.

Here, there were people just like on Earth, but cleaner. They seemed friendlier to one another, sometimes waving as they passed. He also noticed things like cat-people, aliens (at least they were to him), and so many different species and races. There were individuals in robes, colored outfits, military-esque attire, guards patrolling streets, children, and he thought he saw a few pilots.

She was taking him to a large building. There were two guards all dressed in red with a bit of armor. The guards that did not wear armor, carried swords on their person or some other form of melee weapon. This appeared to be a heavily guarded area, however, upon seeing Victoria, the soldiers stepped aside and let them pass. It was a grassy area with the large building dead center, completely surrounded by a wall, but it did not make the area seem unpleasant. Victoria approached the black and red door and knocked lightly before the door was opened by a girl with red hair, green eyes, and a large smile. She also wore an orange jacket, a dark grey tank top, black skinny jeans, and brown ankle boots. She had a big smile and seemed to be expecting them.

"Oh, thank goodness you've arrived! Ever since he left it's been chaos and I was about to put Chris' file to the side and probably lose it!" She said to Victoria as she handed Chris his file.

"Please don't lose that, just go over to that desk and sign some things where the red markers are!"

"She seems...stressed and... worked up," Chris whispered to Victoria. "Who is 'he'?"

"The headmaster has been gone for a while on peace talks and relief efforts. You see, this is also a school where all students learn how to use magic. You can work a normal job, or join the military force, which isn't currently mobilized at all. Your sister is under General Nick's command...actually, she is one of the higher ups like me." Victoria explained. "It's really a lot to explain and it'll give you a headache. Just sign, okay?" She advised.

"I'm not signing my soul away for something you don't explain." Chris protested.

Autumn was about to say something, but before she could, a voice spoke.

"Is someone here?" the female voice asked. "Tori? Is that you? Give me one second, I'm just in the library."

"Who is that?" Chris asked, somewhat recognizing the voice. "Is it her?" Chris turned himself to look at Victoria.

Victoria shrugged and smiled. Chris rolled his eyes as she began to laugh. Emily came out of the large brown doors to the right of the room. She wore a black sheer t-shirt, black jeans, and white and red shoes. She was carrying brown folders, but she nearly dropped them all upon seeing Chris. After quickly placing it all on the shelf against the back wall, she ran up and hugged him. He hugged her back, but something was slightly bothering him. She let him go and held him by his shoulders.

"I've missed you so much. You got taller and your voice sounds so different..." She commented as she looked him up and down. "It's so good to see you again..."

"People do tend to look different when you haven't seen them for a year or more. Especially family, he muttered after her remark.

"Yeah, but...here you are. I know it's weird seeing me-"

"Alive and after more than a year, yeah."

"You seem mad."

"No. So what exactly is this place?" He quickly and skillfully dodged her last comment to avoid anything that might have followed.

Emily seemed slightly hurt, but she began to explain. She told him about the Alliance of the Light and the Empire of the Dark, who they could be at war with soon.

"The Alliance has a school here to train students and magic-sensitive individuals to properly use the powers they were born with. You probably know by now we have a military of magic users and soldiers? It is the job of a Wizard to protect anyone we can and serve the Alliance, myself included. The Terminus Academy has been teaching people about Partners, never to kill unless necessary, tactics, and everything you would need to know. It is rare to enter the military at your age...unless..." She paused and clearly skipped over something, "You don't need to know that. I'm not letting you join at this age."

"Why? You dragged me all the way here, didn't you?" Chris pointed out angrily. "Without explanation why you left."

"I was needed because the conflicts between Sorcerers and Wizards...the Empire and Alliance have been escalating...and soon we do believe it will be war." She admitted. "I had no choice...they told me Earth would be in danger...so I joined up in the military to protect you and our home...But I would have been told to join them regardless."

"And you couldn't tell me?"

"There was no time and Earth does not take kindly to either side. They prefer to stay neutral. I couldn't-"

"Dammit, Emily that's not the point!" Chris exploded. "I thought you were dead!"

The room went silent. Victoria made a move to calm Chris, but Emily held up her hand to tell her to stay. She nodded and left with Autumn to the library and shut the door.

"Do you even realize how long you were gone?" he asked. "Go ahead, tell me."

"Three..." She replied quietly.

"You don't even know!? Emily, it was almost two. The last time you saw me was when I was-" He continued.

"When you were eleven..." She answered. "It felt like three years being apart from you...believe me, I wanted to see you again."

"...Just keep explaining."

Emily paused a moment and regained her composure. She seemed a little bit shaken and uneasy, "Once you sign those papers, you can begin your classes and eventually be assigned a partner...classes are simply about combat and magic...and I'll give you a bit of Lumen to make sure you have a little money...you get a steady income as long as you are a student..."

"Stop." He finally said. "I missed you, yeah, and I'm glad to see you, but I just...really need time to breath and think it all over."

Chris moved over to the desk with his folder and signed everywhere he needed to. Inside of the manila folder, he also found a dorm key with a number. Emily made a move to stop him, but he had already left the building and proceeded on his way. He made his way back down the steps of the building and ran as fast as he could past the guards and into the crowd with his key in hand. He didn't know where he was going, but for some reason he wanted to get away from Emily. He felt so much anger directed only at her, and he knew he didn't want to take it out on her. So why did he?

Chris stopped in an area of town unfamiliar to him, there was a small park to his left and to his right was a set of homes. Then it occurred to him that he had gotten himself lost. He looked around a moment for help and noticed a girl with long black hair, a black top, a black skirt, black gloves, and although she didn't have any weapons, he could tell she was a Wizard. Chris quickly ran up to speak to her, managing to grab her arm lightly before she proceeded.

"Excuse me?" He inquired. Somehow he felt he recognized her, but why did he approach her so easily?

She turned to face him, looking curious and uncaring all at once. She didn't really have an expression.

"Why did you grab my arm?" She asked.

"I'm lost." He admitted.

"Why did you ask me?" She asked in a slightly annoyed manner. "Why not anyone else?"

"Well...I'm new and you seemed nice..." he admitted, internally reevaluating that opinion.

"Oh...well why not just say you are new?" she asked, calmer. She immediately withdrew her question and continued on. She glanced up at his hair. "Emily's brother..." She said to herself.

"Yeah..." he muttered. "I'm looking for my dorm." He showed her the number.

The dorm was number 12,658. She raised her eyebrow for a moment at him before turning and leading the way. She took them through the many streets of town, explaining to him that he was very far from where he needed to go. She told him that his dorm is by the smallest park in the city with the least lights at night. It was toward the west side of town.

Chris thought she was very different than everyone else here...she seemed...detached and uncaring. He decided to try to close the distance a little.

"My name is-" He started.

"Chris," She said. "Emily talks about you a lot to Victoria."

"You know Tori?" he asked her. She ignored this, but she clearly heard him.

Chris made a mental note, *attempt to be friendly...attempt number two failed...attempt number three engaging...*

"So, what is your name?" he asked.

"I'm... trying to find your room. This is the area it's in. Actually, I live near here too so it works out." She dodged.

She began to count the numbers on the doors. The dorms were all side by side and were all around the city, according to her, but Chris wasn't sure how he felt about living near this girl. He noticed his dorm room number and went up to it.

"Well thanks for helping me...See you around." he said as he turned to unlock the door.

The girl said nothing, she had one hand on her hip and the other was rubbing her chin. Chris unlocked and opened the door. He noticed an unmade bed and a few female articles of clothing and items.

Chris was tackled to the ground by the girl. She held his throat with her left hand and held up her fist with the other. He began to blush, but he also got slightly startled.

"You have five seconds to explain yourself!"

"What do you mean?" he asked in a panic, looking for someone to help him.

"How did you get into my dorm?!" She asked.

"It's my dorm too!" he insisted. He was panicking now. "I swear!"

"Out with it!" she demanded.

"Seriously, I got this from a girl with red hair in the headmaster's office!"

The girl punched him anyway and put him into a daze. Everything got slightly disoriented for him for a moment.

"Tori?" He heard her ask without context for what was going on.

"Sis?? What did you-" he heard Victoria's voice too, she sounded panicked.

"He broke into my room." she said simply.

"Oh...you found out about that...Penny, he's your roommate." Victoria told her. "You didn't kill him, did you?"

"No. Not at all. Wait, he was telling the truth? I punched him for nothing? Oh..." Chris regained his vision slightly to see Victoria with her arms folded.

"Good. You are going to stay with him until he wakes up." Victoria told Penny.

"No way, he's no help to me and he's a boy in my room."

"He's Emily's little brother." Victoria pleaded.

"He's going to take part of my room," Penny replied. They began to argue by now.

"You're staying with him until he wakes up."

"Or...I could just leave him."

"I'm your older sister, so I make the decisions here," Victoria pleaded. "He's a new student and my friend!"

"He was weak enough to get knocked out by a punch!" Penny said, raising her voice, but using the same emotionless voice.

I'm going to hate this place, aren't I? Chris thought to himself as he blacked out.

<hr />

When Chris woke up, he saw beautiful, brown eyes staring back at him. He felt comfortable, unsure where he was. Penny stared down at him as he stared up at her, he rubbed his head.

"Are you okay?" she asked quietly. "I'm sorry...I didn't know you had the same room..."

"I thought I heard Tori say you were supposed to watch me anyway?" he asked.

"Um...Well yes...but...You seemed uncomfortable, so I held you in my lap all this time." She admitted as he sat up and got up. "Are you mad?"

"After today, I don't think anything bothers me. Your name is Penny, right? Couldn't you just say that instead of attacking me?"

Penny hid her face in her hair before once again looking back at

Chris and opening her mouth again to say something and then once again closing it.

She finally decided on her words and spoke, "I didn't think it would be important to know my name and it's not exactly a pretty name to me. Maybe on my sister, but even the last name is a bit much. Let me make it up to you. There are shows at a place we call the Dome and I think you'd like it. It's free every night they do it, so let's do that once you get settled in."

Chris blushed once again and shook his head, *she would be cute if she didn't try to kill me.*

"Yeah, just let me get settled in," he agreed. "I don't have my stuff-"

"That's what Victoria was doing...She teleported them for you, your clothes and everything else you need. I don't think everything came, mostly everything important," she told him as she pointed at the door. "Emily probably got the rest."

When Chris entered, he saw a room with tan walls. On the left side there was a bed with dark purple sheets. The room had been cleaned up on the right side, so it was empty besides Chris' things: a few pictures, blue bed sheets made up nicely like Penny's bed. The bathroom was to the far left, and a small kitchen to the right side.

"I cleaned everything up and set up your side for you. It's my way of saying sorry." Penny lowered her head a little and looked away slightly.

"Well, because you did, we can go. Just give me a moment," he told her as he entered the bathroom and shut the door.

He took a deep breath and leaned over the sink, splashing his face with water and looking into the mirror. So far, in the span of two days, he has won an impossible dodgeball game, climbed a wall faster than everyone but a magic user, survived a Sorcerer attack, and beat a Sorcerer. After recovering his sanity, he went off with Penny.

Penny showed Chris the parts of the town on their way to the

Dome. They didn't get to see much, but she showed him the shopping district, the outdoor market, a few restaurants, other dorms, weapon shops, potion shops, and many other things. Chris asked Penny along the way what type of magic he might have. She told him he would find out later and that she has no clue. She explained that she was a necromancer.

They approached the Dome. It was massive with a large entrance, and according to Penny, there were more ways in. It was getting dark by now, and as they went up the steps and into the Dome, it became clear that it was even darker inside. In the center of the walkway, there was a subtle light just bright enough to be noticeable. They could hear a crowd by now, and as they entered, he could see a large stage in the center of the structure, and it seemed like it was about to start. He saw a girl with lightly colored lavender hair that was currently in a messy bun with curly strands on both sides. Her one-piece pilot outfit was a black with a blue phoenix symbol on the right-side arm. She held a pilot helmet under her right arm and waved with her left.

Chris moved forward, but he did not yet take a seat. Every light focused on this girl. She was standing in the center with three other pilots wearing the same outfits with different color visors. She appeared to be the leader.

"Violet Fleur has had fifty confirmed kills and over one hundred completed missions including escort, patrol, combat, and infiltration! She is the best pilot in the Alliance," announced an enthusiastic voice over the microphone. All the while, Violet blew kisses at the crowd and waved more as the pilots behind her stood there at attention and looked about the room and observed their audience. Chris watched as the girl continued to absorb the attention like a sponge.

"Violet, do you have any words for the crowd?" asked the voice.

Finally, a man wearing a blue suit stepped on stage and handed her the microphone. Violet took it and spoke as if she had done this before, or as if it was something she enjoyed dearly.

"We're gonna show the Empire what we're really made of! Everyone here knows a Wizard will always be better than a Sorcerer. You protect, you fight, you serve, you heal, what don't you do besides kill?" she raised her fist as the crowd began to cheer. She spoke louder to overpower them.

"So, I'm here to tell you those no good lousy wannabe's have nothing on you! If they do try anything, we'll go get 'em, bring back that victory, and show them they have no business near our homes!" She cried. The crowd went up in an uproar.

"So, that said, who wants to see their Mages!" The audience went up in an uproar.

Eight figures walked out onto the stage. One was Victoria, another one was a pink haired girl, a boy with short black hair, a girl with curly dark brown hair, a tall boy with blonde hair, a girl with red hair, a girl with blue skin and white hair, and a girl with long brown hair.

Chris looked back to see where Penny was, but she was just leaning on one of the walls back where they came with her left foot against the wall. She was clearly trying to ignore the whole thing and Chris could tell she was hating every second. He approached her, wondering why she hated this so much; she brought him here to make up for what happened when they met.

"Hey. Penny? We should go, I'm hungry and this isn't interesting to me," was the excuse he used.

"Really? We just got here, but alright. Let's go then." she agreed as they left and headed back out and toward the main town.

"Be honest...You have no money."

"No, my sister didn't get the chance to...I was kind of mad at her." Chris told her honestly.

"Gotcha, well I'll pay. I know a good restaurant...it's an outdoor one on the edge of town. It's actually slightly out of town and they serve all kinds of things there. It is Mexican themed, and so they have things from Earth apparently, like tacos. They just recently increased their menu."

Chris was intrigued now at hearing there were things from Earth here, "What's the name?"

"Las Estrellas. The Stars."

Chris thought this name sounded perfect for an outdoor restaurant. He did very much want to go there, but he did feel bad for making Penny pay. She may have been making it up to him, but he wasn't sure how much this would all cost.

"I wish I could help you with the costs. I know you offered, but it is your money." Chris told her as they walked along the pathway.

"No, it's alright. It's nice to have someone to eat with. When Victoria was away trying to get you, I was alone for like a month. So, I'm glad, actually. What about you?" she replied in a softer tone. She seemed sedated compared to her behavior earlier.

"I was alone on Earth for almost two years thinking that was my life. I get what you mean."

It was mostly empty outside. Most everyone was at the Dome, at home, or out eating. The few people remaining out on the streets were heading somewhere, or even out just for a stroll. Chris noticed the lights coming on in the city, they were beautiful and breathtaking. As the night grew darker, he noticed their many bright colors. They were not too bright, but just enough so you could see where you were going, and even better, you could admire them. As they proceeded down the steps, he noticed a bright area in an area slightly outside of town.

Chris noticed that here, the moon was very similar to the one on Earth, but it did not appear to have any craters at this time. The nights here didn't seem as dark because of the lights, but he could tell. If it weren't for them, it would be darker than Earth's nights. Penny explained that when she came to Terminus, she felt she didn't understand why the Wizards and citizens were so happy, but she felt that this world was very appealing. There was something about it that attracted you to it one way or another, if you belonged here, or if you didn't.

"Why is the military not assembled?" Chris found himself asking. "To protect all of this, I mean."

"It's not that it isn't assembled, it's an alliance. Yes, we have a military, and trained soldiers are all over the city. There just simply isn't a reason to go to war. Most of the Light Realm is all Alliance Territory minus small independent pockets of space," she began. "Okay, so like me, I'm a Wizard and instead of doing whatever else, I chose to be a soldier."

Chris stopped and rubbed the back of his head, "You don't look much like a soldier. You honestly look normal," he noted as he looked her up and down. Penny just seemed like a normal girl to Chris, he had never seen a soldier not in full combat gear and wielding a firearm.

"I would say you're not very bright, but you're new and from Earth where you don't see Wizards so I'll explain. Wizards are the field generals and commanders of our military. Sometimes we are higher-up generals, but most are simply above soldiers. So, when you first start, you'll be no higher than a soldier. You work your way up, but you can take and distribute orders, and you are usually in the front." This confused Chris more, but Penny continued.

"Basically, we are specialists."

"Okay...but why no combat gear?" Chris asked, looking at her strangely. Penny sighed slightly, seeing that she would have to explain everything, and on one of the many steps, Chris sat beside her.

"Wizards don't need it. It would only slow us down, and unless you are trying to make yourself durable and tanky, you wouldn't even wear armor. I have a friend that does and he only does so he can go quickly from one fight to another," she continued again.

"Wizards have fast healing. You probably never saw my sister get hurt, right? But if any of us did, our fast healing could help us. So long as we don't bleed too much, it can help...it just has to keep up. If you didn't have fast healing, I might have put you in the hospital...and honestly I'm glad you do or I would have felt bad."

Penny explained that fast healing does not hurt, but it takes mana. She described mana as a form of energy inside of the body.

"It is a second stream in your body, similar to blood. It flows all over your body and allows us to cast spells and manipulate the environment. You have some too, it's clear so you can't see it even if you are bleeding, but without it you'll feel weak. You'll get cold, and it'll feel like you can't hold your hands still or move the rest of your body," Penny noted this as if from personal experience.

"Your fast healing uses up a good bit to heal you, and it comes back, but it takes time. If your fast healing doesn't have enough mana you'll just bleed like any other normal person would."

"I'm not planning on getting into a situation where I'm bleeding."

"You want to stay in the confines of the city?" she asked.

"Well...why would I leave?" he asked.

"I don't know...I feel like I have an obligation to join the fighting force, and I know the Empire will declare war one day...I'm ready, but I wish that day wouldn't come." Penny lightly clenched her hand into a fist and stared at the feet as if she was in deep thought.

"An obligation?" he asked. Penny tensed up. "Too much information?"

"Too much information for when I just met you." She replied. She stood and pulled him to his feet and they continued on their way.

They walked out of the main town and continued along a path of lights and stones. Chris had so many questions on his mind, but he didn't want to overwhelm Penny. He debated if he should consider her a friend, he assumed they were, but what was he to her, he wondered. He could see it now. The restaurant had square tables, wooden chairs, there was also a bar to the right and to the left there was a pit for roasting things. There were waiters that wore blue with white aprons and they cooked the food to the right near the bar.

The restaurant seemed very busy tonight. Penny figured it might be because it is such a clear and beautiful night. However, there were so many tables it hardly mattered. They took a seat at a brown table with a red and black checker pattern on the top. He sat across from her. Penny was simply patiently waiting, but he couldn't help but look around. Chris noticed three guards eating at a table on the far left talking and enjoying themselves. He could hear them from here erupting into laughter at their captain's jokes. The captain was the only guard to wear blue markings on his red attire and sat across from the other two. These guards were clearly off duty or on break, and their weapons lie beside them. A halberd, a firearm that appeared to be a rifle, and a two-handed sword.

"Penny?"

"Yes?"

"What would it be like if I did choose to fight?" he questioned.

"It's dangerous, but you get the right training. Everyone gets training, you'd just apply it and you'd be closer to your sister. You'll get a partner who's linked to your soul, mind, and body, but who knows? I'm hoping I get a good partner, but I don't know..."

"Maybe I'll get you." he interjected.

"That is a possibility actually, yeah. I could probably keep you alive, but you gotta hold your own," she replied briefly.

"I know that, but I think I could be useful...or I hope so."

There was a small crashing noise to his right, like something fell. Chris imagined that it was probably a mistake. There was a louder crash and then a table flipped into the air. All three guards grabbed their weapons and moved to investigate. Penny stood up.

"Where are you going?" Chris asked, entirely confused.

"To help," Penny made it sound like it was obvious.

"Isn't that dangerous?"

"Probably, but it's a Wizard's job, and that means it's your job too. Come on before someone gets hurt."

"But I don't have a weapon and neither do you!" Chris insisted.

Penny summoned a small round blue shield with the Alliance symbol painted on in yellow onto her left arm; its wings stretched proudly to both edges. The shield was only big enough to cover her arm, and she wore the strap on her forearm. The shield was not small enough to be a buckler, but not large enough to be a full body barrier. In her right hand, she held a small sword, only about the length of her full arm. The sword had a blue hilt, and a very clean blade. She handed him the sword and beckoned him to follow her.

"Wait, how will you fight if I have this?" He questioned.

"I have my shield, it wouldn't be the first time I had to fight without that." She declared as she ran off toward the danger.

Chris ran after her and held the sword tightly in his right hand. It was smaller than the last sword he held...or imagined holding, apparently, but it would do. Multiple civilians were tripping over each other to get away; Chris never imagined that he would be the one running toward danger.

There were no less than five grey wolves moving into the zone. Each one was growling and looking as if wanting a fight. Each of the city guards stood their ground to prevent them from moving further. Penny ran in immediately and blocked a wolf that was heading for the guard with the Halberd, and then quickly spun around to smack it away. The guard with the rifle continued to fire, but the bullets only staggered their targets.

"Sir! Look! Wizards!" Cried one of the guards on the right with the sword.

"Won't be the last time you see one, rookie! Focus!" the captain ordered. "New guys..."

Penny blocked a wolf lunging at her, tossing it over her head with both of her arms and blocking another attack with her shield. Chris joined her and began to attack. He was able to injure two wolves that backed off and began to pace in the back while the other three continued to attack. The guards stayed behind them to make sure nothing would get past them.

Chris felt a sharp pain on his left leg, and for a moment, his leg went numb before he felt himself being dragged by a wolf. One of the pack members that had previously backed off had taken the opportunity to bite his leg and try to drag him away. Chris tried swinging the sword at it to free himself or even scare it off, but the sword was so short that the creature simply didn't care enough to even glance up at him.

Penny's shield came flying through the air, crashed into the wolf, knocked it unconscious, and caused it to fall over onto its right side. The shield returned to Penny as she was running over to where Chris was. She extended her free hand and pulled him up.

"You're worrying me." She told him. "Are you okay at least?"

"I'm fine...just stings," He insisted as he got up to his feet and continued to fight.

One of the guards was now on the ground attempting to throw a wolf off of his torso, it was attempting to bite his face. Chris quickly ran over and stabbed it through the back, pressing all of his strength down on one attack. It fell over, but it was not dead, just immobile.

The other three wolves ran off toward the woods and vanished into the darkness of the night, leaving their fallen behind. The guard was helped to his feet by Chris.

"They just ran...we never get wolf attacks much. Did you see how fast they moved?" The captain remarked. "Wolves don't do that. Not even here."

"They seemed tampered with." Penny decided.

As she said this, a teacher wearing white and green approached. She had greying hair and a slightly wrinkled face. With her was a young man about Emily's age with red hair, and a black colored outfit with art to resemble embers.

"Oh dear. Are any alive?" She questioned.

"Both alive, Ma'am. These two Wizards fought them off. We couldn't have done much on our own." He began to give an account.

The boy approached Chris and stared at him for a moment before giving him a slight face.

"Who are you? Did you dye your hair or something?" He questioned.

"No. I'm Chris, nice to meet you." Chris told him as they shook hands.

"Hunter? Did you see all of that?" Penny asked him. "Those wolves weren't normal."

"We got the alert just when it happened. You wouldn't believe how fast some of these civilians ran to the guard station and the Wizard schools just to get help. I'd say at least half." He sighed. "I'd say good job, but it'd get old since you're used to this, Penny."

Penny pointed slightly at Chris with her eyes, "He's new. Actually, he did well. He almost got himself killed, but he still did impress me." She admitted. "I'm thinking I'll train him...maybe. Or I can leave him to you."

"I swear he reminds me of Emily. You wouldn't happen to be her little brother, would you?" He guessed. Chris nodded. "I see."

"Hunter!" The teacher cried. "Hunter! Come over here! Help me transport these creatures to the hospital for study, inform any available experienced life Wizard. I'm going to heal them first."

"Yes Ms. Sapovitts," Hunter replied as he took up one of the wolves and began to leave. "Ciao."

Chris watched Hunter and the teacher leave, and as he turned back to where Penny was, he noticed she was gone. She was over with the manager of the restaurant who was thanking her and shaking her hand rapidly. Penny didn't really react and Chris didn't hear much. As they were leaving the restaurant, Penny explained that they were allowed to eat at Las Estrellas anytime they wanted, for free with their friends, if they liked.

After their brief encounter at the restaurant, the two decided to relax in one of the parks for a while. Penny seemed relaxed like nothing happened, but Chris seemed very tense. He kept rolling up his bloody, torn, pants leg only to see time and time again that the wounds had gone and his skin had healed. Penny glanced over at Chris curiously.

"Did you not believe me when I said you could heal rapidly?" She asked him.

"I did, I just figured it would...hurt...like stitches would." He explained. "I don't even remember it healing. It did feel tingly briefly."

"You did a good job back there, even though I had to save you...You need to watch your back. It's not all about just swinging."

"Hey!" Chris interrupted her, slightly bugged. "I did try! I mean... I don't know how to fight. The most I ever did was beat a Sorcerer in the imagination realm."

"And that is impressive, but nothing if you can't watch yourself," she pointed out.

They both stared off into the water in silence. Chris picked up a rock and skipped it across the water. It skipped halfway and sunk into the pond. Penny looked at him curiously and grabbed a rock and attempted the same; it sank to the bottom of the pond immediately. She sighed softly under her breath and pointed at the water.

"Watch this. In a few seconds that pond is going to light up. I think it's dark enough." Penny told him, she sounded fairly excited.

Chris watched the water for a moment, when all of a sudden, the water lit up a bright blue color, shimmering and shining. Penny explained that this was magic inside of the water that would show brightly at night. It was beautiful to him, but Penny just stared at it, as if she was in deep thought. Chris looked at her curiously and wondered just what was up with this girl. As Penny looked at the body of water, Chris thought he saw her glance over at him and then look back. Perhaps she was wondering about him too.

6

PENNY DREADFUL

The next morning, Chris began to wake up as Penny shook him lightly. He opened his eyes to see her brown eyes staring down at him. She was telling him to wake up. Chris sat up and scratched his head. He was not yet fully awake and was not used to waking up so early (or at least it felt early to him).

"We are training you today. Not on magic just yet, but simple sword fighting," Penny informed him.

"Why so early?" He asked. "Couldn't this have waited-"

"You need to get used to waking up early. I got you food, but it's probably cold now because you woke up so late. I couldn't get you up the past few times and I was about to pour water on you."

"Thank you for not doing that, I guess. Did you at least wait to eat with me?" He asked, however Penny's expression said otherwise. "Okay."

There was a small red and white box with rice. He found it strange that she had gotten rice boxes so early in the morning, but she told him she did not feel like getting anything farther. He simply assumed she wanted it. He began to eat, but he found it slightly difficult because he had so many questions. Last night he could not sleep until much later, he was wondering about everything he had learned the day before and fighting Gatchi, and he still knew nothing about magic. Sure, he would learn how to fight, but where would that get him?

He asked himself why he was here...he chose to come to see his sister of course, but he felt so angry at her, and in turn angry at himself for coming. She had hidden so much from him, but he was still glad she was okay. There was so much on his mind, in fact, that he had given himself a major headache.

Penny was already dressed for the day. She wore a similar outfit to yesterday, however this time she wore a navy-blue belt.

Chris ate his food. As Penny warned him, it was cold, but he couldn't do anything about that. He needed to eat, according to her, to keep his strength up. She also explained that he would probably be worn out and sore. As he listened to all of this, he began to wonder just how long she had been doing this. However, he could not wonder about this long as her voice interrupted him.

"Ready to go?" She asked. "Come on ,hurry and get dressed. You need to get in the habit of getting up early." she left the room. "I'll be back."

Chris got dressed in the bathroom, wanting to avoid an awkward situation if she came back into the bedroom area. He didn't know what he was going to be doing, so he got dressed in jeans, a blue t-shirt, and a light blue jacket. He stepped out and there was Penny holding a sword, but it clearly wasn't hers. It was much longer and reminded him of the imaginary one he wielded when he had fought Gatchi.

"Why the jacket?"

"I usually wear a jacket." he told her. "What's wrong with it?"

"Why?" she asked bewildered.

"I just do- Style, I guess."

"Style won't keep you alive unless you're a model," Penny scolded. "Wait, you're not a model, are you?"

"No way." he laughed as he removed the jacket, threw it on the bed, and followed her out, closing the door behind them and locking it.

They made their way through the city and toward the steps that led to Las Estrellas. She stopped walking and leaned against the wall.

"What are you-" Chris stared at her.

"Thirty laps up and down the stairs," she said. "You need to get warmed up, and it isn't that many stairs."

"What?" He was dumbfounded. She was serious and showed no sign of joking. "There are like twenty or more stairs, Penny. I'm just starting out, isn't that a bit much?" He pleaded.

"That's very true." She agreed. "I'll shave off half then-fifteen laps."

"Less than fifteen!" He tried again. "No way, my lungs will give out!"

"Actually, as a magic user you have more stamina, ability, and if all else fails you could use mana... once you learn how to." she smirked. "Come on, don't you wanna impress me?"

"Penny."

"Chris."

He groaned and proceeded to run the fifteen laps. On the fourth lap, he was panting, and by the tenth, he was struggling to catch his breath. Penny watched and said nothing the whole time. If he started to give up, walked, or slowed from his starting pace, she would threaten to add a lap. In the end, he ended up doing nineteen laps.

When he got to the top of the stairs again, Penny was there with a bottle of water. He had not seen her leave to go get it, but he was too tired to have been paying attention when she did. She gave it to him and giggled slightly. *Is she laughing at me?*

"Don't look so tired, this was nothing. If that was a life or death situation, you would have lived," she punched his arm lightly. "Trust me, the first time I ever did something like that was on a mountain with my mother and my sister."

"Isn't that extreme?" he groaned.

"No, the extreme part was falling down halfway, waiting to fast heal, and even though mom said to stop, I just got up and made it to the top anyway."

She sat there with him until he caught his breath and relaxed even slightly. She made him stretch and then led him over to the training area of the city. There were training dummies, multiple training courses, stands to watch that were currently empty, a shooting range (for magic of course), and much more that he didn't get to see. They were here to meet Hunter, Penny thought he would be a better teacher.

Penny handed Chris the sword from earlier, "Emily told me to give that to you."

"Emily?" he blinked. "Why?"

"Yeah, she got it for you, I guess she figured it would fit you. I ran into her when I stepped out. She's not in the city right now, she's on a mission." She explained.

"What kind of mission?"

"The same kind my sister was on. It won't take as long though, it's only to Iotis...That planet has all kinds of issues, but if anyone could handle it-"

"Wait, why was I harder? If that planet is having issues, I mean..." he asked curiously.

Penny stopped walking and thought for a moment and folded her arms. "I was going to say this nicely, but I'll just say it outright. Your planet's governments suck."

"It does," Hunter agreed, having overheard this conversation. "Your government won't let us protect them even after what happened in Japan-or at least what is left of Japan."

"Pretty much. They don't trust magic users...us or the Empire... the Sorcerers.... No one can get them to listen. We asked them nicely, they said no to both sides." Penny continued on.

"But the Imperials didn't take no for an answer and sent Sorcerers to attack. Your government probably told you Japan was just an accident or a disease...whatever...but that's them covering their mistake."

"But then why? Why not tell the people?" Chris asked. Hunter brandished his sword and stared at it for a moment, debating how to answer. "I mean, that would make it so at least they know."

"They dug themselves in a hole and they don't know what to do, so now they're neutral and trying to basically keep the people in the dark while also defending themselves. It's stupid if you ask me. Picking a side is always better than staying neutral and being caught in the middle. Now they're down a country and still won't listen." he told Chris.

"That doesn't answer my question." Chris said. "Why won't they tell them?"

"They want Earth to be away from the conflict when this all boils over, and your government has always been secretive." he replied again, looking at Chris through the side of his eye. "Since forever, right?"

Chris looked down and took a moment to process this, but before he could, Hunter's blade came dangerously close to his neck.

"Your reflexes are terrible." He said. Penny stepped back and sat in the stands just watching.

"I wasn't ready!" Chris replied, outraged.

"You wouldn't have had a chance to make that excuse if that had landed. I doubt you could have spoken without covering up your neck." He said harshly. "Try again."

Hunter drew back his sword and swung again. Chris quickly brought up his own, blocking it, but as he did, Hunter's elbow came quickly into his forehead. He felt a sudden and extreme pain on his forehead, almost dizzy for a moment. He fell to all fours, but got up, using the sword to lift himself up.

Hunter circled him slowly, "Watch my movements."

"I am." Chris shot back.

"Okay, show me then."

He swung at Chris' knee. Chris parried the blow by holding his sword vertically and swung at Hunter who merely dodged to the left and tripped him so he fell on his back. He held the sword again to his neck.

"Overconfident." He muttered. "It's gonna get you killed."

Chris pushed his sword away and began to swing at him again, but during his third swing, he felt a sudden searing pain on his arm. Hunter had grabbed his arm and burned him with his Fire magic. Chris screamed out in pain and staggered back. Hunter kicked him back hard in the gut, Chris fell over and curled up.

"Over choreographed," Hunter paused for a moment and brandished his sword. "Hard to believe you're related to my ex." He said to Chris. "Can you still get up?"

Chris heard himself saying no, but he still stood anyway, almost falling over. From the corner of his eye, he could see Penny getting up and leaving the stands.

"You can't go on like that. You can give up." He said. "No shame in losing. Just know you would have died, and it would have been pathet-" Chris attempted to jab his blade at Hunter. Hunter stepped back in surprise, narrowly dodging.

"You talk too much." Chris said through gritted teeth.

He was breathing heavily, and he could feel his fast healing helping him out. The pain was slowly dying away. Hunter smiled and began to collide swords with his opponent.

"You're easy to push over the edge. I wonder how long it will be until you lose control." Hunter wondered aloud.

"--op it..." Chris' voice came, shaky, panting, and only slightly audible.

Hunter slashed Chris across his face and let him fall. He stared down at Chris calmly.

"At least Emily is useful. I can tell you'll be a deadweight. You don't even realize how much of a burden you are on her."

"-op it..." he tried again, unable to fully speak anymore.

Chris swung his sword weakly at Hunter's feet, unable to see very well. The blood from his forehead was now trickling down toward his eyes. He half closed them to keep the blood from getting in them.

"Know when you're beaten, Spellcrafter." Hunter said simply as he swung downward.

There was a loud sound of metal colliding. Penny was in front of him, shield raised, blocking the blow entirely.

"I think I should train him," Penny walked closer to him, holding her ground. "That's my decision."

"He needs to learn the hard way, you know. After all, that's how you learned, isn't it?"

"That's not what he needs, and I know. I think it's best you go." She said calmly as she lowered her arm.

He looked at Chris for a moment and then left, ignoring the crowd that they had attracted.

Penny knelt down to Chris, "You can hear me, right?" To Chris, her voice was muffled. "Hang on, okay? Your fast healing is struggling to keep up."

The last thing Chris saw before he passed out was a girl in a white outfit and wizard hat, he did not get a good look at her. She had pink hair and she had asked what happened. As everything went black, Chris once again had a dream. This time, he saw fire everywhere, what looked like to be Penny lying face down on the ground, and two figures towering over them.

As he awoke, he shot up like a bullet, panting. Penny leapt back slightly in surprise, but stayed beside him. Realizing it was all a dream, he relaxed and laid on his back.

"Are you alright?" She asked. "I'm sorry I- well I-" she seemed almost in a panic. "I didn't know he would be so...rough. Do you feel better?"

"Yeah, but why did my fast healing not kick in?" he questioned.

"It failed, because you are not used to being so injured. The more you fight, the more your body will get used to fast healing. In fact, your body will start to use less mana when you heal, allowing you to do it more efficiently. So, one of two things happened...either you burned so much mana that you couldn't even fast heal...or it couldn't keep up and fell behind." She hypothesized.

"You saved me then?" he asked. "Thanks."

"You're welcome for saving you, but I can't save anyone...at least not by healing them. At most, Death magic can heal minds and give a temporary boost, but I can't heal you. You actually should thank Megan if you see her again."

Chris took a deep breath and sat up again, "I guess I suck at fighting, right?"

"No, you're new at it, but you're fast. You surprised the heck out of him when you went straight for him. Off guard or not, he barely got away." She smiled. "From now on, I'm training you and we'll start slow, and we won't train here. I want to go somewhere more private where you can relax."

"I didn't feel fast..." He admitted, "I felt helpless..."

Penny looked at him silently, and quietly. What was she supposed to say after all? It was her fault that happened to him.

"Let me make it up to you."

"You don't have to...I think I just need time to...I dunno...think." He said honestly as he got up and began to walk off.

"Wait! Won't you get lost on your own?" Penny pleaded. "Wait."

"I'll be fine..." he said as he left the training area.

7

COLD WAR

Chris wandered around the city aimlessly, his hands in his pockets. He just wanted space at the moment and he didn't care to make Penny feel worse for just trying to help him. He felt he would only get in the way and that if he couldn't even defend himself, he would die and possibly get other people killed in the process. He sat on a bench in front of a cafe, not knowing where he was, but wanting to sit and think.

How could he have fooled himself so easily? Gatchi was not trying to kill him or even injure him, only convince him to go with her or capture him. Victoria was the one she was trying to kill and they didn't seem to be pulling punches. If nothing else, Hunter taught him that he was indeed being too cocky, and that it would get him killed. If that had been a real battle, he would have died, possibly getting Penny killed too.

He felt where the burn was - healed and gone. The scars were gone, the pain was gone, and his face was unscathed. He dropped his arms and laid back, looking up at the passing clouds. He began to ask himself what Penny meant by having trained in a similar way and not wanting him to go through it. After all, she seemed so calm all of the time...except that one time the day before when she seemed angry during the show at the dome. She seemed like a great fighter, and she was different from everyone else.

His thoughts were interrupted by a male voice, "Man, you look bummed out."

The guy in front of him was wearing a brown collared shirt, dark blue jeans, and black sneakers. His short hair seemed freshly cut. He had what appeared to be green eyes, he had slight facial hair developing but not much unless he didn't want it to, and a slightly cocky smile.

"Yeah, man, I'm talking to you." he laughed. "You look like you got dumped, or lost a bet, or beat up." Chris sighed slightly.

"Oh okay, so it's the last one again," the male said again.

"Look, what is it?" Chris asked, slightly irritated already.

"Oh nothing, just being a good person and checking up on you like I was told." He admitted. "A girl with pink hair who is super bossy told me to check on you because she didn't have time."

"Pink hair?" Chris sat up. "Okay, so you know what happened?"

"Yup."

"What was her name?"

"Megan Fairyhorn...She's an Earthling, actually, from Japan...or what was Japan anyway."

"I wanted to thank her...I almost died."

"Nah, no one would have let you die. Trust me. At least not here. Elsewhere, they might just check your wallets."

"I know. I came from Earth too, but you knew that right? What's your name anyway?"

The guy thought for a moment and then put one foot on the bench and smirked, "You may call me the Presage or Harbinger of Death!" he announced triumphantly.

"No." Chris shook his head.

"Okay fine, then you can call me Ian...before you ask, no, I don't have a last name. Orphaned since I was born." He said casually. "And I am here to assist you!"

"...Okay. That's...different," Chris tilted his head curiously. "I need to get back to Penny. She's probably waiting at our dorm right now."

Ian laughed and wrapped his arm around Chris, "Buddy, you are lucky to be alive. She didn't even kill you."

Chris made a slight face, "I mean she did punch me."

"That doesn't surprise me. Penny was messed with pretty bad when she first came here, her sister too. They had to get used to it, but people warmed up to them and you know."

"Why?" Chris questioned. "They aren't different."

Ian smiled a little. "Man, I forgot you're from Earth, you're new, and you know nothing...It's really not my place to say. Penny will tell you if she wants. I will say I'm not a born Wizard."

"What does that even mean?"

"A little of this. A little of that," he said casually.

"Ian, seriously. Why are you being so difficult? I'm already confused." Chris groaned, feeling irritated.

Ian's smile dropped to an extremely serious expression. "Because I don't want you to think less of her. She's been through a lot and so has her sister...Actually, everyone has. It's best not to ask, but remember this though, the Dreadful sisters are just normal girls. Don't listen to any other crap people try to feed you, got me?"

"I don't fully understand."

"Just trust me and take my advice," Chris could tell he was being very serious, and this was obviously important, so he agreed to take his advice.

Ian and Chris began walking back to Chris and Penny's dorm room. He didn't know the way, so Ian was taking him back. Ian explained that Penny would eventually tell him what he had neglected to, and that it would be wrong to tell him. It had to be her, because she was just that sensitive about it.

It was sometime in the afternoon by now. Chris wondered if Penny might be unhappy that he left so suddenly. He decided he needed to give his mind a break, after all he had been trying to wrap his head around everything that had occurred so far. Perhaps it was best to just go along with it.

"So, have you gotten your magic school yet?" Ian asked him as they walked along one of the many streets, cutting through the grass.

"I wasn't even sure if I would get one. It'll probably be something lame..." Chris laughed. "Like pulling stuff out of my hat."

"What? No... There are multiple schools of magic broken up into subclasses. Elemental...Spiritual...Balance...even Void and Time. But Void is rare. Time...is not for us. There's an organization that manages time actually."

"Are they on our side?"

"Well, I don't know. I don't think they pick a side. I guess they pick the side they deem to be right. They appear, they disappear. They come, they go." Ian explained. "Even Megan doesn't have much on them, but apparently the Headmaster knows a little."

"Whoa wait, so they're like the Illuminati?" Chris asked. "That's scary."

Ian chuckled and elbowed Chris, "They won't hurt you if you're a good person from what I hear. Only a few select people get to become one. I haven't even seen one myself. They blend in. Anyone could be one. We just call them Timeturners. They have their own agenda."

"Okay, okay, you're making my head hurt. I'm already confused. Can you just explain why we are at war with the Sorcerers and leave it at that for today?" Chris pleaded. "I need some answers before my head explodes from all of this."

"Autumn can explain," he dodged.

"Why not you?" Chris persisted.

"She's the headmaster's granddaughter and she's headmaster in training. So, she can give you a history lesson while I get some food." He said casually as he walked off to the market area.

"I'll be back for you."

Chris folded his arms and watched him go, too tired to fight with him. He seemed nice at least. Autumn was nowhere to be seen and he did not know the way to the headmaster's office.

"How am I supposed to find Autumn anyway?" he asked himself aloud. "Sure, find one person out of many. It's the girl that you met when you first came here, best of luck."

"Yes?" Autumn's voice came from beside him. Chris screamed slightly and stepped back. Autumn was now standing to his right looking at him. Unlike him, she was calm. She smiled. "You called?"

Autumn wore a red cloak and black boots, she also wore a red wizard hat, and a golden ring on her right arm. The Alliance symbol was on her back in a light blue color.

"Where did you come from?" Chris asked, completely startled.

"Did you not call for me?"

"Yes?" He managed. "You nearly gave me a heart attack!"

"Chris, if someone calls my name within the limits of the city, I can teleport to them at will. They only have to ask for me."

"Oh, I get it. It's like summoning you," he was starting to calm down now.

"Essentially. I can choose whether I will come, but nine times out of ten I will if I'm not busy. You are new so I took a break from the library and left Emily to finish our work from yesterday."

Chris made a motion with his hand to show he did not want to discuss Emily. He really didn't want to talk about her or talk to her at this time. He still felt angry for her disappearing. She was the only family he had left that he knew of, and he felt he would talk to her when he was ready.

"Chris you can't just ignore her. She really wants to talk to you. I get you're angry but-" Autumn tried.

"How many books are even in the library anyway?" Chris dodged.

"Well...we call it a library but it's more of an archive. I would say somewhere around one hundred thousand books and almost a million other documents. If I was to include the files on students, I would never get it done. Luckily that's not my job. That is the Headmaster's...he wanted to do that personally."

"Geez...bookworms much?"

"I am at least, yes," she admitted with a smile. "So that's probably the best gift you can give me...assuming I haven't read it."

"I'll remember that then."

Autumn regained her focus, remembering just why she came. "Oh right, so what is it?"

"I want to know why Wizards and Sorcerers hate each other." He declared. "There's a war, right?"

"There were multiple wars, Chris. We aren't currently engaged in wartime." She began.

"We've had a treaty for a while. The Sorcerers are doing everything in their power to provoke us into breaking it and declaring war. Thus, causing the neutral worlds to ally with them against us. I won't deny that we have done the same, but we haven't been so easily drawn into another war."

Chris nodded to show he was still following, so she continued.

"Although we are not at war now, there are still conflicts like the one you saw. In the beginning, there was no magic. There are many explanations as to how we got it, all are legends. Only one is deemed as true as far as history is concerned, but we can never be sure." She sat on a nearby bench and patted the seat. He sat beside her.

"Is this going to be a long story?" Chris asked. "My head is already spinning."

"No. It's fairly short. If anything, I'm giving you a head start in your history studies." She answered.

"Mankind used to live on a completely different Earth-by which I mean humans. The Earth you come from is not the original home-world of human beings. That planet is now named Vexusis," Chris's eyes went wide as she said this.

"That planet has no civilization on it now, but your people used to be fairly advanced back then. At some point, they left due to the dinosaurs to search for a new home. Unfortunately, when they arrived, their technology was lost and they had to start over."

"I thought the dinosaurs were extinct," he pressed on.

"Your government isn't very truthful, Chris." she said. "Eventually, in medieval times, magic was discovered. For some reason, this new planet had magical properties and some individuals were given powers. The people back then believed that a magic fountain would give powers to the good of heart, and those that were not would be smote. As the story goes, one day a group of individuals drank from the fountain without the king's permission and thus they gained dark powers. The king attempted to have them killed, however, they took over the kingdom and killed the king, leaving his son to find a way to defeat the sorcerers. Against all odds he worked with the remaining Wizards, defeated the Sorcerers, and banished them into the Shadow Realm."

"That explains the hate for each other...but then what happened?" Chris asked.

"I'm not done," Autumn reminded him. "The man who reclaimed the kingdom for the Wizards then created the Timeturn-ers, an organization devoted to protecting not only Earth, but the Universe. It is said that he began the organization by combining all of the magic types to form Time and vanishing along with his trustees into an unknown place in time and space. We don't know much about them, but I met a Timeturner once."

"Really? What were they like?"

"Well, I don't know. I can't fully remember." She pondered for a moment and swung her feet. "He had blonde, short, shaggy hair, two golden daggers, a black and golden outfit with a dragon engraved on the back, and a super cocky attitude. I don't even remember his name, honestly. I swear it's like they erase your memory."

"I guess they aren't really a secret organization. Ian made it sound like we should be afraid of them."

"They only interfere to guide us along or prevent disasters. There might be one here right now. I wouldn't know or worry about it," Autumn looked away to think. "You keep side tracking me." She tapped her foot. "I forgot where I was...hold on..." she took a moment to try to remember. "Okay, got it! So somehow the Sorcerers escaped the Shadow Realm that was locked and they laid claim to planets near a supermassive black hole...They were uninhabited so we didn't worry about it much, but then they started forcing people off of their home planets claiming that the Shadow Realm was causing them to die. This was never proven, but we've looked into it."

"And?"

"And I don't know. At most we've seen increased aggression and an almost frenzy-like state, but whenever they come into the Light Realm, the universe we live in, their symptoms disappear before they can be seen. So, the Sorcerers blamed us for not caring. They placed an embargo on us, so we tried to negotiate...It never happened. Guns and swords were pulled...magic flew...No one survived. Because of this, the Alliance declared war. The Alliance won the War and the Sorcerers had to give up all of their planets and return to where they came from. So now, both sides are recruiting for magic users and soldiers. We already have weapons readily available; the Empire is rapidly constructing them which has made many military figures on our side uneasy."

Autumn paused a moment and took a breath before continuing

on. "Now we might be going to war because of planets. They're saying that they are dying in the Shadow Realm and we need to help them. We aren't helping because we have seen nothing, and our senate believes that the story is fabricated. We aren't trading anymore, and I would say it's only a matter of time before someone decides to make a move...it depends on who pushes the hardest. That obviously isn't all of the details, but there you go."

"Wow, they really hate each other..." Chris said slightly shocked.

"That's right."

"Is that why I was picked up?"

"That, and your sister felt it was time, yes. Any more questions?"

"No... you and Penny are the only ones to give me actual answers. Thank you, Autumn. I'm still beyond confused, but that helped. Information overload...I'll get used to it."

She smiled and nodded. "I like helping out. You are very welcome. Someone has been trying to call me. Bye, Chris."

Chris looked to his right, she was gone just like that. He thought about how weird it would be to do that every time someone needed you. Ian was still not back so he got up and went to look for him. He was heading in his direction.

"I was coming to get you. Got your answers?"

"They *really* hate each other."

"Even more lately." Ian said. "Let's get you back to Penny. She probably thinks you took off."

Ian took Chris through a part of town that he had not seen yet. They passed by fancy restaurants, a few mansions, large houses, more dorms, and there was construction going on slightly outside of the city. Chris was surprised the whole planet was not civilization, but the Wizards wanted to keep Terminus beautiful.

"So, Ian, how can we tell what type of magic I have?" Chris asked. "I want to know if it'll be something crappy."

"None of the magic types are *bad*, but they are all different and serve different roles...For example, Penny and I are Death magic users. We can take life and give it to another or ourselves, summon dead things, obviously, and we can be Healers, Damage Dealers, or Tanks."

"I get it...but then what are you guys?" Chris inquired.

"We are both tanks. Penny is more defensive using her shield. I'm a little different. I'm like a damage sponge, I heal so quickly that it takes a lot to drop me." He had a smug look now. "I'm pretty tough to kill."

"That's impressive," Chris admitted. "How long have you been here?"

"Just a year... a little over that.... You know, but I guess you've got it rough finding things out, and starting from scratch."

"I'm adjusting...slowly."

"Well classes start tomorrow, it'll help. I heard Penny is trying to train you." He assured him. "So, you're fine."

"Well no, Hunter." Chris explained the entire situation; Ian knew some details, but not all. They continued to walk toward the dorm as they spoke. Ian was a very good listener.

"Well, Chris," Ian said finally after letting Chris vent. "That's not what Penny told Megan, or what Megan told me. Penny is going to teach you personally so you can get a head start on training, class, and maybe magic. I'm not too sure about that last one, but I do know she feels like crap for thinking Hunter could train you. He and Emily didn't end very happily. I dated your sister too, but I never beat up on you."

"Why did she think he could? Err...rather why did she think he could train me?" He queried.

"He's a good swordsman and he's tough. He's fairly good at

magic, and he dominates in competitions out in the training area. To me, he thinks like a Sorcerer...action first."

"He doesn't seem to like me much either," Chris added. "I swear he seemed like he was trying to kill me."

"Nah. Hunter can be a bit rash sometimes, but I don't think he would kill you. He still cares about Emily too much." He moved his hands behind his head and looked up at the sky.

"Still if he messes with you again, let me know, bud. I know Emily is going to tear into him when she gets back. Your sister has some strong lungs, a strong voice, and she isn't afraid to use it."

When they arrived at the dorm, there was no sign of Penny, and so Chris assumed Penny was inside. There were a few people in the park today. A few kids playing with a kite, a parent watching them and reading a book, which had a boy with a scar holding a wand on the front cover, and someone else just running around. Ian knocked at the door three times before leaning on the brick wall and folding his arms. There was the sound of movement from somewhere within before Penny's voice answered from within.

"Who is it?" She asked.

"It's the police, open up!" Ian ordered, using a deeper voice than his own.

Penny laughed. "Do you have a warrant, officer?"

"I do, in fact ma'am," He continued. "I've also found a missing person. Please open the door so I can have a look-see."

"Give it up Ian, you're not getting in here unless you've found Chris." She declared.

"Damn. Okay I'll just take Chris and leave then, ma'am. Good day to ya." He whispered to Chris as he walked away. "I'll give her three seconds before that door opens."

There was the sound of the door unlocking, before flying open to reveal Penny running out. Ian continued to casually walk off and waved his hand behind him, as if to say you're welcome. Before Chris could say anything, Penny hugged him. She seemed relieved to see him, and Chris began to realize that Penny actually did care.

"Are you okay? You know what, stupid question...You obviously weren't. I'm so so sorry...I had no idea he-- I'm sorry, let me make this up to you!" She apologized as she released him and held her left arm with her right hand.

"There's nothing to make up, I'm okay. Thank you, Penny," he said to her as he placed a hand on her head. "It's good to know I have you watching my back. Just don't let me blackout again," he joked.

She smiled, releasing a sigh of relief. Penny then told Chris about how she had begged Megan to help her find him, and so Megan told Ian. However, Ian told the both of them he would find Chris on his own. During this exchange, she had also declared to train Chris. She knew she could train him better than Hunter did, and so she would.

"I'm so sorry," She said again. "I really want to make this up to you."

"No. You did nothing wrong. I'm glad you'll help me get better. I'm seriously glad you're even going out of your way to help me." He told her.

Later that day, after getting something to eat, Penny led him out of the city and into the grassy plains. It was just them, he was not allowed to bring his weapon and she didn't have one either. He wondered how they would train with no weapons.

"I want you to block, okay? I'm not actually going to hit you just yet. Just focus on blocking."

Her palm came near him, but it did not make contact. He tried to block, but it was too late. Her fist came forward next, he blocked with his left arm. They continued, his reflexes improving each time. She began to move faster, he matched her and blocked appropriately. After that, she showed him the "correct" way to punch. She demonstrated as she explained. He would need to turn and use his weight in the punch, but not go overboard. He mimicked her perfectly.

"Well now, you're getting good. I can see you're a fast learner. You're doing great!" She praised him.

"Thanks, but that was easy."

Penny's fist came from nowhere, Chris blocked it just in time. She leapt into the air and performed a spinning kick, this time he blocked with both arms together. He then countered by throwing a punch, which she caught effortlessly.

"Too much. I could have thrown you or even flipped." Penny began.

Chris quickly flipped Penny so she fell; laying on her back, slightly shocked. She smiled as she sat up, "Well no one has been able to do that to me before." Penny admitted, dusting herself off.

"You brought it up. I just used it against you because you seemed slightly off balance, and you were talking."

"I knew you would learn fast." Penny approved. They continued to practice, and each time he got better. He got faster, flinched less, and began attacking more efficiently. Penny was growing more impressed with his prowess.

"You're not allowed to do anything else until you answer this question, Chris." Penny looked him straight in the eye. "Why do you fight?"

He sat there in silence, unsure of his own answer. He was brought here after all so he had not given it much thought. The answer that he had conceived seemed cliché. His reason wasn't anything to marvel at, so he wondered if he should fabricate one.

"Don't think," Penny waved her hand in front of his face. "Just say it."

"To protect Emily since she's my only family and my friends, of course." He shrugged, it wasn't necessarily cool, but it was true.

"You *need* to remember that or you might find yourself fighting worse, giving up, or destroying what you are fighting for."

Chris felt something different inside of him. Not necessarily physically - mentally he felt stronger. He felt like he could do just about anything, if he had remembered his reason for doing so. It was like something had awakened inside of him, it might have always been there or maybe not, but it was there now.

"Reach out your hand. Picture that sword your sister gave you, and focus. Feel it in your hand...and call for it."

"Should I close my eyes?" he asked.

"No, you can't do that in an emergency situation. Just summon it. It will come, hopefully."

He held out his hand and pictured every detail of the sword. At first, nothing happened, but then the sword materialized in his hand. There was a flash of white and blue, a few particles here and there. There was his weapon in his hand, its owner had called it and it had come.

"First try. Not bad...not bad," she clapped. "You're gonna have an advantage tomorrow in your classes. Seriously, many new students struggle or can't do it at all."

"It was easier after you had me say my reason," He shrugged. "Even in the Imagination Realm I couldn't get it to go."

"Well guess what? You just used magic for the first time."

"That was magic?"

"Yup. There is no hocus pocus...you simply cast. You wanted your sword, you called, it came."

"Can you tell me my magic type then?" he asked.

"Probably Ice or Death I guess. I don't have the skill to read you. Megan can and teachers and definitely Mages too...People strong with their magic."

"Can I try casting a real spell?" He pleaded.

"No," She said suddenly. "That's dangerous. You'll be taught by your magic school teacher."

"How is it dangerous?" he questioned, extremely disappointed.

"Boom," She said as she pointed at him.

"I'd explode?!"

"You need to go slow. Imagine a full bottle with no top gets turned over."

"*You said boom!*" he yelled.

"Yes, you would. You wouldn't die, but it would be messy. Nine times out of ten it is an actual explosion. Harmless to the user, but harmful to everyone else. That's why you need training." She tilted her head. "You seem scared."

"*Yes!*"

"I'll protect you. That's why I said no," she smiled. "But I'll admit...that was funny." She began laughing harder than he had ever seen her laugh.

For a moment, the wind blew. The breeze was refreshing, even relaxing. Penny's long black hair flowed gently in the wind. Chris stared at Penny as she laughed uncontrollably, and he realized he was blushing. He was not blushing out of embarrassment at all; perhaps it was something else about this moment. He wondered to himself how to get her to smile like this more, to laugh and be happy like this. Now that he had seen her like this, he figured she was very cute.

8

PER HIS REQUEST

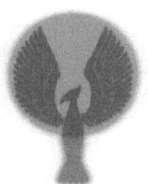

T he next day, school had begun. The school was closer to the heart of the city. It was not just one school; it was multiple schools organized in a neat circle around each other. They were separated into small buildings the size of one classroom. The grass was well kept and healthy. There was a stone path leading to each of the schools and to a fountain in the center, each school had a building color and theme. Teachers were outside of the schools welcoming students in. The fountain was white with symbols depicting each of the seven main schools facing their respective direction; Ice, Fire, Storms, Death, Imagination, Life, and finally balance. However, balance was strange in that the symbol for it was simply a crown with each of the other symbols engraved in it.

It was a rather clear day, there were a few clouds, but no sign of rain. Students were told where to go. Some students were told to go directly to class if they had a partner or were specifically told, and some were told to go to the balance teacher. Chris and Penny were directed to the balance teacher. And so, they reported outside, but there was no sign of the teacher. Chris wondered if this teacher was busy, or if they reported to the wrong place, but all of the other students were here, so that couldn't have been the case.

A twenty-year-old man was approaching from the town. He had blonde hair, orange eyes, and a quaff hairstyle. He didn't really have a beard; it was shaved, but still there. He wore a grey tweed suit, a grey vest, grey dress pants, and white dress shirt. His tie was black and he wore a tan flat cap with tan dress shoes. He had a black walking stick tucked into his right arm. The handle was a brightly colored blue diamond, the collar was golden, and the shaft was brown. In his left hand, he held a large brown suitcase. The class watched him as he approached, and there were a few whispers here and there as he stepped in front of the fountain to attend to the class.

"Alright. Hello, please confirm you are in my class. Can we confirm you all are?" He asked. He had a clear British accent. "Okay... Okay. Good, that saves me a headache. It's a pleasure to meet you all. Now before we get started, I'm just gonna take the role really quickly. However, since there are a lot of you, it won't be quick at all," he said, glancing up as he summed his clipboard from midair.

"Are teachers on Earth like this for you?" Penny whispered to Chris.

"Sometimes. Most complain about taxpayers' money and others just try to help you get by." He told her.

"Tax?" Penny asked curiously. He looked confused and astounded as she said this. "Oh, wait I know what that is, the Empire has it. I wasn't thinking for a moment. They don't have tax here because we generally have enough money to pay for things we need. Other planets sometimes have tax, but in the Alliance, Terminus does not pay. Some of the money from stores and other things go toward that, but it's just not necessary here."

"But what if you owe another country... Err...planet or something?"

"There aren't any other factions, at least in our controlled areas.

We don't have to worry about it. Other planets get wartime tax from the senate, but since we keep the peace right and protect those planets, we get none." She explained. "It's not like countries on your planet, and I am very glad it's not. That seems like robbery to charge those that keep you alive."

Penny seemed rather emotionless. Just the other day she was smiling and laughing after training. Now she seemed to be back to the way she was when he first met her now that she was around these other students. It's like she was a totally different person, and Chris couldn't wrap his mind around why this was.

"Dreadful." The teacher was still going on with calling role.

"Here," Penny replied.

"My dad says Sorcerers don't belong here," one of the students said. "She's not one of us. Why does she get to attend?"

The teacher pointed his walking stick at the student, a warning to mind his tongue.

"Penny has more than proved herself in the past and she will continue to. Many of us here have grown to see her as a fellow Wizard, and if you cannot accept that, perhaps you are not a true Wizard." He said simply, turning his head for a brief moment to nod at Penny. "Her sister has done good as well, and I expect the exact same respect for the Dreadful sisters as you have for each other, am I clear?"

"Yes sir," He said grudgingly.

"Early, Kirkland, Moore, Lynn, Jones." he continued.

"Here," a student replied. It must have been Jones.

"Why is this not fully in alphabetical order?" He groaned slightly under his breath as he read the next name. "Fairyhorn."

"Here!" Cried a female voice in the front of the crowd. Chris did not get a good look.

"Spellcrafter." He said again as he looked up. Everyone turned to look at once.

"I'm here." He replied nervously, avoiding the people looking at him from all directions. Why was he so important? He just got here. Maybe his name stood out...

"Bright." He continued on as everyone turned back.

The teacher continued on until he went through every name and got a reply. There were only a few who had been relocated or did not show up. He simply assumed they overslept.

"Okay. First of all, my name is Alleyne Atalanta. Please don't try to pronounce my name, you will fail horribly and I'll shun you. Therefore, you can call me Alleyne. Thank you all for coming on time," he started to look them all over.

"Sir, why were you late today?" One student asked. "Just curious."

"I was in a meeting. A meeting regarding that one." He said pointing his walking stick at Chris. "And that one," he said as he shifted over to where it now pointed at Penny.

"They've been working very hard and training well together. They might be taught faster than some of you. This boy was seen in the outskirts being able to do things most first years can't do. This girl has never gotten along with someone so well, minus her sister. She even cracked a smile, and she does have experience. Both will be learning at the same level as the older students and are able to enter the partner competition," he told them. "I'm not supposed to tell you, but whatever. It's impressive, so I did."

"Why though?" Chris asked.

"Hmm?"

"Why me? I get her, but why me?"

"They think you two might be partners," he answered. Penny looked over at Chris and he looked back at her. Penny was in shock and so was Chris.

"You'll still be in my class from time to time, however, if you become partners, you will attend each other's classes. Your sister

didn't like the idea of you already getting a partner, and she especially disliked the idea of your entering, but that is your choice, Spellcrafter."

Two students came running in, adjusting their clothes as they ran
into the crowd. The teacher shook his head. He marked them as tardy
and folded his arms.

"First day...coming in late. Come on guys, do better. I'll let it slide
today, but you're gonna get me in trouble if you do that later...Break
your legs." he said jokingly.

"Now before we get started on this first lesson, I want you all to
know what an amazing achievement it is just being here. You were
selected to become Wizards. You protect, you serve, and you are not
just soldiers. You are artists, healers, scientists, animal and nature
experts, and you all have skills and talent. It is my job to feed your
minds so that talent does not starve, like the Death teacher's soul
does on the first day of every year when he has to deal with the fresh-
man." Some of the kids began to laugh at this remark. Alleyne set his
suitcase aside so it did not get in the way and scanned each student
over.

Alleyne then made a clicking noise with his teeth as he thought
about his next words. "Okay class," he began.

"I'm going to need volunteers for this next part. You will be
summoning your weapons. No instruction yet, we are going to try
before anything else." He set his walking stick against the fountain.

He pointed at Chris, Penny, Ian, and a girl beside Ian that Chris
couldn't really see. He pondered a moment and then began to select
any child who made eye-contact with him. Some went up groaning,
some nervously, and some confidently.

"Okay, so raise your hand if you don't have a weapon with you
already. Whether it's with you or not, if you own one."

He gathered a bundle of fairly good swords...they were not as
good as the one Chris received from Emily, but they would get them

by until they got better ones. He placed their weapons on the table and made sure everyone could see them.

"Okay, listen up. You need to summon your weapons to you. I don't expect you to get it the first time, it is a very difficult skill to master, but once you do, there will hardly be any situation where you cannot defend yourself," his eyes moved across the sea of students.

"If your weapon is at home, then that's even better. Call your weapon to you, picture it in your hand, feel it's weight." He said as he grabbed his walking stick once again. "Now," he said as he pointed the walking stick at the four of them.

Chris, Penny, Ian, and the girl summoned their weapons. Chris summoned his sword he had obtained from Emily. Penny summoned her small sword and shield. Ian summoned a broadsword with a black and grey hilt, and the girl beside him summoned a dark and light green Jian sword with a yellow hilt guard. Chris' sword had a white and blue shimmer around it, Penny had black, Ian had grey, and the girl had green. They had all summoned their weapons at the same time. The class began to clap, and the teacher clapped the top of his hand that was on the walking stick.

"See, there you go! All four of them were actually able to do it! I understand you all had prior experience, right?" he asked.

"Yes sir," Penny answered. "Chris just learned yesterday." Chris nodded.

"Wow alright," he applauded. "Megan, you were trained personally by the headmaster, correct?"

"Yes, indeed." He heard the girl on the end say.

At this point, Chris just really wanted to know who Megan was, and so he leaned forward slightly. Megan was a girl with pink hair and blue eyes. She wore a white shirt with a black line going down the center, a white jacket, a white skirt with a black trim, white stockings with black bows, and white boots with a black underside and a slight incline in the back. Her sword was elegant and even in the sheathe; he could tell it served her very well. She appeared to be experienced, and Ian would occasionally glance over. He thought to himself, *so this is Megan?*

The rest of the class began attempting the same, but only a few were successful. Out of the entire group of maybe fifty or so kids, only fourteen were successful. The teacher told them they would eventually learn, but he wanted to see where everyone was. Then he explained the schedule for the day. Before going to their next classes, everyone would be checked for their magic type. Chris was a little nervous this might involve needles, but the teacher simply explained that he would only need to touch their wrist, similarly to how you check a pulse. Since he was experienced, he could tell a person's type just by touching them near their veins. So, he checked the students who did not previously know.

"Ice," he proclaimed as he placed his hand on Chris' wrist. "You have Ice magic." Chris held his hand up and stared at it. He began to ask himself questions like if he had always had this ability, why had it not surfaced before? Perhaps he just never thought to try, or Emily had protected him yet again. He couldn't help but remember back when he and Emily were living together. There were hard times, and he drove her crazy, but she still loved and cared for him. She had taught him how to defend himself a week before she left, and he supposed that was why.

"Does anyone want to try to shoot the target? You only need to hit on the board."

"I can try," Chris volunteered. "But I don't know how to do it."

"You will." He said giving Chris a light pat on the back as he stepped forward to see a target with the smallest red dot he had ever seen.

He held out his right hand and wondered how this would work. Nothing happened. He became a bit disappointed and looked back at Penny. She nodded and gave a gesture with her hands for him to focus. Everyone was watching, he couldn't just fizzle out now.

A blue shard of ice came from his hand. It did not exit his hand, nor did it hurt him. It simply appeared there. There was a massive gust of wind as it left his hand, spinning rapidly like a bullet and cutting through the air. He had managed to hit the board, in fact, he was near the center. His hands felt cold and tingly, almost numb. Everyone started clapping, but he felt slightly fatigued.

"Good job. Now I want you to try to hit to bullseye just twice," the teacher instructed.

Chris tried, but missed every shot, and the last shot seemed to be the wildest, veering off course and flying into the fountain. One shot bounced off of the fountain and flew at Alleyne who caught it effortlessly and dropped it to the floor, letting it shatter.

"You will be taught how to better control it, I assume the first was just luck," he told Chris. "Anyone else?" he asked the class as Chris went back and stood beside Penny.

"I'll teach you later today," Penny whispered under her breath as the next person went up. "There's a trick to it. It's all in the mind."

After a while, the teacher instructed them to go to their respective classes. There was a transition of the students in each school going to the center where the fountain was and students going to each school. Penny followed Chris to the Ice school. There was a blue color to the school and it seemed almost like it was covered in frost. There were icicles hanging from the roof. There were about ten students in the class.

The interior of the school was actually rather big. It was only one room, but it was sizable. The wall was blue with intricate snowflake designs, the roof was a snowy white, and the desks were brown and long so two people could sit together at each one. The chairs were white with black padding, the teacher had a desk in the center of the room that was also brown. She had a small baby blue lamp on it with a pile of neatly stacked books.

The teacher was twenty-three, she had white hair that went over her shoulder, grey eyes, and an excited smile. Chris could tell she was a nice teacher simply by her smile. She had a wand in her hand (or at least he thought it was a wand, it was more of a scepter). It was rather thick and appeared to be shimmering slightly; there was a blue crystal at the end. She wore an elegant white shawl over her shoulders, a cyan blouse, a long cyan skirt that touched the floor, and dark blue shoes that couldn't really be seen. She held her wand up to her chest, watched as students took their seat, and waited.

Chris and Penny sat in the front. It took a few minutes for the class to become settled, and all the while the teacher just waited. She gave Chris a courteous nod when he made eye contact briefly. She pondered her words as the class grew silent. She called role, and did her very best to remember names by repeating them back.

"Hello class, good afternoon." There were a few replies back. "Come on. First day and everyone seems too uninterested. Good morning class." She said again with excitement.

"Good morning," the class replied.

"My name is Ms. Norora. Most people call me Ms. Nora because it's shorter and easier. I have been teaching here for all of two years now, so I'm still pretty new, but I do my best! I want to know more about my class before we do anything. Any volunteers?" She asked as she looked around. No one volunteered, she seemed slightly disappointed, but that did not stifle her determination to get the class involved.

"You," she said pointing at a boy with brown hair in the back.

"I'm Princeton Gavvry," he replied back. "I like computers and this is my first-year learning, but not my first year in the school...Uh I can already use my magic very well. I've been in this class before.

This is my third year here...and yeah, I'm a mage," he said as he smiled. The class applauded.

The teacher scanned everyone again, this time at the front of the class. "You and then the girl next to you." She said. "You are new. I know who Penny is, but I don't know much about either of you."

Penny shrugged. Chris shifted around nervously. He did not expect to be second, nor did he want to be. He decided to just say it as best he could; it was only an introduction, after all.

"I'm Christopher Spellcrafter. Most people call me Chris. I'm new here...I don't know much about this place, but Penny has been helping me out. I'm getting used to it. It's very different here from Earth. I'm an Earthling...I've only used magic once so far. My sister is Emily Spellcrafter, and I hope I didn't just embarrass myself," he said as he sunk in his seat. The class clapped.

"Wow an Earthling? We don't get those really; there are only three in the whole city. You, your sister, and Megan Fairyhorn. I think you'll love it here. I'm glad Penny has been able to assist you, and if I can in any way, you just let me know." The class clapped again.

Chris noticed Penny grip her skirt slightly as he finished his turn. She was lightly tapping her foot, and looking down at the desk. Chris smiled at her and so she gave back a small smile. Penny spoke quietly, even Chris could not hear her. The teacher asked her to speak up. The class spoke in whispers as she attempted to speak. She finally found her voice after some time and began to speak.

"My name is Pennelopie Dreadful, but people that are close with me call me Penny. I uh..." she glanced around for a moment before taking a deep breath, and continuing on.

"I know magic and fighting, but I'm still learning to be a Wizard. I don't like to talk or think about my past much. I don't like to talk about my family unless it's my sister...I don't know if I'll fit in, but I think I made a friend...he's an Earthling." She glanced at Chris and smiled. "I'm a Sorcerer. A Sorcerer by blood, but I chose to join the Alliance along with my sister Tori. I just hope I do well." The class clapped, a few kids snickered, but she didn't pay them any mind.

Chris smiled and Penny nodded back as if to say thank you.

"Well...you two seem very close already. I'm glad you help each other, that is the biggest thing most partners I see have to work on. If you two do end up being partners, I think you will be rather impressive. I'll be keeping an eye on how awesome your performance is, thank you for sharing."

The class went on, she told about what they would learn and eventually when they got partners they would attend the class together. She emphasized how Ice is graceful and strong with a team, and that many Ice magic users would focus on being able to take damage rather than attacking. Most Ice users were hard to even injure, and nearly impossible to knock down. Most were either leaders or strategists, but some were also scientists.

"Normally I would have my assistant with me to demonstrate and help, but he was assigned his own class. We called him Mr. Ed, he retired, but he comes in as a substitute sometimes. I hope I'm not ever sick, but if I am, just know you have a good teacher in the meantime. She paused for a moment, scanning the class. "Now that we are done with the introductions, formalities, and protocol, let's have some fun!"

She pointed her wand up and smiled widely. Snowflakes began to descend from the ceiling. There were no clouds, it was simply magic. She then flicked her wand to her left and created a snowman with a smile and a hat, and almost immediately after that she pointed her wand at one of the windows and froze it. She smiled and bowed as the class clapped (the ones that had seen magic before like Penny gave a golf clap or didn't applaud at all). She moved her wand again and undid what she had done only moments before - but she left the snowman of course, she was rather proud of it.

"Now that was just for show, you will learn defensive and offensive spells, especially if you wish to continue on and become a Mage. Otherwise, you will do sparring and combat training. Mr. Ed will come and assist with that, he is very good at instructing students in melee combat. He is also well versed in the history of the Ice school, the Alliance, and whatever questions you may have." She explained.

Chris raised his hand, "I have a question."

"I have an answer," she replied, waving her hand as a go ahead.

"What happens if you choose to focus on damage as an Ice Wizard? Why is it so difficult and if I chose to could I?"

"Well, yes...but," She emphasized the word but. "I think it's best to focus on taking damage, Ice isn't as good at damage as the other schools, especially Storm. Not to say that it can't be done, do what you want, but it will be difficult. I think you'd want to have Mr. Ed help you and practice on your own, should you choose that path. Once you choose it is difficult to change." She answered. "That is not to deter you...I'd say make sure you're confident. Ice has to work harder to be damage-dealers. But they can take damage more than most."

"Okay," he replied.

"Mr. Ed will be here...I think...tomorrow. I'll check on that for you."

After a few minutes, class change occurred, and they left the Ice classroom and made their way to the Death class. It was a black color with a bit of grey. There was a white skull symbol on the two doors. The doors were grey. They entered. The interior was dark with lit candles on each desk, there was a rug that led down the center of the classroom that was black and with red flower designs on the rug.

The teacher wore a black and red cloak with a grey jewel in the chest area. His hair was brown and slicked back, it wasn't long at all. It was about the length of his neck. His eyes were a pale grey, he had a chin curtain style beard, and a neutral expression. Unlike the other teachers, he was actually the most calm so far, he was writing on the board and not paying any attention to the class as of yet. A name resided on his nameplate on his desk, it read *Silas Mendelson*.

"Class, what is Death?" he asked without turning.

No one replied, there were a few whispers. "I know what the majority thinks and it is not learning how to kill things faster. It is mastering one's life force and other's life forces, even the enemy. To take life from one and give to another. To revive using nothing more than a person's time...The amount of years they theoretically have left. It is also the ability to allow your body to take heavy amounts of punishment, only to still be standing or even strengthened by it. Although it is a relatively new school, it is powerful. It was not allowed by the Wizards some years ago, but now that it is, it can be finally used for good. Now I've been here almost ten years now, I'm forty and I haven't had a student fail yet. But I do not tolerate slackers, liars, or any other disorderly behavior. You are Alliance Wizards, you are here to learn so you may fulfil that role, this is not social hour."

He turned to the class, those pale and cold eyes darting through the crowd. He did not seem mean, perhaps strict, but not mean. However, his eyes gave Chris a certain chill, he couldn't breathe for a moment and found himself taking a deep breath, as if he was momentarily under water, or his lungs were closed off. The teacher raised his eyebrow, noticing Chris immediately.

"Ice is the cousin to the Death school, and so it is not strange to see an Ice Wizard get paired with a Death Wizard, what IS unusual is to see Life and Death join as one. It is rare, but powerful. I have seen both, and they make the best partners. You have already had the partner talk, but you probably did not know that as you and your partner grow closer, you can communicate mentally, without your lips ever parting and speaking. You can sense each other's emotions, and if you are close enough, you may experience one another's emotions. If you are too far, this will not work, but as a Death Wizard, this is essential. You do not have partners yet, and when you get one it will be a bumpy process, but as you grow used to each other, so too will your abilities." He continued on, "Death is not only a part of the life cycle, Death is emotion and an understanding of all life. You are not life Wizards, you do what they cannot."

Chris began breathing normally again as the teacher looked away. It was as if his gaze was death's cold stare. Not necessarily scary, but he forgot how to breathe. Penny placed her hand over his; she noticed his uneasiness and was trying to help. She seemed calm, maybe even a little at home.

"Now not to worry. We will not be killing any animals or anything of the sort in here. You will learn how to achieve the path that you commit to. I expect hard work. I expect questions. Some of you are farther ahead than others," he said referring to Penny. "But you all have something to learn."

9

SCARS

T he class dismissed and everyone left. Penny asked Chris if he wanted to do more training and he hastily agreed. They stopped to get something to eat and then headed on their way to the city outskirts. Along the way, he wondered what the Headmaster was up to and who had seen them in the outskirts practicing, and most of all, Penny was wondering if they could actually be partners. Chris was still trying to understand what a partner was, and Penny just explained that it was exactly what the word's definition said it was. She told him it occurred when two people had souls that fit together so perfectly that they became linked, they fight better together, and usually if one dies, the other is less effective. She also told him that the headmaster may have just been trying to see if they could be partners, it did not mean that they were because they had not gone through any tests, and they had not even done the competition.

Chris did not think Penny would be his partner, he thought maybe someone like Ian would be, or maybe Emily, but she had a partner already. Victoria had been her partner for over a year now. When they became partners, they quickly became stronger. Emily became the Headmaster's right hand, and because of this, Victoria rose with her. Emily was not as strong as the Headmaster or Autumn according to Penny, but she was near their level.

When they arrived at their spot from yesterday, they found Victoria there. She wore a black tank top, a purple jacket, a black choker, a purple and white skirt, purple stockings, and maroon shoes. Her hand was on her hip and her orb was casually orbiting her like a planet. She turned and looked at them as the orb flew under her arm. She smiled.

"Sister?" Penny asked. "What are you doing here?" she questioned.

Victoria smiled and stepped forward, "So I can't see the new kid and my only little sister? Wow that's harsh."

"You know that's not what I meant." Penny laughed a little and rolled her eyes.

"I figured I would help. I mean I don't have anything to do, I'm bored, and he has a lot to learn."

"You could pick up a book."

"Haha...No."

"Okay." Penny shook her head and looked at Chris. "Are you okay with this?"

"Yeah of course." Chris answered. "Does that mean you were the one who saw us practicing?"

"No."

"What?" Penny questioned.

"It wasn't me, I was only told. Emily did, she was checking up on you." Chris made a face. "Come on...You gotta let it go...She means the best."

"Anyway?" Chris interjected.

Victoria sighed softly and nodded. "You'll talk to her eventually. You love her too much and she's all torn up over the whole thing, but I'll leave that alone. What were you gonna teach him today?"

"Disarming, dodging, and maybe have him find his own style." Penny replied.

"Oh that? That's easy. Okay Chris, I want you to try and attack me." Victoria told Chris confidently.

"Just like that?" he asked, astounded.

"Just like that. Don't hold back. Use everything you know so far to try to beat me."

Chris summoned his sword with the flick of his hand. He took a moment to decide on how he would attack her. She was very experienced, and that orb would also be attacking him. He lunged forward, attempting to slash upwards. She stepped back with her right foot to avoid it, he tried to come down. She dodged again and ended up behind him. The orb came quickly, he blocked with his sword and redirected it away. Then, he took his opportunity to go in for a slash. Victoria caught the blade, pulled it from his hands, and took the hilt, and quickly jabbed it into his stomach. He fell to his knees and held his stomach trying to regain himself. Victoria spun the sword around and pointed the hilt toward him so he could take it.

"You don't always have to kill someone, in fact, if possible, you should try to incapacitate. Killing should be a last resort, or if there are too many. Never the first choice. You should always practice some self-restraint," she helped him up and placed her hand on her hip. "You saw how I calmly waited for my chance. You can't disarm me obviously unless..." she thought for a moment. "Okay don't laugh at me; my sword skills are rusty, when I became a Mage I never touched it again." She summoned a sword with a silver hilt and a grey blade.

She ran at Chris before he could react, he raised his sword. She flipped over his head, attacking in the air, he blocked a few blows, turned to face her, and collided swords with her. For a moment, they stayed like that. She pushed back against him, he was the one to pull away and immediately began attacking, but pacing himself so she had no opening. She made a mistake, he got his blade locked with hers, and sent his hand to the right. Her sword flew away and impaled into the ground a few feet away.

"Are you done?" Chris asked with a smile. "You don't have a weapo-" she tried to punch him and so he used his hand to push her back and stagger her, and when she got her balance back a few seconds later his weapon was to her neck.

"Well, well..." She sounded impressed, nodding and rubbing her neck. "Ow. Very good...You certainly learned quickly."

"I just did what you did."

"No, you did more than that. You didn't just stun me, you disarmed me, stunned me, and if I wasn't a Mage that would have been the end of that...I'm rusty with my sword fighting though so..."

"I'm rusty with my sword fighting though so..." Penny mocked her. "I never lose because I'm Tori." she folded her arms and began laughing.

"Sis, don't make me knock you on your butt." Victoria warned, placing her hand on her hip. She stuck her tongue out, and so did Penny.

Chris watched them go back and forth. They weren't arguing, they were simply being siblings. Victoria had now gone over to Penny and engaged in their conversation. He felt that he was missing something. Although he was mad at Emily, he did miss her, and wanted to be with her again like they were before. He wasn't sure how things could be normal since none of this was normal to him yet. He had already gone off on her, and things were very weird between them.

"Chris?" Victoria called to him. "We're gonna head back to the city. I haven't really spent much time with Penny lately since I got back, is that okay?"

"That's fine, I know my way back. Go on." He waved, after they had gone, he lowered his hand and went into a deep thought.

He felt empty, not necessarily lonely, but more so as if he was a jerk. Emily had been so excited to see him, and he was upset that she was gone, but he shouldn't have been so hard on her. Did he go too far? He closed his eyes.

When he was younger, he would always sit in her lap and watch tv with her. He didn't think about their long-gone parents or what the future would hold, only the fact that she was there with him. One night they had been watching TV after they had dinner. She had taken him up to sleep in his room, only tonight she did not read him a story like usual and left in a hurry. This could only mean one thing: a date.

He would get out of bed, quickly steal her favorite red shoes, and hide them under his bed. Then he'd take her cream purse, hide it under the bathroom sink, and then climb back in bed pretending to sleep. She would come in, fold her arms and question him, but he maintained his story of innocence. She would usually just go anyways without any of that stuff, put on one of her other pairs of shoes, and just leave; however, tonight she stayed. She had not left to go on a date, she talked to someone. After they had gone, she returned to his room, sat on his bed, and looked at him. She assumed he was asleep, and although it was two years ago, he remembered it vividly.

He did not have his eyes fully closed, but they were closed just enough to give the illusion of sleep and he also slowed his breathing. She ran her fingers through his hair, and apologized for not being there for him enough, for letting them lose their parents, and for 'not being a better sister.' She rubbed his arm lightly since he was laying on his side, and then stayed there a long while - as if she had all of the time in the world. After about an hour, she finally got up, she left a picture of them on his black dresser and got up to leave. She turned one more time, looked at him, and took a deep breath before shutting the door and leaving. He never saw Emily again after that. Not until he came to Terminus.

When he woke up, he was frantic, she was nowhere to be seen. He wasn't sure what to do, and so he went to the neighbors even though he was always told not to go to stranger's houses. Not every neighbor was a stranger, but some were. No one knew where she went, but Ms. Wayne called the police for him and let him stay at her place, fed him and did her best to comfort him. Mr. Wayne had gone out to work further in the city and was working on construction of a new building.

When the police arrived, they searched the house, but never found a trace of Emily, not even a note. They received a call saying Chris had a legal guardian who would come down and live with him for the time being, and because of this, they took him home in their squad car and left him there to wait. This person never came, but Chris would receive food, money, clothes, and everything he needed from someone he never saw. He came to accept these things simply showing up. He did not have any family to turn to, he was alone and miserable. Until he met Jackie and Ty, he was the most quiet and depressed person he knew.

He stopped reminiscing to find himself just taking deep breaths. He reopened his eyes and drew his sword. He found the nearest tree and approached it, gripping the hilt tightly in his hand until his knuckles were white.

"Dammit!" he cried as he began hacking at the bark.

He left scars all across the tree. He wasn't even sure what he was doing. He just kept swinging, each swing was harder than the last one. Random blows in every direction. He yelled out. He stopped for a moment panting and staring at the tree. He wasn't sure why he was doing it, but he could no longer stop himself, he felt so much anger and pain. It was an old memory, but it was fresh in his mind. Seeing Victoria and Penny so happy only made that worse for some reason. Once again, he began attacking the tree, harder this time, switching to a reverse grip and cutting diagonally. He began to move faster, this time attacking the rear of the tree, now every side had scars. He screamed out, one last vicious slash onto the poor victim tree. It fell to the ground and rolled before coming to a stop. He panted; he did not feel any better.

It was getting late, he had been at this for a long time now, all of the emotions he had felt from all that had been happening were swirling in his mind. He dropped his sword and sank to his knees. His eyes began to sting, his heart heavy, and then he began to weep. The tears burned his eyes, descending from his face and falling into his lap.

On the way back to town, he wondered what he would do. He was here learning to be a Wizard. He got here because he wanted to see his sister; he found her and then met Penny. He only really knew a handful of people here, and he wasn't sure what would happen to him. He looked up at the darkening sky and imagined Earth's sky. He could not tell a difference. *Maybe their sun is different, or there are more stars,* he thought. *There's no pollution, the people here are so different, it feels nicer, my sister is alive- and yet I feel so strange. I don't think I have the same reason for being here as everyone else. I found what I came for - Emily.*

The lights were on in town now; it was much darker than before and the streets were much less crowded. He was half expecting Penny to appear out of nowhere and start asking where he was, but she didn't. It was a clear night, some of the city folk were out looking at the sky, going to late night shops, heading to one of the outdoor restaurants, or heading home. He decided to take a different route back to the dorm. He walked passed many of the other dorms, passed the guard station, and was coming up on the school grounds. Alleyne was still in the area, he was checking to make sure each school door was locked. He turned in time to see Chris.

"Spellcrafter, you're wandering around late for a new student. Seeing the sights?" he wondered.

"What? Oh, you could say that." Chris shrugged.

"It is a nice night for it, one of the clearer nights recently." The school lights came on with a different set of lights by each school. A ghostly white for Death, a bright green for Life, an orange and dark blue for Imagination, a cold blue for Ice, a purple and yellow for Storm, a passionate red for Fire, and finally, in the very center inside of the fountain, all of their lights created rainbows, altering the color of the water.

"What's with the downcast expression?" Alleyne asked him.

"Mr. Atalanta?" Chris asked, unsure of how to phrase his query.

"Alleyne."

"Mr. Alleyne? Why does the headmaster think Penny and I could be partners?" he questioned.

"Because you are so in sync from what he explained. You seem to work well together, and he isn't sure yet, but we'll find out in just a few days. Should you choose to enter the partner contest, you'll find out sooner. You may want to talk to Penny about it."

"That's not what I meant," Chris said as he held his arm, shifting his feet, and slightly furrowing his brow. "I mean...Why not put Penny with someone who has been here with her longer?" He asked. "I really want to know. Is it because he has plans?"

"The man always has plans. But not only that...Penny isn't really like you and I or even Headmaster Brood," he admitted. "I assume she hasn't told you out of fear you'd turn on her or leave." Alleyne stopped to let Chris think on this.

Things were silent for a moment. Chris realized how she had been treated this whole time by the other students. Even when she introduced herself, people reacted horribly. He wondered what she could have done and why she deserved it, she couldn't have. He thought she was nice, sweet, maybe even cute.

"You are probably one of the only if not the only one here who makes sense to be her partner, in fact, I am convinced you are the only one who would be willing to try. You only get one partner, and if you choose not to work together, then you both suffer."

"Then...what did she do?"

"She's...done a lot in her past, but she does her best to make amends and help people now. It wasn't her fault, it was how she was raised. Victoria saved her. She brought her here, and since then she's changed. It's not really so much about what she did even though that is a huge part of it. Penny and Victoria are Sorcerers."

"Sorcerers? But you said-" Chris interrupted, trying to make sense of all of it.

"They are Wizards by allegiance, pure-blood Sorcerers by birth. We've never really allowed Sorcerers to become Wizards and fight alongside Wizards. The belief that they could get along has always been taboo since magic began. There has never been a partnership of a Wizard and a Sorcerer. People think it's absurd. Many people here truly believe Penny should not get a partner. They believe she should have been partnered with her sister."

"But Emily and Victoria-" He interrupted. "They're partners."

"It is not official. The only ones that know are myself, a select few of their friends, and the Headmaster. They were never paired. They discovered they were partners during a mission when they were alone. They nearly died, but during those few days, they became closer and stronger and survived. Apparently during that time, they fell in love," he explained as he gathered his things into his briefcase.

"What...?"

"You would be the first. I will not tell you much more, as a teacher I shouldn't go into the personal lives of my students, but it's worth talking to her about."

"Why did you insist that...I'm probably the only one who could be her partner if she has her friends?" he interviewed.

"Because you accept her, right? If you accept her and you match, that means you are partners. No one here so far meets both of those requirements."

"I feel bad for her..." he admitted.

"Look out for her. You may not be partners yet, but somehow I can tell she's looking out for you."

"Yeah...She has a lot. That's why I could do what I did in class...I probably would have shot someone by accident or not been able to summon my sword."

Alleyne smiled and placed his hand on Chris' head and ruffled it, "Goodnight, Christopher," he said kindly as he collected his things and headed the way Chris had come from.

Chris continued on his way. He had learned the town in his spare time, and so he mostly knew where things were. He was remembering the things Penny had said to him when they had first met. She didn't trust him, and was rather weary. It was because of them.

"Why did you ask me? Why not anyone else?" He still remembered what she had said plain as day. She had even thought he was trying to break into their room to hurt her, she was never given a roommate. No one had ever approached her like that.

It was true that he was starting to care about her, and he wasn't sure in what way, but he did like seeing her happy and impressing her. Knowing all of this new information only made him want to do it more. He would make up for the people who paid her no attention or mistreated her. Being her partner wouldn't be so bad. He was hoping it would happen now and if that meant people looked at him differently too. Well, it would be just like it was on Earth then.

"Megan, I think you've received enough instruction," he heard an unfamiliar voice say ahead. "I don't have any more to teach you. Sign up for the partner competition and we'll go from there. You've come a long way since Japan, and I'm proud of you."

"There must be more I can do," he heard Megan's voice more clearly as he grew closer.

"Megan, you are strong enough and smart enough to take me on in a fight. You nearly matched Autumn in combat, and although you lost to both of us, that is a massive feat. When you get a partner and a team, you'll be essential. You will be their lifeline."

When Chris rounded the corner, he saw Megan and a thirty-seven-year-old man in a large red coat with two golden rings on both arms. The coat was blue on the shoulders. He had on a red Wizard hat with a blue line just below the golden Alliance phoenix symbol. His shirt was a grey color with blue buttons connected by golden link chains. His pants were blue, and his boots were red with golden wings - the same wings that had been present on the Alliance symbol. He had white hair and red eyes.

Megan nodded in agreement. Her eyes were hidden by her hat a moment. She lifted her head to see Chris. The man looked as well before walking off.

Megan spoke, "It's you...I never got to say hello in class. I'm glad you're okay. Why are you out so late?"

"I was out training and I guess I lost track of time...what about you?"

"Oh, just getting ready for the partner competition, I want to be well prepared," she answered happily. "I'm surprised Penny isn't with you."

"I was going to go see her next," he answered truthfully.

"Want me to walk with you? It's on the way back to my house."

"House? You mean dorm?"

"No. I worked two jobs and saved up enough for a house," she said, correcting him and proudly folding her arms. She turned and began to walk, and he followed her.

"So, Megan? Did I hear that man say that you came from Japan?"

"From what was once Japan, you heard correctly," she replied solemnly. "I was there when it was destroyed by the Empire of the Dark. There's nothing left there. I'm better off here, and I'm honestly happier."

"Nice to meet another Earthling. Actually, I think one of my teachers mentioned that you were from Earth like me and Emily."

"I haven't been back to Earth in like…A year. How is it?"

"Same ol' same ol'." He admitted.

"This all must be weird for you. I'm here if you require me at any point." Megan said as she adjusted her hat.

"I think I'm used to it now."

"That's good. Still, after what happened with Hunter, I'm utterly mad at him."

"I dunno how I feel toward the guy right now."

"Emily got back today. I heard her screaming at him actually…"

"What?"

"Yeah. She had some words to say. She didn't censor herself. They made a scene by the school earlier."

"Oh man…"

They continued walking in silence. They were nearing his dorm. Megan told him her house was only a little bit after his dorm. He noticed that she had her sword on her side. She must have preferred to have her weapon nearby in case of emergency so she could draw it rather than summon it, or perhaps she had summoned it recently for use and has not put it away. They arrived at his dorm and said their farewells for the day.

He put his key in the door, turned the knob, and entered. He saw Penny, still fully dressed, asleep on the bed. Her lower body was on the bed, but her upper body was slightly dangling off, so she must have been exhausted to have fallen asleep like that. She had coffee on the nightstand in between their beds.

"You were trying to stay up and wait for me…" Chris said this aloud in a soft whisper as he came toward her.

He slipped one arm under her and held her legs and his other arm behind her back as he lifted her and laid her on her pillow, tucked her in, and headed to the bathroom. He changed, brushed his teeth, showered, and climbed in bed. He looked over at her, she seemed very peaceful, and she slept silently like a princess. He laid down on his pillow and felt something - paper. He removed a note that was left for him in his bed, it read: *Signing up for the partner competition tomorrow morning, I hope you'll go with me. Just let me know when you wake up, we can get breakfast on the way. I tried staying up to wait for you, but I'm exhausted so if I fall asleep, I hope you find this. -Penny.*

10

PARADOXES AND PARTNERS

The Partner Competition was to be held in the outskirts of town. Over the past few days, people from all over the universe came to watch, construction of the course was almost complete. It had only been 6 days, and they had to tailor the course based on the amount of people that entered. The course would have thirty starting gates, so that's twenty-nine people that could possibly end up being your partner. There was also the chance you could go through and right at the start be disqualified, because you don't get paired. It would seem like you ran through a maze only to end up back where you started.

The course was magic, and so it was no surprise when they were told that there were 200 possible paths and one massive exit. There would be dangers littered throughout the course, and there would be a special team of professionals whose only job was to hinder partners - whether that be to eliminate them, trap them, or drag them out of the course.

There were stands being set up at the entrance, and a large monitor that would monitor contestants as they progress- show who is eliminated, and who has been partnered. They will also see who has a potential to be partnered; their portraits will shift on screen before attaching to another. Partners can also fight another partner group, and the course may force confrontations. This will also display on screen and a red "conflict symbol". Partner groups that are temporarily helping each other will have a line connecting them, and it will vanish as soon as they separate.

Once it started to get dark and the moon was in the sky, all contestants had to make their way out to the contest area. It took up a massive amount of space. There was a band playing loud and proud, it was the Alliance of the Light's chosen song. Once that was finished, a group of students who volunteered and students who were in the chorus began to sing. Their conductor was Autumn. Once the song was finished, there was loud applause.

A man in black military attire, a black beret with the Alliance bird symbol on it, and combat boots. He had two holsters forming an X shape across his chest, a sword in its sheath, two pistols in each holster, and a dagger in his belt. He was not at all young. The man appeared to be in his late forties or early fifties, he had five stars on his torso. His soldiers wearing similar colors stood at his sides, with one arm across their hearts.

A girl with pink hair and blue eyes came up and hit Penny's shoulder lightly as the man was talking, "You're trying for a partner? That's great!"

"I won't get one, Morgan. I know how this works," She replied.

"Pft...You've never tried the competition so you can't talk. I've already got my partners, so I won't be joining you. It is 'unfair for a Mage to compete'." She said in a hush tone as she pointed her finger at the headmaster's special seat that would preside over everyone else where he could see everything. Another chair was to the left of that. Autumn's. The chair on the right was reserved for Emily.

Penny made a face and looked away. She did not believe she

would get a partner, and she refused to get her hopes up at the foolish thought that she would. No one would be her partner because of her being a born Sorcerer. She glanced at Chris and tilted her head slightly, wondering why he was so interesting to her.

"Are you still listening to me?" Morgan was waving her hand in front of Penny's face.

"Wait...Ooooh Penny..." She smirked.

"What? Oh. No, no...."

"You have a crush?"

"No, I do not."

"Are you sure?"

"I don't know what I feel. He's strange and I dunno. I guess he's interesting. He's my friend."

"What's his name?"

"Chris...But don't start-" She tried.

"Chris and Penny kissing in a tree..." Penny glared at her. "Okay, okay...just poking fun. You're my best friend. You know I'm kidding."

"I know. I just...don't know...It's like he's weird. Part of me feels bad for him getting dragged into this, part of me relates, the other part of me thinks he's really interesting..." Penny looked down at what Morgan was wearing: a pink jacket with a bit of black, a black under-shirt, a pink and black skirt, and pink shoes.

"What?" she seemed rather confused.

"Too much pink...Your hair is pink too..." Penny looked away and scrunched up her face.

"It's always been pink."

"That's my point."

"I like it. I just got it!"

"Not judging...Personally though...you look like bubble gum," she laughed a little. Morgan pouted and turned her attention back to the event.

A female announcer began to speak, "All contestants please report to your starting gates. Five minutes to start."

Chris began to make his way to his gate before someone caught his arm...Emily.

"Do you have a minute?" She asked politely. "If not..."

"Yeah...Yeah, I do," he replied.

"I'm sorry...Not just for not being the best sister, but all the years you had no sister at all. I wanted to say sorry for leaving you...making you think I had died...That wasn't my intention...After our parents died, the last thing I wanted was to leave you. You had no family left to go to...No one at all. I had to heed my orders, but I felt sickened at the thought of leaving that night. It was not that I didn't care..."

"I...Know..." he rubbed his arm. "I was being a jerk."

"No. You were justified. I'm not a very good sister...Well I was, but not now...So I'll find a way to make it up to you. Just be careful...You can't die in this competition, but if I see you in the medical building I'll raise hell."

"Emily," Chris heaved a sigh in exasperation. "I'm fine, I promise." He glanced up at the large clock on the screen. "Look," he gestured with a thumb toward the time steadily ticking away. "Let's walk and talk."

As the pair made their way toward Chris's destination, Emily began to assess her brother's physique. He had a bit more muscle, but he didn't change much.

"I see you've gotten more capable."

"Penny trained me."

"Your roommate? I've been inform- Sorry...*told*...still talking like the 'Headmaster's right hand'." She placed her hand over her face.

"Don't like the title?"

"It's not that...I just have to be professional anytime I can and so I'm losing my casual nature."

"Oh yeah you were really casual on those dates you went on." He had a sly expression now.

"Um, excuse me, you stole my shoes and hid my purse, my pocket book at times, and you even cried when you were younger."

Chris flushed a pale color out of embarrassment. "I don't remember that last one."

"I do. You balled your eyes out, I told my date Jeremy I couldn't go out that night and held you...up until you fell asleep in my arms. I couldn't get up to move, because you would wake up every time and cry again."

"So anyway, the contest is about to start, Emily," Chris interjected suddenly.

"I'll spare you your embarrassment little brother." She burst out laughing as he walked off. "We'll talk after, just be extra careful!"

He smiled as he walked up to his starting gate labeled number seventeen. He hadn't talked like that with her in a while, and so it was nice. He knew it would take quite a while for them to grow closer again, especially after the way he'd treated her. Chris felt heavy amounts of regret. At least their conversation seemed to cheer her up. She was beaming brighter than he'd ever seen her before and that was more than he could ever ask for. He saw her taking her chair and smiling wider than before.

Autumn was also in her chair by now with her right arm on the arm rest, her cheek against her knuckles. She was bored and obviously impatient for it to start. She was tapping her fingers on the armrest and tapping her foot. She seemed more impatient than Jackie, if that's even possible.

Chris glanced over to see where Penny's gate was...*Number thirty-two*. She had her eyes closed like she was counting. She was anxious, Chris could tell, but it couldn't have been about the dangers of the course, she has handled worse. It seemed like the audience and spectators were setting her off. Not only was she a sorcerer, but crowds were clearly not her strong suit.

"Contestants!" Chris jumped slightly and tried to prepare himself.

"Be aware that cheating is prohibited, you are being monitored." *How? There are no cameras. How can they see us?* He thought, looking around for cameras that weren't there. He had learned not to question it; nothing was really the same here.

"Due to the fact that this could take up to a minimum of 1 day depending on your skill, you are advised to get some form of rest. This course is not short and will test your skill, intellect, teamwork, problem solving, calm under pressure, and is designed to push you closer together." He was ready for this, it was unlike anything he had to do on Earth, but he was confident now.

"If anyone would like to back out or ask questions, please do so."

No one did. All of the contestants looked around at each other. Penny was the only one who didn't, she kept looking forward. She did not want to distract herself and was avoiding looking at anyone. She also seemed tense. "Ten seconds to start."

"You can do this little brother!" Emily broadcasted behind him.

"Seriously, Emily?" He asked under his breath, embarrassed. Still, he took comfort in knowing she was rooting for him. It was nice to have his sister back.

"Ten. Get ready." Chris looked back again.

There was now a man in the headmaster's chair. He was a man (possibly in his late thirties) in a large red coat with two golden rings on both arms. The coat was blue on the shoulders. He had on a red Wizard hat with a blue line just below the golden Alliance phoenix symbol. His shirt was a grey color with blue buttons connected by golden link chains. His pants were blue, his boots were red with golden wings-the same wings that had been present on the Alliance symbol. He had white hair and red eyes.

"...Six." He nodded at Chris and smiled, as if to assure him.

"...Five...Four..." Every contestant took position. Chris looked to his left, he noticed Megan's hat. She was here after all. He couldn't fully see her, but if she was here, Ian had to be.

"Three...Two..." His heart began to race in anticipation for the moment when he would hear the word..." "Go!"

As the wooden gates opened with heavy force, Chris' vision was flooded with darkness. The contestants each ran at full speed into the maze. It was extremely dark by now in front of him. He could only see the green of hedges as he ran; the cool night air was hitting his face as he sprinted forward. *Which way?* he thought as he turned right. The path closed. He doubled back and headed straight instead. Right next. Where was the exit?

After a few minutes of running in circles, he plopped on the ground with a groan. "Oh my god" He swore to himself. "I've been here before... at the same crossroad! Why can't I get out..." Chris drove a hand through his emerald green-colored hair.

"Alpha team has been formed," the announcer cried. Twin brothers appeared on screen.

"I can't get out...Wait." He came to a realization. He headed back to the right; the hedges began to close again. He rolled under it, summoned his sword and slashed the next few hedges that were meant to stop him. He stood up and began walking cautiously.

"Did I do that right? I don't know if resourceful is taking my sword and going full gardener..." he asked aloud to himself.

As he continued along the path, he saw a shimmer in the distance. A light? A scope! He quickly ducked behind the hedge just as the shot flew by. It was either a trap or one of the hunters meant to stop them. He lifted his sword and pressed his back against the foliage, inching out just enough to where he could see a reflection: it was a man with a sniper rifle. He was crouched behind a few boxes and camouflaged. He turned the blade slightly to where he could scan the environment. Everything was hazy, but he could still make out the important things. There was a way out of the area to the right beside the shooter. He would need to run for it and dodge as best he could.

"Did you turn tail and run?" he taunted. "Scare easy?" Chris gritted his teeth. *Just go.* He bolted around the corner.

"Oh, okay you're choosing the flight option then?" The man said again as he fired another shot. Chris ducked, catching himself with the ground and continuing to run.

Another shot came, this time grazing his left shoulder and whizzing by with a loud buzz in his ear. This time, a volley of shots came as he neared the exit beside the man. He lifted his sword and on instinct he turned to the flat side. He blocked one, two, then three. He then went straight for the man.

He went to reload his sniper, but he knew he couldn't reach it in time. He instead drew his sidearm. Chris cut the barrel of his gun, spun, and kicked him hard so he fell back. He then turned his attention to the exit and made for it. That man wouldn't be after him again anytime soon. He put all of his force into that blow. He continued to pant and gasp, he had more energy due to his training, and because he was a magic user, but that still wasn't easy for him.

He continued on his way. Before him was a hallway of hedges and at the very end was a red light. Progress. He jogged halfway and then walked the rest. He wasn't sure what it was, but he felt like he needed it. As he approached the light, it became more and more purple. He entered the room. It was more open like a small room or a clearing. There was a floating necklace in the center emitting a bright purple light. There was a sound. Footsteps - extremely close footsteps. He drew his sword and pointed it to his right. A smaller sword was pointed at him. Perhaps he had gotten the drop on them.

"Partner group Bravo and Charlie have formed," the announcer informed the crowd. Cheering could be heard.

"Chris?" Penny lowered her sword and smiled, relieved.

"Penny," Chris smiled back. "I went through all kinds of things to get here. What does that necklace mean?"

"I have no idea. I came over because it had a blue light, but then it started turning purple as you came closer. I didn't know it was you so I didn't take chances.

"Have you been attacked too?"

"No. Were you?"

Chris chuckled humorlessly, still out of breath from his escape. "I almost got *shot*." Penny looked at him, raising her eyebrow and then shaking her head.

"You're here so that says something." Penny said as she walked up to the necklace.

"That I'm pretty good now?"

"That I'm a good teacher," she answered. "But that too." She extended her hand and grabbed the necklace. She pulled. It did not move. "What?"

Chris placed his hand on the other side of the necklace. It split into two identical silver necklaces. One necklace had the name Chris carved into the ring and the other had Penny. Chris' was blue with a purple outline and Penny's was a light purple with a red outline. Both of them felt a slight jolt - something awakening or changing inside of them. Then once again the announcer's voice came, "Partner team Delta has formed!" Their names and portraits displayed on screen just as the others had. Above their names it read, *Delta.*

"Delta?" Chris questioned.

"It's a callsign. It was assigned to us. It's going in order. Echo should be next." Penny answered. "We're one of the first partner teams. Now we just need to find a way out of here, I guess."

"Yay, more dead-end rooms." Chris said, his voice thick with sarcasm. "Man, I wish Megan were here. She seemed really smart." He admitted.

"Partner team Echo has formed!" the announcer cried again. Penny looked up at the screen as the biggest grin carved itself across her face.

"Oh man, they'll kill each other," Penny laughed and hunched over. Chris looked up at the screen to see the names Megan and Ian. Their portraits were above their names, and *Echo* was right above them.

"Wait...Aren't those two opposites? I don't know much about Megan."

"Megan is the brains. Ian is the brawns...I suppose it's a good match."

"So that's good?"

"I guess we'll see. Come on. We have a contest to win. Watch my back okay?"

"You seem like you're already used to being partners."

"No. I just want to get through this. Since you're trained this should be a breeze."

There was a loud explosion in the distance followed by a cloud of smoke. The board flashed red for a moment before marking out one name. The other name remained. Sounds of combat could be heard in the distance. There were mostly just gunshots, the remaining partner was a girl. Her male counterpart was defeated in combat and would most likely need a healer to tend to him. They could not see the fray but the sounds were quite loud.

"Trouble," Penny said. "I say we go the other way."

"I think we should go toward it. If they need help, we should help. They could help us too."

"Chris..." Penny started, her voice was very quiet. "There is a low chance of making it that way in time, and if we did, she could turn on us to protect her partner, or worse, we get caught." There was another explosion. Chris pointed in that direction. "They won't last long if we don't move now."

"If we are too late, we turn around and take the long way," Penny compromised.

"That works for me." Chris agreed. Penny summoned her shield. She ran ahead of him, he followed behind her. They weren't far and the sounds of battle only grew louder.

"Crap, crap...Hang on Tatsumi! Once I handle these guys I'll heal you!" She was in an open area with lots of cover.

She had yellow hair, a red bandana tied to her arm, denim shorts, a white crop top, and a pistol holster on her waist. It was like a battle-field. They were out of the maze now and it seemed like many other groups could run into each other in this area. Her partner, Tatsumi, was lying face down in the dirt. He had brown hair, a yellow shirt, tan jeans, and brown boots. His sword was full of bullet holes. He was still moving a little. The girl was crouched down behind cover, reloading her two pistols. They were being attacked by six gunmen. The attackers were wearing white coats and masks to protect themselves.

"Keep firing, pin her down! Don't let her peek her head out!" one attacker barked. "Don't hurt her partner anymore. His fast healing can save him, but not if we injure him anymore. Careful not to kill them!"

"Chris, I'm going to draw their attention. You go around and back her up."

Penny threw her shield like a frisbee and hit the two nearest to the girl in the head. She extended her hand, caught her shield, and held her sword at the ready. She began advancing. The other four began firing on her.

Chris rolled around and took cover as he went. One of the soldiers was firing at him as he made his way to the girl. The girl stood up and began firing again, taking out the one that was firing at Chris. He ran over to where she was hiding and slid into cover.

"You?" the girl stared at him. "Emily's brother? Why are you helping?"

"You were in trouble. Is your partner okay?"

"He will be if I can get to him, but first we'll have to get these guys to lay down."

Chris dashed out from cover and dashed straight through two of the attackers, cutting them as he went. Both collapsed. Penny finally closed in on the last one, slashing with her sword to disarm him, kneeing him in the chest, and then finally spinning and kicking him against one of the large rocks in the area. She relaxed and let her arms fall to her sides.

The girl had already run out to her partner and began healing him with Life magic. She took a deep breath and sat on her legs. "If only I had specialized in healing instead of damage we wouldn't be in this mess. You're going to be okay."

Penny stepped forward beside Chris and watched the girl work. Her partner's wounds began to heal, but he was still in very bad shape, and she told them he had a concussion.

"Can you guys go on?" Chris asked.

"I won't risk his life. It sucks, but I don't think he'll make it. Why did you help us?" She wondered. "You could have just run by."

"Wizards don't do that," he replied. "My sister never would, so I won't either. I'm sorry you're out."

The girl glanced at Penny for a moment and then looked away. "She's your partner?"

Penny walked away upon hearing this remark. "Yeah, if it weren't for her I couldn't have helped you out. I was hoping to help keep you in the game."

"Seriously? "the girl scratched the back of her head. "I mean, yeah I guess she did take out a large set and keep them busy," She seemed to have mulled over the situation. "Okay, maybe she isn't so bad."

Chris smiled at these words. The girl turned to Penny's direction. "Hey, Penny? Thanks," she tried. Penny said nothing, only replying with a nod.

The girl shrugged and returned her gaze to Chris. "You too."

"No problem!" Chris smiled. "We need to get going so we can stay on time, uh-"

"Zoe, my name is Zoe. Get going, I gotta lug my partner. They should just let us walk out. They can probably see us honestly."

There was a loud rumbling sound as another path out of the area opened. There was the main gate that led into a dark forest full of thorns, and now there was a cave opening.

"Looks like they rewarded you. Good luck...This is brutal." She murmured as she stood up, letting her partner lean on her for support. They slowly made their way out of one of the many entrances.

"Partner team Bravo forfeits!" The announcer cried. "Medical please make your way to Entrance 21!"

Chris walked over to where Penny was and smiled, relaxing quite a bit and feeling calm. "Well that was an easy fight."

"That wasn't a fight. We didn't struggle, we tore through them. I don't expect to run into anymore anytime soon." She replied, turning back to look at him.

"Speaking of fights...I've been meaning to ask," he began as they walked. "Remember those wolves? Did they ever find out why they acted so weird?"

"...No. They're baffled. There have been multiple strange occurrences. I'll tell you if we have time to rest, ok? Now is the worst possible time."

"Yeah...you're right...So... we're going into the cave? Is it a shortcut?" They walked inside, the cave closed behind them. "No!" Chris groaned.

"It is now." Penny started, looking at the trap he obviously had his foot on. "Great."

They wandered through the cave for a few minutes, holding hands so as to not get lost in the dark, and feeling along the walls. Penny found a torch, managed to light it, and guided Chris through the cave. She wasn't sure where it was taking them, but there was only one way to go. Penny seemed slightly irritated. She was moving faster and not responding to anything he said minus a noise occasionally.

Chris apologized for setting off the trap, but Penny insisted that she wasn't mad about that. She didn't like the idea of helping the other partner group. They could have attacked them, it may have slowed them down, and she wasn't sure if this shortcut would be a boon or slow them down.

She told him to avoid taking unnecessary risks, "Even if it was the right thing to do, it was reckless. I knew I couldn't convince you though...You have this look you get when you're determined."

"Well if we work together we can place really well! I bet we could make it into the top four!" Chris said, attempting to ease her worry and brighten the mood. "We're a team now so you have someone watching your back."

"Watching my back?" She seemed amused, continuing to follow the cave.

"Yeah, you've protected me, and now I'm strong enough to protect you! Nothing will happen to you! You're the shield and I'm the sword."

"I have a sword."

"I mean-" Chris searched for the right words. "I'll fight for you if you protect me." He explained. Penny's lip curled slightly.

"You're weird...But you're a good friend. Still, I didn't expect to be partners. I know they were anticipating it, but still. You have bad luck having a Sorcerer as your partner."

"Nah... Imagine if I would have gotten someone else. I trust you. I care about you. Why do you always act like you're on your own?"

"Because if the people I care about die, that's the way it is. I don't lean on anyone. Not even my sister. I just protect who I can. Including you. Which is why I was upset about earlier. We're partners now. You're my responsibility."

"Yeah, but you don't need to carry *everything* yourself, that's why I'm here!" he said, sounding rather upbeat.

"Yes. I do. I trust you, but it's easy to die."

"But my training-"

"Isn't enough!" Penny snapped back, Chris jumped slightly. "Chris, you're getting good and that's great, but the more you get cocky, the more I worry. I know it's easy to die because I've killed more people that I can count and it haunts me. Many were magic users. You aren't invincible."

They continued walking in silence. *Killed more people than she can count? She must have tried to spare them. Penny doesn't seem like the killing type. So far, I haven't seen anyone get killed. I haven't even seen Sorcerers kill. You just need skill and you're fine. If Penny has killed so many people that she doesn't know how many then...I'll just have to avoid killing altogether.*

Chris wished Penny understood he wanted to protect her too. He wanted to protect everyone. He could protect everyone if he tried hard enough. The reason he wanted to train so hard was to make sure they were all safe and to wipe the floor with Hunter. Chris was not a novice anymore, once he mastered magic, he could defeat anyone.

Penny stopped and covered Chris' mouth quickly before he could ask why. She handed him the torch and advanced. There was a red scorpion the size of a person walking toward them. Penny slowly lifted her sword; it had not noticed her yet. As it turned, she cut clean through its tail and then stabbed downward through its body. She casually stepped over it and continued.

Chris shuddered and swallowed hard. He stepped toward the scorpion and quickly stepped over it and ran after Penny. He tensed up heavily and handed her the torch. "Are you afraid of scorpions?" she asked.

"Terrified."

"It's okay. It's very dead. I'm not scared of them. Bugs don't scare me much."

"Bug? That thing was a demon!"

"It's a dead demon then. Come on, there's light."

They poked their heads above ground and scanned the environment. No one. Nothing. Just a forest. Chris started to climb up, but Penny pulled him back down. She scanned the area further. Tripwires, nearly impossible to see. She could not see what they activated, but she felt uneasy. She took a rock and threw it. A net sprung from the ground immediately and lifted up into the trees.

"Watch where you step. That rope is too thick to cut. So, if we get caught, we'll waste time."

They made their way across the area and back into another hedge maze. This maze had sixteen different paths. Penny sat down crisscross and closed her eyes. She insisted that they should rest, because otherwise they'll be tired when danger comes along. Chris told her he wasn't tired, but he actually fell asleep first. Penny kept watch. They switched after two hours, Penny told him she only needed one hour.

Chris glanced up at the leaderboard again. Only four partner groups were left. Alpha, Delta, Echo, and Gamma. He needed to stay focused in case of danger, but his mind kept wandering back to what Penny said about having killed many times before. He imagined her killing people and protecting others, or at least for good reason. She didn't seem like a cold-blooded murderer to him, she seemed like she didn't enjoy fighting. He would ask her another time.

A day had passed. Chris and Penny had stopped to rest in a nearby cave, but even so, they were both exhausted and worn out. They had gone through multiple challenges by now, but lucky enough they never ran into any partner groups that attacked them. Both were dragging themselves along. When they saw the large exit gates, they ran for it. Neither of them were running at full speed, and Chris kept tripping. They ran out of the course and across the finish line. The crowd in the stands was silent. The headmaster stood up, Emily sat forward, and Autumn's eyes widened.

"Are we late?" Chris whispered to Penny.

"I don't think so...I don't think we're first though. They aren't clapping."

"Do you know what you've done?" The headmaster asked. His voice carried over the entire area, Chris felt himself shaking a little. What had they done wrong? "Turn to the leaderboard and check the last fastest time prior to you."

On the leaderboard they saw their names along with their call sign; their time was one day and eight hours. The previous time Jacob Brood and Elizabeth Mcmanus. Their time was two days and one hour. Chris stared at the board in disbelief, they had taken so many detours, and yet they came first. No one else had made it. On this screen they could also see the progress of the other contestants. They weren't quite there yet. The crowd began to clap and cheer, Chris turned and smiled widely. Emily probably cheered the loudest.

Penny turned and looked around at the cheering crowds. She had never seen so many people delighted to see her. It was a strange feeling, and her feeling of uneasiness increased. Chris nudged her and laughed. "Loosen up, we did it!"

"Yeah. We did." Penny said as her big brown eyes scanned over the crowd.

"Aren't you happy?" he asked, concerned. He stopped celebrating and focused solely on her.

"I am, but, they're cheering for you."

"*Us.*" he corrected.

Penny smiled for a moment. She seemed to have loosened up a little more. She was glad to have finally gotten what she was told she could not have. She did what many Wizards could not do, and she had a partner who cared about her. He really did have her back; she wasn't sure how long he would, but he did. However, her joy was cut short as a soldier ran up and whispered something into Autumn's ear. She went completely pale, leaned over, and whispered it to the headmaster. His smile faded as he stood and announced something right as the other contestants arrived. No one was cheering anymore. It was silent. Terror painted the faces of everyone who had heard the news.

11

ZEUGE DES TODES

That night, security was raised in the city and surrounding planets. There were guard patrols, soldiers, and teachers were told to patrol near dorms. Students were recommended to stay inside, but they were told they were allowed to leave if it was necessary.

The headmaster's instructions were very clear: "The Empire," he began, "Has a fleet of warships stationed near Terminus. The Alliance has lost three supply convoys meant to arrive in Terminus, and we believe they will attack soon. As of now..." he continued as he scanned over the crowd. "We are on high alert. The Alliance is not at war, thus, we do not believe there will be an attack. However students, you are advised to stay near your dorms. Civilians, try to stay near your homes tonight. Teachers, guard the dorms. Guards, start a patrol. We will not let his city fall."

Chris still remembered his intense expression. He laid his head on his pillow and turned so he was laying on his side. His mind was racing at the thought of the Empire being nearby. No one had reported them or detected them, which meant one thing: they were killed. No one had noticed due to festivities and the influx of new students. Things were so tense that some of the guards seemed more fearful than the students.

Victoria and the other Mages were instructed to help the teachers. They would not only guard the schools, but they were also to patrol near the homes and restaurants. They were more advanced students, and in the case of an emergency, they were the most capable of saving lives due to their studies. She had told Chris to stay with Penny at all times and, if an attack did come, to stay in the dorm. She also told him that if he had to fight to make it as quick as possible and watch for multiple attackers.

He remembered what she had said before she left. "Chris," One last very important thing. "If you see a man that even looks like he's wearing a black coat or red mask," she started. "Run. Don't fight. If he even *looks* like he has a sword with a red blade, I want you to run." She looked away for a moment. "Every time he draws that thing, someone dies."

"Red like blood?" He asked, slightly unsettled.

"It's not blood. Its attacks tend to suck the mana from targets so their fast healing becomes useless and their magic becomes limited. He can change its properties to envenom targets, paralyze, and a few other things. My point is stay away. That is their leader..."

"Stay away from the scary guy." He said to assure her he was listening.

"He's- also my father. He's one of the reasons Penny and I aren't sorcerers among other reasons. "

"Your father?!" Chris stared at her, his eyes widened a little.

"Yes," Victoria let out a sigh and slowly nodded her head. "He's extremely dangerous. Few people can match him. He's an expert sword fighter, and his Fire magic is also extremely dangerous. Armor is extremely useless and I've seen it burn through the most reinforced doors. Please...promise me you'll stay away."

"I will." Chris hugged her and nodded. "You have my word."

"And Chris?" she spoke again, softer this time and more urgent. "Don't let Penny fight him either. I know she'll try if she's near. It's probably best to avoid his generals and top guys. I can match their combat ability, but you probably can't. Even for me, it'll be a challenge," Victoria paused for a moment. "We'll be okay." She smiled as confidently as she could and left.

That was the conversation. He was slightly unsettled by it actually. Penny's father sounded like he could take anyone who went against him. His generals could be coming at any given time and just anticipating the damage their commands could bring made Chris shiver. He took a deep breath and reminded himself that he was more capable than before; if a situation required him to fight, he would be able to protect himself.

He glanced at his sword given to him by his sister. *You won't let me down.* Chris thought in regard to her. *You haven't just yet, I'm still alive. It's going to stay that way, and I'll protect whoever I can. Then...Maybe we can be a normal family again*, he thought.

Penny had gone out to get something to eat for them, and to check on her sister. She said she would be back in thirty minutes and it had only been twelve. He wasn't worried at all. *She's a badass. If anyone could handle them she could. I'll still keep her from her father if they do show up. Penny seems like she can do anything. Maybe she just isn't afraid of anything*. He stared over at the clock and went into a slight daze. It was eleven o'clock. It couldn't hurt to close his eyes for a moment, right? He drifted to sleep.

'Get up!' a male voice boomed from outside; Chris shot up like a lightning bolt. "Get up!" he repeated. He did not fully register the voice until someone began violently banging on the door to get his attention. *"Get up! We're being bombed! We're being bombed! Get up!"* The booming voice broke suddenly, and grew more powerful.

Chris quickly swung out of bed and grabbed his sword. He opened the door. It was one of the guards. "The alarm isn't working!

Tell everyone you can!" And with that he sprinted as fast as he could to the next dorm over.

He was right. Chris's eyes widened as he saw the beautiful city lit ablaze. There were black and red planes flying overhead, and some were currently bombing the guard station. Embers and screams filled the air. Chris ran as fast as he could to where Victoria was stationed. He had to find her and Penny.

Violet was taking cover behind a building. She was firing a yellow pistol with blue lasers for ammunition.

"Chris! I need you to help me get to the airfield! I need to get to my plane so I can get those bombers out of here!" She took a shot to the arm, but her pilot suit produced a shield that protected her.

He sprinted forward, running on the wall of the building and began tearing through the soldiers. They couldn't keep up with him. He had cut them in as many places as he could so they would fall to the ground.

They continued on their way. "I saw Fairyhorn up ahead. They dragged her out of her house, and she made the ones that attacked her pay dearly," Violet fired a few times in the direction of two soldiers wearing black and red that fell to the ground. "I don't know if she's still there, but I'm not worried."

Then Chris saw her. Megan was fighting three sorcerers at once. She spun her sword and slashed low, tripping one by cutting the back of his leg. She spun, blocking an attack coming from behind, side-stepped, and roundhouse-kicked her assailant, he staggered back a few feet. When she held out her hand, a strong burst of wind erupted from the palm of her hand. A scream came from her attacker as they were flung into the lake. Megan turned and saw Chris and Violet approaching.

"Chris, I'm glad you're okay," she said. She didn't look tired at all, but she was slightly injured on her knee.

"Are you okay?" he questioned.

"I'm fine. I didn't even really take many hits. I was lucky that I wasn't killed in my sleep." she dusted herself off. "I was about to go find Ian."

"It can wait. I really need to get to my plane. None of the planes have launched. I don't think any pilots are nearby. I can handle everything if you get me in the sky."

"I don't think finding my partner comes second."

"We'll be bombed to ashes if I don't make it to my plane," she argued. Stepping closer, she urged, "People are dying, Megan!"

"I see that." Megan scoffed. Chris took note of Violet's attempt at guilt-tripping. "I'll help you, Violet, but I won't be nearly as effective."

"You and Chris will be good enough. Clear a path," she ordered.

The three made their way to the airfield only to see a firefight had broken out. "I don't think you're getting to your plane..." Chris told her.

"Like hell," she said as she began running in. "I've got this!" Other pilots were at the airfield returning fire at the invaders. Violet joined them.

"Violet!" one pilot cried.

Violet quickly shot one of the soldiers in the head and two in the chest. She turned just in time to dodge a magic attack. The other pilots began firing at the magic user who Chris could not see from where he was, but he assumed he had fallen when he saw them hurrying to their planes. An enemy plane began to descend rapidly and fire on them. They dodged as best as they could, but some of them were shot and fell motionless to the ground. The plane came back for another pass.

"Shoot him down! Shoot him down!" Violet ordered. The aviators began to focus fire on the plane. It took damage, but it still managed to take out at least seven more pilots that fell to the ground hard.

"Megan?" Chris asked, concern in his voice.

"Violet is a show off, but she is capable. All of those pilots have over two-hundred hours of combat experience. They'll be fine. Trying to help now would be a hindrance. I don't think I can take any of these planes down without being in one myself. I would never get in my plane without Ian," she replied, her gaze pulled from the battle for a moment to address him, but then went back to watching.

The pilots that were remaining got into their planes. Each plane was a different color. Chris could see Violet quickly buckling up and then beginning to take off. The plane was coming back again. He could see Violet duck down and cover her head as the plane fired again across all of them. The plane in the very back of the line exploded and flew up and into the air. They began to take flight. The Imperial plane tried to retreat, but Violet and another pilot pursued it. The rest went immediately after the bombers and attack planes.

The plane that was with Violet peeled off and tried to cut off the Imperial aircraft. The air cracked as Violet flew over them. A few shots were fired from Violet's plane, and with that, the enemy plane was no more. It exploded mid-air. Megan smiled, "See? Training."

"I don't know who's more impressive, us or them!" Chris cheered, watching the parts fall to the ground in awe.

"We fly planes and we fight on the ground so... us," Megan answered. "I'm going to find Ian. You better find Penny. She'll probably be where Victoria is." She began to run away full speed. "Stay alive!" She called back to him.

Chris began to run back the way he came, occasionally stopping to fight. He saw his teacher using her wand to block other magic attacks and redirect them. She then fired a flurry of hail in their direction. He debated if he should help her, but when he saw her take out ten at once he figured she would be fine. She was protecting a man who had wandered outside before the attack. He saw the Life teacher healing an injured woman. Emily was with them.

"Emily! More incoming!" The Life teacher warned.

"They'll pay," Emily hissed.

She ran directly at two Sorcerers, then she summoned her weapon. Emily's weapon was a green and blue halberd that could change forms to any weapon she needed at the time. One was wearing grey armor over his clothes, and another was wearing a red hood. She began relentless strikes on both at once. She tripped the armored attacker and tried to finish him, but his garb protected him. She used magic to tie him to the ground with vines. Emily then changed her weapon to nunchucks. She held her ground as the Sorcerer charged, sword at the ready. She quickly corrected by changing her weapon to a flail, wrapping it around his weapon, and yanking it from his hands violently. She then changed her weapon to a metal bat and hit him as hard as she could as he stumbled forward. Her weapon returned to halberd form.

She happened to glance over and see Chris. She looked relieved, but also bothered. She had a wound on her arm, on her stomach, and her leg looked bloody. She ran up and took him by his shoulders and asked him if he was okay, he explained that he was.

"Where's Penny?" he asked urgently.

"She ran by a while ago looking for you. She went to the dorm, but when she couldn't find you, she ran by again." Emily told him. "Don't you dare try going that way. We're losing control over there."

"If she went that way, so will I," he said, looking her straight in the eye. "I won't let her go alone."

"Fine," she reluctantly agreed. "Myra! I need you to help my brother!" she called to a girl with her hair dyed a teal blue.

Her hair was curly and long, her eyes were grey, and she had a very serious expression. Myra wore a blue shirt with white sleeves, white shorts with a little blue, leggings, and black shoes. She ran over and looked Chris over for a moment. "Your brother?"

"Help him get to his partner. She went toward an area where

Sorcerers and Imperial Soldiers are everywhere," she explained. "Get him to her by any means."

"Yes ma'am," she said with a gleam of confidence in her eye. "I'll eliminate anyone who gets in his way."

"I'm counting on you to keep him alive, Myra," Emily told the girl. "Go, Chris. Myra will make sure you have an easier time. Don't expect her to be in the middle of the fighting though."

Myra dashed off and Chris followed closely. He noticed her reaching for her dagger. She stopped and took cover behind a crumbling wall. Chris joined her. There were five sorcerers and three soldiers all talking. Myra looked at Chris. "Stay," she told him simply. She climbed to the top of the destroyed wall, leapt to the next building, and moved to the one closest to them. She leapt down, pulled two soldiers into an alleyway and killed both. She then crept over to one of the Sorcerers, stabbed him in the back quickly, then threw her dagger into the other Sorcerer. He screamed in pain. The remaining sorcerers and soldiers turned to see her standing there calmly.

"Gonna have fun with this one. She thinks she's tough because she can sneak up on us." A female Sorcerer said. Chris couldn't quite see their faces.

Myra used her Storm magic to strike the soldiers with lightning. The Sorcerers engaged. Myra rolled quickly and retrieved her dagger.

She's amazing. She took out most of them before they knew it. I don't know if she can handle the others though, he thought. *I should help.*

"Hey over here!" Chris shouted as he charged in. Two of them looked away to focus on Chris. Myra's lip curled. She drew throwing knives from her belt and tossed them into both of their backs. They didn't get up, but they also weren't dead. *Paralyzed,* he thought. The remaining Sorcerer lunged forward with a strong swing. Myra leapt into the air, doing a slight flip. She landed on his back, plunged her dagger downward into his back as her feet landed. He let out a yelp as she leapt off of him and replaced her dagger into its sheath.

"I said stay," Myra said simply. She pushed her hair behind her ear.

"You were in trouble so I tried to get them off of your back."

"Sweet," she said as she smiled. "And selfless I see." *She's extremely short spoken*, he thought as he ran with her. It made sense, she was the stealth type.

Myra stopped and looked at the sky. She smiled and said simply, "Mages." Chris looked up at the sky and grinned. She was right. The Mages were hovering above the city watching and seeing who needed help. They were standing on what looked like a spider web above the battlefield.

One of the Mages was Victoria holding her arm beside another Mage: Morgan, who confidently beamed with her hands on her hips. A boy with short black hair and a yellow overcoat was squatted down, holding the web together beside them. Next to him was a girl with curly, dark-brown hair holding a flute to her lips. Behind her was a tall, blonde-haired Mage with a magic staff behind his back and a girl with long brown hair juggling a fireball. Another Mage with red hair walked forward and lunged off to a section of the city as soon as he saw her, her cloak flapping in the wind. Finally, there was a girl with white hair and blue skin. The girl with white hair began pointing down at the battlefield and saying something to Morgan. In response, Morgan leapt off and rejoined the fighting.

Those are the Mages? Wow, Chris thought to himself. Though out of all of the Mages, he couldn't help but notice Victoria who seemed to be staring right back at him. He couldn't see her face very well from this distance, but he felt it. This must have been the sector she was told to guard. *That's so cool...*

"Chris, there are more coming. We'll need to deal with them quickly," Myra's voice came suddenly, snapping him back to reality.

"Uh-huh," Chris agreed. He held his sword in reverse grip and made his way forward.

A sorcerer with a polearm swung at him. He blocked it, but was knocked back a bit. He winced. *He hits hard. I'll need to just avoid those.* He swung again but this time Chris jumped back to dodge it. He charged in and got a good hit in and as the attacker fell, he continued on his way. He could see Myra fighting in a crowd. She needed help. He had remembered what Emily said about her not handling crowds very well. "Hang on Myra!"

"Behind you!" she warned. The polearm user was back for more. He dodged out of the way of his blade. The pole of the weapon came around to hit him; he had no time to dodge. He barely blocked it, but it still caused him to fall over. His sword fell out of reach. *This guy is really tough and annoying.* One of Myra's daggers came from seemingly nowhere. She was getting overwhelmed, but she still prioritized him. He retrieved his sword and brandished it. The Sorcerer attempted the same attack as he did before. Chris dodged and elbowed him as hard as he could in the stomach. When he saw an opening, he cut the man across his chest. He saw him fall and knew he would not get up. He was in too much pain to move.

"Myra!" Chris called to her as he turned. "I got him hang-" He choked slightly as he saw her get pierced deeply by a blade. Then another. Then another. He charged forward to help her. "Myra!"

"Save your partner," she whimpered. "I can hold them." She threw out more daggers, backed off. Her wounds weren't healing fast enough. She retreated for a moment to evaluate her next move.

"Myra! No, don't!" She began to cut through as many as she could to clear a path for Chris, but she was slower now.

She knelt down and tried to catch her breath. A cold steel sword pierced into her chest. Her eyes widened.

"Myra!" She fell forward. Myra hit the ground with a 'thud', she was gone. Chris' jaw dropped and his eyes widened. Myra died right in front of him in seconds. She was doing just fine a moment ago and now she was dead. He couldn't help her.

Victoria's orb of energy flew through the crowd and knocked them all back in different directions. It was like a car had crashed into them all at once, causing them to topple over. She landed down beside Chris and gazed down at Myra's unmoving self.

"What happened?" she asked, anger was in her voice as she watched a group of Imperial soldiers approaching.

"She protected me and then she got overwhelmed and-" he struggled to speak.

"I understand." She flicked her hand to the left. The orb smashed into the new group causing them to crash into a building, and through the brick wall. She seemed angry that so many people were being killed.

"They didn't even declare war. They attacked us without warning. Even worse they probably have a spy in the city. Someone disabled the alarms and early warning devices. When I find out who, I'm going to make sure they end up either in the prisons or dead."

"I'm trying not to kill these people, but it's like they don't give up." he told her.

"They're not going to. You can't always spare everyone, there are too many. You can try, but you've got to kill some." She folded her arms and looked at Myra again. "And I'm starting to want to, more and more."

A man wearing a black general's outfit, black boots, and a hood was walking toward them. Victoria sent her orb toward him. He merely raised his sword and blocked it effortlessly.

He drew back his hood with one hand. He looked to be in his twenties or early thirties. He had short black hair that seemed slightly unkempt, purple eyes, and a twisted grin. His physique was compact, but still rather built. He had some armor under his black cloak, but it did not look very heavy. There was a sword with a stylish red hilt at his side. *Is this their father? He doesn't look like Penny or Tori,* he pondered. Much to Chris's relief, only the hilt of his sword was red, the blade was silver. Chris figured they had a chance.

"Victoria! My dear! How have you been?" he asked as he drew his sword, his grin creeping more across his face. "I had one hell of a time trying to find you. I asked those Wizards and poor guards back there where you were and they just didn't know." He began to laugh maniacally. She clenched her fist harder. "So you see, I kind of killed them all out of frustration. I would have killed this one too-" He kicked Myra's body out of his way as he approached. "Unfortunately, these boys beat me to it! Why Imperial training has come a long way, hasn't it?"

"Tori? Who is this guy?" Chris questioned.

"Vedi Der Ritter. He's one of my father's generals, in fact, he's basically the top general. If he's here, my father can't be far behind. We need to get help," she answered.

"Why can't we take him?"

"Chris, he'll kill you," she warned.

"Can you take him?" he questioned. "You're a mage."

"I'm not sure...He's unpredictable and fast." Victoria admitted. Chris stood at the ready to fight.

"Aww, how sweet of you to say. If your sister was here, I could take you both with me to your father. Lord Chaos misses you. He told me to ask you nicely before doing anything drastic."

He began to play with his sword's blade and run his fingers across it. "You see, after your little run in with Gatchi and stopping her from completing her task, she went missing. We heard about the whole thing and how it cost us a new recruit."

"Gatchi never came back?" Victoria repeated.

"She never returned. Either she was afraid of punishment or she's gone rogue. Incompetent if you ask me," he laughed. "Now come along."

Victoria did not move. Chris stood with her. "Oh-ho so you're being rebellious now?"

"You're talkative," Chris said.

"*You're* going to die next," he shot back. He ran toward Chris.

Victoria moved forward to stop him, but he merely shoved her aside forcefully and continued toward him. Chris raised his sword and blocked his first strike. His second strike came faster striking him in the arm and then across his cheek. Victoria's orb came around and hit Vedi's sword so Chris would have a window of opportunity. Chris switched to reverse grip and slashed as fast as he could. Miss. Vedi had ducked under his attack and had cut his leg. Chris fell, and as he jumped to deliver a crushing downward blow, Chris blocked with his sword and threw him off. He couldn't walk.

He suddenly heard the soothing melody of a flute in his ear. The girl with the flute was extremely far away and yet he could hear it very clearly. She was facing his direction and playing a soft tune. His cheek, arm, and leg healed rapidly until they were perfectly fine. She bowed in the distance and began to play in other directions. One of the mages had brought him back into the fray.

"You're up again? How wonderful! I had hoped I couldn't finish you that easy!" Vedi laughed as he flicked his sword to rid it of Chris' blood. "Look at him struggle, Victoria!"

Victoria and Chris rushed him together and began attacking from both sides. He blocked everything and then swung his sword once again to knock them both back. He made for Chris again. Chris blocked every attack, keeping his sword near his midsection to be ready for anything.

Victoria fired her orb again and ran toward Vedi's rear. He turned to redirect Victoria's orb into the ground where it became stuck. She attempted to kick him. He blocked. Chris tried to go for his head, he knocked the attack away. He prepared to finish Chris. Chris raised his sword to block the incoming death blow, but he could not raise it fast enough. Victoria threw a punch to try to save Chris. Vedi's lips drew back to reveal his teeth in a sinister smile. He reversed his sword and stepped back, dodging under her punch and impaling her through the chest. Her eyes widened as she let out a barely audible scream. Vedi then turned to slash her across the arm hard, and finally kicked her away as hard as he could so she landed with a loud thud, facing the sky.

The girl with the flute ran over to look down and see if Victoria was okay. She turned and was probably telling the others what had happened, but they were too busy with the rest of the city. The only one that was left up there with her was the boy with the black hair. She tried to play her flute, but so many people were in trouble that she had no time to help Victoria. The civilians came first.

Chris ran over to Victoria and took her up into his arms. He cradled her and pushed her hair back to see her eyes. She had blood trickling down her forehead and around her ear. She appeared to be going into shock and her healing wasn't keeping up at all. She glanced back at Vedi who was merely laughing, and then she looked back at Chris. She must have been cut across the throat at some point because she could not speak. Chris covered her throat and held her chest where she was stabbed.

"Chris?" she asked, sounding faint and weak. "Is it bad? I can't feel most of my body right now. The parts that I can feel I don't feel very well." She was bleeding all over him.

"You're losing a lot of blood, stop talking...You'll be okay, you'll heal," Chris told her frantically. "Hold on... I can maybe use something...."

"No... It's done...He isn't known for not getting a clean hit, and I left myself too open when I tried to stop him from killing you," she began to choke slightly and grip onto him. "It hurts."

"I know it hurts... Just... hang on-" Chris pleaded, his eyes starting to sting. He was forcing back tears, biting his lip to stay calm.

"Can't. I'm sorry...Do me a huge favor? Protect my sister...She means the world to me," she asked. "Run away from Vedi and get as far as you can. Emily can help you, she isn't far." Victoria placed both of her hands over his arm.

"Tori..."

"Tell Emily... I love her so much, and that she's the sweetest girl I've ever known..."

"Tori..." he choked, beginning to cry, his tears sliding down his face and mixing with the blood on Victoria's outfit and on her skin.

"Chris," She managed once again. "It's okay...Just don't let them die please stay alive as well..." she asked. She tried to smile, but it was barely noticeable.

"You can't go!"

"You really are just like Emily, you know?" She laid her head back slowly and shut her eyes. Her hands weakened around his arm before letting go completely.

Chris began to cry harder, his tears mixing with the red already on her. The orb of energy that she had used so often glowed brightly for a moment before going dim and finally dying out. The orb was now black and empty. Victoria was no more.

1 2

CHAOS AND ORDER

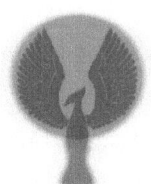

W as she really gone? Did he just hold her and see her die in her arms? Why were these good people dying? Myra died and she was only trying to help him find Penny and make sure she was okay. Victoria died just trying to protect him and fight off a maniac. What did they do wrong? He must have missed something. Maybe it was all a nightmare that he would soon hopefully wake up from. A lie? A sick joke? Victoria did like to mess with him frequently, but this was different. She felt cold and soulless, her magic orb had died out; its master now gone.

He tried to force himself into a false reality where she was still alive. She would wake up and begin laughing and say something like: "Now let's get this guy! After this you should talk to Emily, and then maybe we can go see a show at the Dome!"

What was happening? He had spent all of this time making himself ready to fight, to solve puzzles, to handle disputes, and more...And yet it had never occurred to him that there would be death. In war people die, but Victoria seemed invincible; in fact, everyone close to him did in his eyes...until now. He made so many promises that he would protect people: Emily, Victoria, Penny, and everyone who he had grown close to. As the thoughts in his mind began to assemble the event that had occurred, he realized that it might be impossible. Unlike with Myra, he was right there. He was right with Victoria, and he watched her die when he could have done something.

He was screaming her name. He didn't even remember beginning to scream. He had simply started at some point and was just now coming back to what senses he had. He was crying hard and holding her closely against him, squeezing her as if he had hoped it would bring her back. He gripped a bundle of her hair tightly in his hand. This magical world was perfect, but now these invaders were destroying it. Chris slowly rose to his feet, laid Victoria safely out of the way by a red building, and summoned his sword. He turned to Vedi, his eyes showed rage.

"Does it hurt?" Vedi asked him. "You know we aren't so different. I see that now, but at the same time..." he continued. "We're opposites. I recall my first taste of reality. It was...bittersweet."

What was he doing? She had told him to run as fast as he could to Emily, but when he imagined Emily's horrified and hurt face, it only gave him more purpose. He wanted to stop Vedi, he wanted to defeat him. Chris ran for him, blind with anger. He wanted to kill him. They collided swords, Chris ignored his attacks, only blocking what was necessary. He was focused on attacking, constantly going for his head.

"That's it. You see?" Vedi laughed as he cut Chris in the leg once again and kicked him over. "We aren't so different. Are we?"

"I'm nothing like you! You're a monster!" Chris winced as he tried to sit up. Vedi placed his foot onto Chris' chest and smiled. He leaned down slightly.

"I'm a monster?" he smiled.

"I'm going to end you!"

"I almost don't want to kill you! So much potential! Yet you waste it trying to protect...Protection fades boy." He told him as his smile dropped slightly. "You're a fool if you think they won't die one day anyway."

"Then I can kill you, so it wasn't for nothing!" He attempted to sit up, but Vedi stomped down to stop him.

"You *really* do remind me of myself...In another life maybe...Poor, poor you." He shook his head.

What was he supposed to do? No one could come and save him now. Emily was busy and probably unaware. Megan had gone to look for Ian and the Mages were busy. There was nothing he could do to free himself. He wasn't going to die though. Vedi didn't seem to *want* to kill him and he was going to follow Victoria's last instructions. Then it occurred to him what Ian and Autumn had told him only a few days before.

"Autumn!" he cried out. "Help! I'm going to die!" he yelled at the top of his lungs, loud enough for his words to be heard.

"Really? Damsel in distress?" Vedi removed his foot from Chris and kicked him over to where Victoria was. "I thought you would actually do something. Man..."

"That's enough, evildoer," a female voice echoed off the walls in the area. Vedi turned and his smile dropped slightly. He did not seem as joyous. Autumn stood before them at the end of the street. She had appeared just as she did before. She stood with her feet together and her hand out.

"Leave or be destroyed." She sounded so different to him.

Before she sounded so shy and kind, but now she sounded confident, angry, and even a little scary with her commanding voice. Autumn wore a red long-sleeved top, a white collar with an elegant yellow and white tie under it, a white hat with a red lining in the center similar to the headmaster's, a yellow belt with a white and silver Alliance symbol, a long red skirt with yellow lining, and red shoes.

"I didn't know the headmaster let his little sidekick out at all!" he taunted. "I don't see any training wheels though! And a golden mark on your arm-" Vedi glanced at the golden band that she wore on her left arm. "Almost like the golden bands on his! You're growing up!" Autumn looked over at Chris and smiled.

"You're safe," she said kindly. "You did your best, let me take it from here." she returned her attention to the madman in front of her. "Leave. Now."

"How rude! You tell your guests to leave when they've only just arrived!" He shrugged. "No wonder you don't get many visitors on this part of town. I mean look how deserted it is! Not to mention you keep dead bodies lying around!" He shook his head as if disappointed. "Horrible. Just awful."

"Very well," she said simply as she fired out a gust of wind from her hand and sent him back a few feet like Megan had done. She then moved her hand downwards and surrounded herself with diamonds of different colors. Vedi leapt backwards as she launched a volley of shards in his direction that missed by inches. He moved right and made his way toward her to attack. She placed her hands in front of her and shielded the attack with a barrier of Ice magic just large enough to block the blade.

"Well, well little tike. You know what you're doing," he began to applaud her.

"I am the headmistress in training. I will become headmistress next, and thus," she continued on. "I cannot allow you to harm anyone else. Even if that means I have to subdue you."

"I'll just have to kill you too," he said simply as he began to try to attack her from all sides only to be blocked with the same Ice shield every time.

"You will not." She began to shoot Fire magic at him. If he wasn't so fast, she would have hit every shot. She summoned more to protect her and fired lightning bolts at him. Occasionally, he would get hit, but she had not taken a blow. Chris watched, his chest tight. He was nervous Autumn might die too, but she was holding her own. She appeared to be winning.

A figure appeared behind her. A sword was drawn from its sheath. The blade had a malevolent red glow to it.

"Autumn, move!" Chris cried. She glanced behind her for a moment and then evaded as the sword came crashing down, destroying the part of the street where she was previously standing.

Autumn landed soon after and stood at the ready once again. The newcomer had on a long black coat, armor on his legs, arms, and chest, he also wore a red mask with a skeletal version of the Alliance symbol. *No... It's him. Autumn...*Chris felt himself trembling with both fear and anger. His fast healing had healed him enough to move, but if he did, they would kill him. He stood no chance.

Autumn fired crystals at the both of them in midair. Both dodged immediately. Vedi moved quickly behind her and kicked her out of the air. Autumn landed gracefully still. She summoned more diamonds to protect herself. Chaos moved in and broke through her barrier, the shards of the crystals began attacking them. Vedi took a hit in the shoulder, he removed the shard and threw it aside.

Chaos spoke, his voice was deep and chilling. "You believed that to end us?"

"I only need to inconvenience you," she admitted. "You have moments at best to leave."

"Vedi," Chaos spoke again. "If she is telling the truth we must kill her immediately. We cannot fight them both."

"Mess or no mess?" Vedi asked.

"Vedi." Chaos sounded irritated now.

"Alright, no mess this time." He let out a low grunt. "The next one then."

Chaos turned his head to Chris. Autumn's eyes widened. Vedi quickly bolted for Chris as Chaos fired a blast of fire at Autumn. She dodged the blast and quickly extended one hand to shield Chris with Ice. She turned back to see Chaos bringing his sword down again. She took a hit and immediately knelt down. The location where she took the hit on her shoulder wasn't healing as fast as it would have. He had drained her mana. She had just enough to fire shards of Ice magic to force him to retreat.

"We're running out of time," Chaos told his general.

"No, you're out of time," Autumn corrected. "I've been stalling some time now."

"You're one annoying kid," Vedi chuckled. "Great."

The Headmaster was approaching from down the street where Chris had come earlier. Autumn stepped aside and went to Chris. Vedi took a step back as if he was slightly unnerved. At least twenty Sorcerers came marching to backup Chaos. The headmaster took a step forward, and for some reason this one step caused a massive shockwave. Autumn put a barrier around them. Every last Sorcerer except for Vedi and Chaos held their heads briefly and then suddenly fell unconscious.

"Vedi, fall back," Chaos ordered. Vedi began to run. A figure fell from the sky and landed behind him and ensnared him in a wire string. He had his arms and legs caught by the wires. The mage with black hair and a yellow coat was now restraining him with the same wire he had used to construct his platform.

"Marvelous..." Vedi muttered. "I have to kill you too?"

"I wouldn't try if I were you. If you move too much, it'll cut you," the mage warned. "It could take something important off."

"Good to see you, Miyato." Autumn sounded relieved. "Don't let him get away."

"Oh, trust me," Miyato pulled back his hand that was sprouting out the wire to prevent Vedi from moving. "After what I saw him do to Victoria, this bastard is going nowhere."

"You're a lifesaver," she replied.

"No. I wish I was," he glanced at Victoria. "Don't call me that."

Vedi managed to free his sword and cut through the wire holding him in place. Miyato produced more wire with his Imagination magic and sent it after him again. Vedi sliced clean through it and continued to run. Chris tried to stand to give chase, but Autumn held his arm and told him it was too dangerous.

"Miyato will handle Vedi," she told him. "You stay with me. I'll keep you safe. That's my priority right now."

Chris turned his attention back to the Headmaster who had an extremely displeased scowl. Chaos removed his mask and smiled. He looked to be about thirty with graying black hair, brown eyes, and he had a scar across the right side of his face near his eye.

"Brood, you couldn't help yourself, could you?" The headmaster said nothing. "Not even for an old friend. Not even when you know our cause is just."

The headmaster looked up at him slightly. Chris could not see his whole face. The right of his eyes were being covered with his hat and the other of his red eyes showed fury. He stepped forward and raised his elbow to strike. Chaos raised his sword horizontally and blocked it, a shockwave came soon after. The headmaster began effortlessly blocking Chaos's attacks and redirecting his fire back at him. All the while Autumn was continuing to shield him from harm and Miyato was trying to restrain Vedi. The wire was digging into Vedi's arm slightly and cutting him as he struggled. He pulled back hard in an attempt to bring him closer, but Vedi took his opportunity to throw a hidden dagger at him. Autumn quickly shielded Miyato and called out to him to ask if he was alright.

"I'm fine," he turned back to where Vedi was. "He got away."

"It's fine, just get over here into my shield!" she urged. He made his way over and knelt down beside them.

"It's not fine. He killed two people. One was a mage," his wires dissolved in his hand. "The headmaster can at least deal with Chaos."

"Since it's a one on one, he can. They're evenly matched and my grandfather knows Chaos very well," Autumn reassured.

Chaos slashed his sword hard and sent flames over the area. Autumn struggled to hold the barrier up, but she managed. The headmaster launched himself into the air and fired down water, which removed the fire, and then froze it in an attempt to stop him. Chaos slammed down his sword which erupted fire to prevent himself from freezing. He shot a storm of fire at the headmaster who merely absorbed it into his hand. Chaos used his fire to cover the area in flames; once it cleared, he was gone. The headmaster extinguished the flames once again and adjusted his hat. He said nothing, he looked at the children huddled together under the shield, and then the dead soldiers, Sorcerers, and students.

"Well done, Autumn..." he said, Alliance planes flew overhead.

The enemy bombers were gone and their remaining forces were in full retreat. A few more planes came into the atmosphere bearing golden Alliance symbols. They began dropping off troops and Wizards from other worlds.

The headmaster extended his hand and healed Autumn's injury. He let out a long sigh and lowered his head in frustration. Chris noticed that the whole time he had not spoken. To be fair what would he say? What would anyone say? This was horrible.

"What happens now?" Chris asked.

"Now I guess we clean this place up and work with the other worlds," Miyato said. "War is completely unavoidable now."

Chris noticed something in the alley behind the headmaster. It was a girl. She had black hair, brown eyes, a red dress, and black shoes. She smiled at him before vanishing. She looked just like Victoria; his heart sank.

"What? You look spooked."

"I just saw...I thought I saw Victoria," Chris told them. "It looked just like her."

"What?" The headmaster turned quickly to see and began running in that direction.

Chris looked over to where the Headmaster was standing and felt sick to his stomach at what he saw. Penny was standing there with little to no emotion on her face. She looked rather injured, but mostly okay. Tears were running down her face as she approached, "Chris? Is that Tori?" She managed, her voice shaking. "Is that my sister...?"

FANTASY'S LIE

A large funeral was held on the outskirts of the city. There were about 1000 deaths on their side alone, some were civilians. They made sure every person had their own coffin. Victoria was buried in a separate area since she was a Mage. Chris left purple flowers on her grave since she seemed to like that color; she always did wear it a lot. Ian left a gift that she had previously given to him, Autumn left a plaque commemorating that she was a Mage, and Megan apologized that she was not there.

The dead were put to rest and that was that. It didn't stop the feelings of those in the city or those who had come only to help stop the attack, but it gave them some peace of mind. The only person who did not attend the burial was Penny. In fact, Penny had not said a word since she found out about Victoria's death. She didn't talk to anyone and he didn't recall seeing her eat. She just stayed in the dorm under the covers laying there, occasionally getting up to go to the bathroom. He had to force her to at least drink, which she had done reluctantly and after a bit of arguing.

In truth, Chris felt guilty. He couldn't save Myra or Victoria. He blamed himself for it, and the simple fact that he had witnessed both stung even more. It felt like everything he had accomplished when he came here was for nothing. He trained, he fought, he got his partner, and he made friends only to watch the person who brought him here in the first place get struck down. He had given up hoping that he would wake up from this dream". He walked over to the nearby tree that casted a bit of shade over her grave and sat down in its shadow. Ian sat with him.

"You alright?" Ian asked.

"Is it weird that I don't know how to answer that?"

"Nope."

"I just don't know what to think. I feel sick," he replied as he stared at the grave.

"It's normal. I get it...Want to talk about it?" he offered.

"No, no... I uh don't want to talk about it," Chris replied. "But thanks." He paused a moment and then looked at Ian. "I've just never seen someone die right in front of me before...Her blood was all over me...She told me to protect everyone and apologized for dying, but it was my fault."

"You can't blame yourself. You're still new, and anyone can die at any time. All you can do is keep fighting," he admitted. "It's a bittersweet deal that they kill us, but we don't kill them. The moral high ground sucks sometimes, I know." He placed his hand on Chris' back. "But think of it this way, because of you, Autumn was able to find one of their generals and stop him from doing damage. On top of that, she located their leader and the headmaster had time to come help."

"He's right," Megan assured him as she sat across from him. "You did really good."

"I guess."

"Is Penny okay?"

"I don't know, she doesn't want to talk to me...I think she blames me," he told them. "Guys, I don't know, I think she hates me."

"She doesn't, she's just hurting. She's not blaming you at all," Megan told him.

"Man. This really sucks," Ian said quietly as he looked at them both.

"I think we should get our minds off of this...After this, let's go train. Maybe we can try to distract ourselves," Megan offered.

"Good idea..." Chris agreed reluctantly.

He wasn't sure how excited he was after all of this. In truth, he didn't want to train. He really just wanted to forget everything that happened. He looked over the people at the funeral. He noticed Emily.

"I'll be back," he told his friends.

Chris walked up beside Emily and looked at her for a moment and then at the grave.

"Emily?"

"Yes, little brother?" she answered quietly. She was holding Victoria's orb in her hands, running her hands over its shape, perhaps for comfort.

"Are you okay...?" he asked out of concern, stepping closer.

"Of course," she faked a smile, he could tell. "It's just like her to leave without saying goodbye, but still, thank you for this. I'll probably keep it in my room."

"Emily..." he tried. She was walking away already. He debated going after her, but he figured she needed time like everyone else who had lost someone that night.

Later that day, Chris was called into the Headmaster's office. Autumn told him it was because of what he had seen and to ask him questions. The main room was red with brown lining along the walls, it wasn't too particularly bright, and it was extremely organized. His desk was brown with the Alliance symbol on the front. He sat behind it. The hat he usually wore was hanging on the nearby coat hanger.

"So, you saw Victoria?" he asked. "Even though we know for sure she died?"

"Yes sir," Chris replied with a nod.

"Then that confirms my fears," he placed his face into his hands. "That was a Shadow."

"A Shadow? I don't get it."

"A Shadow is an inverse of yourself. Some things may be the same, like looks or personality, but more often than not it's like looking in a mirror," he continued on. "They may walk, talk, and fight like you. They may be completely different and only share looks and name; however, they are extremely dangerous."

"So, I have one?"

"Yes. I don't know where it could be, but they come from the Shadow Realm. Everything in there is, for the most part, a mirror of the Light Realm which is our universe," he explained. "If your Shadow kills you or is nearby upon your death, it will take your powers and begin to use your powers and its own."

"Can you kill your Shadow at least? Then-" Chris began.

"No. If you kill your Shadow you will be erased from existence. No one will have any memory of you, and although the events in which you took part in will continue, no one will know who did them," he warned. "I will have everyone I can go on the hunt for Victoria's Shadow. She's off world by now, but I can almost guarantee that she will not use her new powers to help us."

Chris shifted uncomfortably in his seat. The chair was extremely nice, but because he was so nervous, he was hardly sitting back in it. This whole situation had him completely on edge. There was a darker version of Victoria somewhere out in the universe now and that really didn't sit right with him.

"Also...I am sure you've noticed the rather strange happenings as of late?" Headmaster Brood asked Chris, a serious look in his eye. "The wolves, the alarms not going off, and now the local village may need our assistance," he stood up and faced the wall. "I believe there is a traitor in the city."

"A traitor?"

"Yes, I am all but certain. Don't worry I don't believe it is any of your friends, but we will do a full investigation. I'm having the Life teacher check the alarms and the wolves for any signs of who it may be," he turned back to Chris. "You may go. Times are hard, but we will heal. Protect your partner. I can tell she's not doing well."

"Yes sir," Chris replied, taking his leave.

The headmaster recommended that he see a grief counselor, but Chris insisted that he was okay. He had told Megan and Ian that he did not want to train, and that he would another day. Penny needed him, and he felt responsible for the way she was. If he had been better, Victoria would still be alive.

As he made his way through the battle-scarred town he saw reconstruction taking place. Most all of the buildings had been repaired (minus the guard station that was in shambles.) He was trying to avoid going near the part of town where it had all happened. What reason had he to want to go toward it? That street held so much sorrow.

Chris arrived back at the dorm and knocked. No answer.

"Penny?" he asked. "Are you in there?" There was movement from within, but no answer. "I'm coming in okay?" he said as he turned the knob and entered.

The room was dark and lonely. It was rather cool and although he couldn't see much, he could make out Penny's figure. He turned on the lamp on the nightstand between their beds and sat on his own, focusing his eyes on her.

"Penny?" he began. "I'm really sorry..."

"It wasn't your fault. It was bound to happen..." she replied emotionlessly.

"I know but I could have... something... anything," Chris struggled to find the right words as he continued on. His voice was thick with resentment as he clenched his fist in an attempt to calm himself.

"Chris...Please. It's alright. I'm fine."

"Fine? This isn't fine though. This is--"

"Chris..."

"Yes?"

"Please? I don't want to talk about it anymore..." she mumbled from under the covers.

"But...I'm worried about-"

"Chris," she snapped back. "Stop. This is why I didn't want a partner! I'm fine on my own, just leave me alone," she yelled. Chris saw her fingers curl into fists. In a small but fierce voice, she hissed, "I don't need you okay?"

"...Sorry..." he answered, somewhat hurt.

"Just...talk to your sister. You never know when you will lose her like I did mine. You're mad at her, but once someone is gone they are gone," he saw her shift, she must have turned the opposite way. "Just. Please - leave me alone. I don't want to eat and I don't care to do anything else right now. That's all I need-- To be alone."

"Okay," he turned out the light and headed out of the room, leaving her to be alone as she wished.

Her words stung but she was right. He had been avoiding Emily and ignoring her. Victoria had died and her and Penny were very close. He needed to fix things with his sister. He had a feeling he knew where she was, but she would be busy helping repair the city. So, he waited for night to come and headed out to find her. She was probably back at the new cemetery where Victoria was buried. He was afraid to try to speak to her, but he knew he wanted to. It had to be done before something bad happened.

It took him a while to get there, but Emily was in fact in the cemetery. The sun was starting to set by now and she was just out there alone. She wore a long black dress. She usually wore bright colors, but not at this time. She was holding purple flowers close to her heart and she wasn't really moving. He figured she was still saying goodbye.

He came over to where she was and sat beside her. He didn't say a word. He would wait for her to speak first. If she wanted to talk to him she would, and if she didn't he would try again another day. Chris knew Emily had lost more people than he had so she deserved time to mourn. Even still he couldn't just leave her, and Victoria was someone she loved.

"Hey."

"Hey," Chris replied softly.

"What got you to come out here? I thought you would be with Penny," she admitted. She seemed to be sobbing slightly, but he couldn't tell because her hair was covering her face.

"I was, but I came to find you. I wanted to say-- I'm sorry," Chris told her. "For being an insensitive jerk. I mean this is hard for you too and I know you were excited to see me--"

"I wasn't mad. I just want to be a family again, Chris," she admitted. "I didn't care if you hated me for life if it meant you were safe and alive and happy to some degree," Emily wiped her eyes and sniffled. "If I could see you...That was enough. I wanted to be a family again."

"I'm sorry..."

"Don't apologize for my mistake...I wish I could have taken you with me, but it was too dangerous...It was my decision to leave you..."

"Why?" Chris questioned. Emily glanced at him for a moment. She said nothing as she returned her attention to Victoria's grave. He understood now. "Because...You were afraid I would die?"

Emily nodded and took a long breath before releasing it again, "You don't have to force yourself to talk to me."

"I'm not...I wanted to. I just didn't know how. It's been a while along with this," he used his Ice magic to craft a snowball in his hand and threw it backwards.

"Yeah...abracadabra..." Chris said quietly.

He paused a moment to think of a way to make her feel better. He thought of as many past memories as he could to help her. Which one would help her the most? He really wasn't sure, but he had to try something. Chris was probably the best one to do this.

"Speaking of magic, do you remember when you always tried to trick me into thinking you made things disappear?" he asked her.

"That was so lame."

"Nah... It was funny."

"Really?"

"Watching you struggle."

"Brat," she laughed as she pushed him slightly with her elbow. "God, I remember when you used to steal my stuff too!"

"Hey, I was helping you," he said jokingly.

"Okay, whatever. I had so many dates lined up and going out with friends--"

"And I helped you catch up on your favorite shows and focus on your little brother," he finished for her. She returned her attention back to Victoria's grave.

"I don't know if this is weird for me to ask as your sister--" she began. "But do you think she thought of me before she died? Or maybe she's in a better place...I mean I honestly don't know if there is a heaven, but I hope so...She'd go there. And be all goody-two-shoes there too..." she was crying silently, but he could hear it in her voice.

"She did...She told me to protect you and everyone else and that she loved you," he explained. "She really did love you."

"Yeah..."

They sat in silence for a moment. Her weeping continued for a few minutes before she was too exhausted to cry anymore. Emily had never really cried in front of him. She usually tried to stay positive, and in control of her emotions. She never hid how she felt, but she never let herself get out of hand.

"You know...I get the feeling you made a home here," she finally said. "I'm really glad."

"I have...and I've changed."

"No, you're still my short little brother," she smiled as she ruffled his hair.

"I'm basically getting to be your height."

"Which is why I'm sayin' it now," Emily smiled at him. "Thanks, lil bro."

"You haven't called me that in so long," he said. He was admittedly feeling nostalgic and excited about having that pleasant nickname again.

"Well get used to it. I'm calling you that again," Emily bubbled. "Listen why don't you stay at my place tonight? I know you have Penny, but I haven't had the chance for...two years, was it?"

"Sure, but--"

"No buts or butts. Only yes," she said quickly.

"...*Sure*," Chris continued. "but I'm also going to ask you for advice. Is that okay?"

"Is someone crushing on Penny?" Emily teased.

Chris began to blush at the thought. He never thought about it before. Emily was very good at reading him. Her lip curled as his expression began to display embarrassment. Chris wasn't sure how to respond. Penny was only a friend up to this point, and someone he knew here. He wasn't sure what he felt, but when he thought about having any romantic feelings toward her he almost wanted it to occur.

"Oh my god you look like Tori when she admitted that she liked me!" Emily began to pinch his cheeks.

"Stop--" he whined. "Emily..." he tried. "Don't start."

"No now you have to tell me everything!" she declared as she dragged him back toward the city by the arm.

Emily's home was closer to the magic schools. It was on the same street and had a view of the administration building where the headmaster and Autumn were. Her house was a tan color with an upstairs and downstairs. The interior was extremely nice. A grandfather clock was ticking beside the door. She had a black sofa and a brown wooden coffee table. There was a game of chess on the coffee table that had not yet been finished. The white pieces were winning, but the queen was gone, the king was in danger, and the black pieces still had their king and queen. This must have been Emily and Victoria's way of passing the time.

Emily sat on the sofa and put her hands behind her head. She still seemed very off. She wasn't smiling and she was staring up at the ceiling. Chris sat beside her and lightly shook her.

She smiled at him and nodded. "Sorry," she apologized. "I zoned out."

"No, it's alright...So, you and her lived here together?"

"Yeah...Victoria was here. You see, I was losing to her in a game of chess. She always managed to win. I never saw it coming."

Chris studied the board, "You left yourself defenseless..."

"I was trying to get her king and queen, but I didn't notice that she made it so every move I made my pawns couldn't save them," Emily explained to him. "Oh yeah...That reminds me..."

She removed a black watch from a black and silver box. He had seen a similar one on Victoria.

"They don't really use phones here as much so this will help you. They have a really big range and you only have to press the right name," she began to attach it to his arm.

"Thanks, Em," he smiled a little.

"Penny has one so until you learn to talk telepathically this should be useful. And I want you to use it if you're ever in trouble."

She went silent. Chris looked at her, but she seemed distracted. She was looking at a picture hanging on the wall across from them. It was her and Victoria. Emily was carrying Victoria on her back while Victoria took a picture of them. Victoria had her hair long at that time. She seemed like she was trying not to fall off.

"She told me she might die one day, because she wouldn't stop until she set everything right. I knew she could die...But it never occurred to me that it would happen so soon," she said as she turned to look at him.

"What was she trying to set right?"

"She wanted to stop her father. He had already done a lot of bad, but once he attacked Japan she knew she had to do something. So, she took Penny here and fought against her own people with her sister," she began. "She said that when their mother died Chaos was never the same. When she first came here she was treated pretty poorly...I didn't really know what to think of her and then..."

"Then?" He urged.

"I dunno...One mission went wrong and we were the only survivors from our group and we well...something clicked and I felt...calm despite the worse. I ignored it until she confessed to me. And man did she stutter..."

"She always seemed so confident..."

"That's her brave face. Deep down she was unsure of herself too, but she was always trying to make things easier for others. She told me that when she met you that you spared Gatchi."

"Of course, I don't want to kill. I've so far avoided it. It's not easy when the people I fight are going for the kill," he admitted. "I'm sorry, but after Tori died, I swear for a moment I--"

"Wanted to kill?"

"Yes..." he summoned his sword. "I tried to kill Vedi. Tori said that if I have to kill then I should, but to spare as many as I could."

Emily nodded her head and smiled a little, "I won't be nearly as effective now. With Tori gone my powers will decrease. I'll have to work harder...If I had two partners like Morgan it would be fine."

"Decrease?"

"Without your partner your magic powers will begin to become less effective. You'll have to hone your skills like a Sorcerer to be able to survive without one. Sorcerers work hard so they don't need partners."

"Makes sense...I'm sorry I couldn't save her."

"You still say sorry too much," she told him, taking his sword from his hand and holding it in her own before setting it aside.

Should I talk to her about Penny? She might understand, he thought.

"Emily? About Penny? I'm really worried about her."

"I know you are. I haven't seen her for a while," she noted.

"I don't know why I'm so worried I just feel like I need to be a good friend and partner and..."

"There's something more isn't there?"

"Yes," he nodded his head. "I think I might like her just a tiny bit."

"I noticed...You need to just keep trying. Penny is stubborn some-times, but she cares about you," she began as she wrapped her arm around him. "She'll listen to you. You'll know the right time to try again."

"What about--" he started.

"Your crush?" she said before him.

"Yes..."

"That'll come...I can't tell you what to do," she ruffled his hair. "Penny hasn't been in any relationships. She was never interested in it."

That night Chris slept on the sofa. He was having trouble sleep-ing, because he was worried about Penny. She probably wasn't sleeping again. She just didn't listen to him and as her partner he felt responsible, but more than that he just really wanted to see her happy again. It was already rare to see her smile, but now it did not show. He rolled onto his side and placed his arm under his head. He couldn't stop worrying,

Did she really mean what she said about not wanting to be partners? he wondered. *Maybe she was just upset about everything, but maybe she's mad at me for Tori...Maybe she'll find another partner...*

Three days passed by and Chris had still not spoken to Penny. She was keeping to herself. He rarely ever saw her move, and he would bring her food, but she never touched it. She drank what he would bring, but nothing more. She just didn't seem to care about anything.

Megan and Ian had invited Chris to come training with them. He agreed, but only because he wanted to get his mind off of everything. Emily wanted to come watch but she had no time. Without Victoria, there was much more work to be done, and until another staff member was added she would have to do double. She seemed like she was in better spirits. They were talking again and so even if things were harder, he knew he had her.

Chris was wearing a white jacket with a red shirt, blue jeans, and red shoes. Megan was wearing a pink long-sleeved, a light pink skirt with a bow on the front, and brown shoes. She was wearing a bracelet on her left arm. She had her hair in a ponytail. She was tapping her foot.

"Ian," she groaned. "We were supposed to start an hour ago...Where are you?"

Wow she's mad...I thought those two were getting along by now. I guess not, he thought as he watched her.

Chris could see Ian walking toward them. He was wearing a tank top and torn jeans. His muscles were rather large. He didn't seem to care that he was late and Megan really seemed like she was going to blow a fuse. She started toward him. This couldn't end well.

"Where were you, dumbass?!" she demanded. "You're *unimaginably* late! I was about to start without you."

"Hey, I overslept," he said nonchalantly.

"I woke you up! The whole point of you moving in with me was so we could function as partners! I thought it would be an advantage, but clearly not," she was yelling rather loud now.

"I fell back asleep. Cut me a break," he slicked back his hair.

"Ugh. Idiot," she summoned her sword and relaxed herself. "Let's get started, Chris?" she called to him. He was looking at the ground, not really paying attention anymore.

"Christopher?"

"Yo, Chris come back to the world of the living!" Ian said. Chris snapped to attention and looked up at them. "You look like hell are you alright?"

Chris nodded and summoned his sword. He wasn't all there at all. He wasn't sure how he could fight when his mind was roaming. Not only was he still worried about Penny, but his mind was still giving him images of Victoria's death. He couldn't stop himself. He didn't think he was traumatized, but it was like she was haunting him.

"Are you certain you want to train? You seem pale," Megan noted. "I also sense that you are trembling."

"Me?" he was taken aback by this statement. "Yeah I am just a few things on my mind. How could you tell?"

"I utilize Life magic and I practice extensively. I can see your mental state," she informed him. "And yours is not very good. You're extremely worried about something and feeling guilty." *Okay the fact that she can read my mental state makes me uncomfortable.*

"Let's begin then," Megan attacked once.

Chris's sword flew from his hand and fell to the ground. He looked back at it. He had not been disarmed so easily before. Megan relaxed her arm that was holding the sword. She placed her other hand on her hip.

"My point exactly. You got disarmed in one hit. I barely even struck you." Ian looked a little confused, but he seemed to be in perfect agreement with her.

"Yeah, Chris you are really acting weird," he observed. "I really do think you should stop."

"I can do it." he insisted.

"No. You're worried about Penny," she decided finally. Megan glanced up at Chris and her expression showed that she was sure of that much. "I think you should go help her."

"She won't talk, trust me."

"No Chris, "she smiled. "No one else could do it. She's my friend, but she won't even talk to me. You're the only person she even said a word to. She was mute to the rest of us."

"Megan?" Ian questioned.

"What?"

"You got all of that from his mental state?" he asked, disbelief in his voice.

"No. His expression and his behavior gives it away more than anything. Mental state can't tell me all of that, idiot..."

"You think you know everything don't you?" Ian surrendered.

"I don't actually," she shot back. "But I know more than you." She turned back to see Chris leaving. Megan smiled a little, she seemed proud of herself.

Chris stopped to pick up a box of rice for Penny. She had gotten it for him the second day he was here. He figured she liked it. On the way back to the dorm room he began to ponder what he would say to her. *Maybe I can try to convince her to eat, or better yet I could beg her to listen because I care.* He wasn't sure what he could do. He finally decided on a plan and began to walk at a brisk pace.

In his hurry he had forgotten his sword back with Megan and

Ian. He summoned it and continued moving. The street that he was taking wasn't as crowded, because there was a lot of reconstruction going on that way. He made his way passed the administration building, and followed along the path he first took with Penny. He cut across the grass in the park and headed straight for dorm 12,658.

He outstretched his hand to touch the cold doorknob. He felt a slight jolt. Indeed, he was nervous about seeing her. He wanted to help her, but if his plan failed he wasn't sure what he could do. If Victoria was in position she wouldn't have hesitated, but he wasn't her. He had to bring Penny back. He turned the knob and entered.

Penny was no longer under the covers. She was sitting up in her bed against her pillows. She had a book in her lap and she was flipping through it, the cover was purple. Penny glanced up at him and quickly tried to hide her book under the sheets. Chris sat beside her.

"I didn't expect you to come back so early," she admitted.

"Well I'm back," he assured her. He placed her food on the nightstand. "What was that?"

"It's-- It's just a photo album...."

"Of you and your sister?" he asked.

"Yes, of course..."

"Can I see?" he extended his hand. She brought it out from under the covers and placed it into his hand.

There were words engraved in golden text: *Victoria and Penny's memories.* He felt his heart sink for a moment, but he shook it off and smiled. He turned to the first page. There were a few notes scrawled on it such as: *Victoria became a mage; I'm glad but a little jealous, she's always so busy now, I wish we could be a full family again,* and so on.

"So, you kept it like a diary and a photo album?" he wondered aloud.

"Kind of..." she confirmed. "Tori had her own photo book too. It's identical so we always mixed them up. We had the same pictures and everything," Penny watched as he flipped the page.

They had many pictures of what appeared to be happier times. He saw a man with short black hair, amber colored eyes, a trimmed cut beard that covered his jawline and around his lips, and a large smile. He was wearing a black and red long-sleeved shirt and grey khakis. To his left was a woman with long and beautiful black hair, brown eyes, and a soft but happy expression. She wore a casual purple dress, and seemed to be attempting to fix her hair before the picture.

The little girl closest to her mother had on a pink polka dot dress. She had her hair in a French braid. She had a very joyous expression and didn't seem to have a care in the world. Her hand was on her dress, lifting it up slightly as if she was taking a bow. Next to her was a shorter girl who had black hair that fell to her shoulders, a purple and black polka dot dress, and flats. She was hugging the father's leg and trying to hide from the camera. She was doing a very poor job of avoiding the photo and she had a very shy smile.

"That's me," she pointed at the girl trying to hide behind her father's leg. "I was a little camera- shy..."

"So, the other girl is Tori?" he raised an eyebrow. "Right?"

"Yes," she cracked a smile. "She loved being on camera. I tried dressing like her in this picture...In a lot of them actually."

"Penny?" he asked as gently as he could.

"Yes?" she turned toward him a little more.

"I want to help you...I really care and I hate seeing you like this," he set her book aside and looked her directly in her eyes. "If you push me away, I'll always come back."

"Chris," she started. "I'm a Sorcerer."

"Okay?" he shrugged. "So?"

"I'll cause you trouble," she lowered her head. "I'm trouble."

"Well..." he placed his hand over hers. "I don't think you're trouble." Chris gave her a warm smile.

Penny didn't say a word as tears began to escape her eyes. They rolled down her face. He reached out to wipe them. Penny lunged forward and hugged his arm. She was crying harder than ever now. She was squeezing him rather hard, but it didn't hurt. He simply continued his attempts to comfort her. Her tears were getting all over his arm, but he still did not care.

"I wasn't blaming you, I'm sorry!" she bawled. Chris did not reply, he began to pat her head gently to calm her. He smiled and let her vent. "I hurt everyone..."

"Penny..."

"Yes?" she replied shakily.

"I will never leave you," he promised. "Not for any reason. Do whatever you want to me and say whatever you want; you'll still have me."

"That can't be true...If you die-" she stammered.

"I won't die," he responded immediately. "There are too many people that I have to protect. Emily, Megan, Ian, and so many others..." Chris slipped his hand under her chin and lifted it gently. "Especially you. You're my partner."

Penny looked at him in disbelief. She didn't seem to understand why he was trying so hard. She shook her head and smiled. She hugged his arm gently to her chest and laid on his shoulder. Penny continued to try to wipe her damp face. She took an extended breath before releasing it. She ate the food he had bought for her rather quickly. She must have been very hungry.

"Hey Chris?" Penny asked. She was still sniffling.

"Yes, Penny?" he replied softly.

"Can you tell me about Earth?" She sounded somewhat shy. He agreed, because he figured that it would help her. He talked to her about his home planet.

Chris told her about the streets, the lights, the sounds, the people and the cities. He then moved on to explain exciting things like fairs, and deferred more dull things like school and boring jobs. Her eyes seemed to light up the more he told her about it.

"So... there are five oceans, three countries, and seven continents?" she asked. "Wow, it's like someone tore the planet apart..."

"Yup! Some people think all the land masses used to connect like a puzzle," he took both of his hands and connected the index finger to the space in between his middle and ring finger. Penny was watching him intently.

"Yeah you're right. I never really studied the planet much," she admitted. "It didn't really cross my mind."

"Well it has multiple climates on the planet and animals. Like a penguin... an elephant," he explained.

"What the heck is that?"

"Which one?"

"What is a penguin-an-elephant?" Chris exploded into laughter. Penny began to pout and squeeze his arm hard to get him to stop laughing. "What?"

"They're two animals. An elephant *and* a penguin," he corrected. "Not a... Whatever you said." Penny squeezed his arm hard, Chris yelped. "Why?" he questioned. "What did I say?"

"You teased me," she said as she stuck out her tongue. Chris rolled his eyes. She squeezed his arm again and giggled quietly. He took his finger and flicked her in the head.

"Ow," she glanced up at him. "That was mean."

"Okay, Penny," he smiled.

Chris continued to tell her about Earth. She smiled when he told her about the creatures known as bats. Penny remained quiet the entire time. He gave recounts of his time on the planet and some of his favorite experiences. Penny sagged against his arm and closed her eyes.

Chris continued on for an hour or so before noticing that Penny had not been talking for a while. He glanced down to see that she had indeed drifted to sleep. She was still attached to his arm and had a rather peaceful expression on her face. He figured she looked really cute even though she had been crying, and even more so now that she was asleep. He attempted to gently remove her from his arm, but she clung to it tighter as if she didn't want to let him go.

He laid back and gave it a few moments to see if she would let go. She did not. In fact, Penny seemed to have wrapped herself around his arm so much that he couldn't even free it slightly. Her sleepy face was nuzzled against his arm. He gave up. She was not going to let go, and he didn't want to wake her. Chris was feeling pretty tired as well, but he was using what energy he had left to help Penny. He felt he had succeeded at least for today.

As he drifted to sleep his last thoughts were of Penny. Not necessarily on the fact that he had helped her, but that he was actually pretty comfortable with her on him like this. He actually found it really nice. She was soft, warm, and smooth. She slept like a princess too: quiet and delicate. He knew now more than ever that he had to protect her. Not because he was told to by her sister, or because it was the right thing to do, but because he wanted to. Because of the way she was making him feel.

14

MIYATO

Chris awakened the next morning to Penny staring at him with her big brown eyes. He was honestly relieved to see her. Last night, he had a nightmare about fighting Vedi again and losing horribly. This time Vedi had not killed Victoria, but he had killed Penny. Chris then managed to defeat him, but he felt empty after. Thus, waking up to this face made him feel many levels of relief.

Penny appeared to be mostly awake, and so he assumed she had been up for a while. Why had she not moved? She could have easily left or let go. She didn't even go get food like usual.

"You're up," she said. "Good morning."

"How long have you been up?" he questioned, yawning.

"Um," she pondered for a moment and then shrugged. "I don't know. I've just waited for you. We fell asleep together."

Chris started to blush profusely. Penny tilted her head and stared at him, baffled. She knew he was blushing, but didn't seem sure why. Penny uncoiled her arms from around his and slipped out of bed. Chris stayed in bed for now. After some time passed he also climbed from Penny's bed and got dressed. He wore a grey long-sleeved shirt, blue jeans, and brown boots.

Penny stepped out wearing a black and purple top, a black skirt, and black and purple boots. Chris stared for a moment before playing it off. He stood up and smiled.

"What? Is there something wrong with this...?"

"No!" Chris replied instantly. He got a bit shy. Penny looked surprised that he had answered that so fast. "No... You look great."

"Are you hungry?" Penny asked.

"Yup!" he answered.

"Then let's go get something to--" Penny paused for a moment and stared off. She must have realized something now that she was back to her normal self.

"What?" he asked.

"I need to talk to Autumn, come with me okay?" she urged. She took his arm and took him straight to the administration building. They made it to the library where he had arrived on his first day.

Autumn was wearing a red top with grey shorts and white shoes. She was sitting at her desk reading a book. She looked rather down actually. Autumn was laying her face on her knuckles as she read. She jumped when the door opened.

"Chris. Penny. What brings you two here?" she asked as she closed her book. "I'm actually glad you're here I was going to call you down--"

"Autumn wait," Penny requested. "Have you seen Hunter at all since before the attack? Not even during the attack just at all?"

"...No..." she placed her hand on her chin. "Actually, he wasn't at his post before the attack..."

"I just thought about it. Not because of what he did to Chris, but because he's been acting weird. Especially when those wolves attacked..."

"Actually Penny..." Autumn took a deep breath. "I was going to ask if you two had seen Emily."

"What?" Chris asked as he stepped forward.

"She never came to help me and she never went home last night," she was in deep thought, her tone indicated that much. "I-- I will talk to my grandfather about this..."

Chris felt his heart sink. He had just made up with Emily and spent time with her. Now she was missing and so was Hunter. Deep down Chris was terrified; he tried not to worry too much, but even Autumn didn't know where she was. If she didn't know Emily could be in a lot of danger. He turned away from Penny and Autumn who were still talking and walked away to think.

"In any case...granddad has been informed that-- Well..." Autumn paused and tried to find the best way to say this. "The Senate found out that you and Chris were made partners. They don't seem to want to listen that you two are a good pairing, and the fastest yet in the competition..."

Chris turned back to Autumn, "Don't say it." he seemed crestfallen. "They don't like Penny having a partner."

Penny folded her arms and shifted her weight. Autumn nodded and looked at Chris and then Penny. "There will be a hearing about it. You will both attend. It's tomorrow...That's why I'm so worked up. Not to mention everything else," Autumn told them.

Chris looked at Penny who merely hid behind her hair. He could not see anything but her mouth forming a straight line. " Why now? Isn't there enough going on?" she said. She was nearly inaudible.

"They prioritized it...They think you are a traitor."

"What?!" Chris barked causing Autumn to jump slightly. He immediately grew angry. "She helped fight them off and her sister is dead!"

"Chris, this..." Penny sighed, reminding him, "this is what I meant..." She gazed at him with a calm expression. "It's why I said I'd cause you trouble."

"I'll defend you," Chris stepped forward, determination in his voice.

"We won't win," Penny breathed.

"No... I just got you happy again..." Chris gritted his teeth.

"Let it go...What about Emily?" Penny returned to the problem at hand.

"Right, well, until we have proof that it's Hunter, I can't do much. I mean you can't just make accusations like that." Autumn brushed her hair back. "I'll investigate into it and get the general to interrogate the Sorcerers. We don't have time to chase whims."

"But if they see the traitor is Hunter they might--" Chris tried.

"They'll still put Penny on the spot. They don't want her to have a Wizard partner," Autumn corrected. "I'm sorry, she'll just have to defend herself."

"I'll defend her too," Chris reminded her.

"I know," Penny smiled and looked back at him. She still seemed really shaken up again. Chris figured Penny was expecting them to be separated. He wasn't going to let them take her away or hurt her.

"I would recommend consulting Hunter's partner," Autumn continued. "She'll probably help. Just don't accuse him. There isn't much proof right now."

"Who is his partner?" Chris asked.

"Morgan Nightgem," Autumn answered.

"She's my friend," Penny told him. "She was my first friend when I came here. She's very... colorful-- she loves to wear pink and she's a Mage."

Chris recalled seeing a girl of that description the night of the attack. She was standing nearest to the middle with her hands on her hips. He had also seen her just before the partner competition talking to Penny. She seemed like a social butterfly. Penny got along with her very well from what he could tell.

"I will also have one of the investigators check out her house--" Autumn began.

"No point," Chris interjected. "She never went home, remember?"

"Right...Well, go find Morgan. She should be with the other Mages. They are being briefed in the war room. It's the building to the left of this one. Third floor," she handed them both silver pass cards. "Don't lose these. If anyone asks, you're bringing important information.... which isn't a lie."

"Thanks Autumn," Chris smiled. "Seriously, you've already taught me a lot, and now you're helping me again."

"Anytime," she smiled shyly. "Now get going-- tomorrow, most of your time will be with the senate..."

Chris and Penny made their way across the lawn and toward the brown building. When they arrived, the guards stopped them for a moment. Penny presented their passes and explained that they had important news about developments. The guards stepped aside and they continued inside.

The interior housed a marble floor with unique designs, white columns, and some furniture. There were military personnel engaging in their own conversations in each corner. Some looked around warily when they heard the door, but upon seeing that they were mere students, they continued with their conversations.

There were a few soldiers and officials that had different attire. Instead of the normal black uniform they had grey, dark blue and proud gold, and many other colors. Chris figured that this building acted as an embassy. The alliance was said to have been made up of different militaries along with its own. It was rather fascinating to him to see them all gathered together.

Chris and Penny made their way to the stairs. They descended about thirty or so stairs before reaching the third floor. The third floor was dimly lit with a soft baby blue light that pulsed along the walls. It was built into the wall and there seemed to be almost a pulse that trailed down the hallway every few seconds. Penny stopped for a moment and checked each door to see what the sign beside it said. *Conference, interrogation,* and finally the one they were looking for: *war room.*

"This is us," Penny told him as she moved over to that side of the hallway.

Penny held up her card to the right of the door. A light projected from the mechanism and began to pan up and down the card slowly. After a few moments it beeped quietly and flashed green. The door slid open to the right and allowed entry. Once they stepped through it closed behind them and sealed.

Faint voices could be made out in the distance. The room was extremely dark with a path leading forward to a large room with multiple seats. There was a circular table in the center with a hologram of three planets. The only ones in the room appeared to be the Mages. There were seven of them now, previously eight.

Miyato was wearing a black shirt, a grey coat, black dress pants, black dress shoes, and he appeared to be checking some sort of tablet. Chris recognized his voice immediately.

"Everyone listen. We can't keep arguing about this. It's obvious that we have a security breach, but the war takes precedence, right?"

"Right, but if we're going to war the last thing we need is a backstabber," a female voice replied. It was the girl with the flute. She was wearing a light pale green jacket, a dark blue top, skinny jeans, and brown boots. "I mean we seriously can't be expected to go fight when the city is practically still licking its wounds."

"And without Tori we're down by one and until we get a replacement..." the boy with the staff began rubbing his chin. He walked away from the table and faced toward the wall to think.

Morgan hunched over the table and stared at the diagram laid before her. She was wearing a similar outfit to last time he had seen her.

"Enough, everyone," Morgan's voice came, the entire table silenced. Her hand came down onto the table, demanding attention. "I say we search the city again. We keep searching until they force us to go fight on these other worlds. The Empire is still nearby and can attack anytime they want. We have more defenses and we're ready for them, but that doesn't mean they can't do more damage," her eyes began to scan them over one by one. "We already know that we have two planets under attack. Liana city has been lost on Penrose, and the fighting has advanced to the jungles. Our people are using guerrilla tactics, but eventually we *will* be deployed there."

"That's going to be hell for everyone involved," Miyato noted.

"Not you," she corrected. "You're staying here. If anything at all happens to the city I want you to keep the people safe. We won't be long, but I'm sure you don't mind since you want to find the traitor so bad, right?" she somewhat smiled at him.

"Gladly," he replied in a laid-back manner, slipping his hands into his pockets.

"Then it's decided. Now the military will get the support they need out there, and we have a Mage here," she concluded. "You five should probably look over the battle plan again."

"Morgan we aren't new jacks," the girl with the flute began. "I'm offended."

"Melody I have to beg you just to study," Morgan countered.

"Fine," she groaned as she turned back to the maps. "I'll study the gosh dang plans."

"Hey," Morgan said as she turned, surprised to see Chris and

Penny standing there. Morgan hugged Penny. "What are you doing here? You're not breaking the rules, are you?"

"Me? Have I ever broken a rule?" Penny asked her.

"No, but I don't want you to get in trou-" she paused when Penny held up the silver key cards. Morgan nodded.

"It's really important we need to talk to you."

"Okay go ahead," Morgan agreed.

"Have you seen Hunter lately?" Penny said under her breath. "At all?"

"No. I've only seen Jerard today. I haven't seen Hunter."

"You haven't seen Hunter at all? Not even last night?" Penny pressed on.

"I have two partners, I struggle to keep up with one. Sometimes I curse the day I got two because I can hardly keep up with one," Morgan mused. "Wait did he do something wrong?"

Chris started to say something, but Penny silenced him by flicking him discretely. She pulled Morgan to the side away from everyone and began to speak to her privately. Morgan seemed to be protesting slightly from what he could tell. Penny didn't want Chris to interfere.

"So, Chris," Miyato's voice came out of the blue. Chris turned his attention to Miyato who had now turned toward him, and was leaning against the table. "How's your morning?"

"Man... I don't even know," Chris replied honestly.

"I'm sorry you came here at a time like this. It's messy right now. Hell, I'd be wanting to leave by now," he paused a moment. "How's Emily?"

"Oh uh--" Chris wasn't sure how to answer. "She's around..."

"Oh okay, I was just wondering. She was supposed to help me with my half of the cleanup in the southern part of town. She never showed, so she owes me next time!" he chuckled and smiled. "I'm sure she had a good reason."

"Miyato right? What brought you here?" Chris asked him.

"I was in the Empire..." he made a straight face as he said this.

"Really?!" Chris was stunned for a moment.

Miyato began to laugh a little, his facing forming a smile, "No that's Penny's story. I transferred from another one of the magic schools. I just happened to get noticed as a student excels with his mind and imagination. Because of that I got to be a mage."

"So that string you had was summoned..."

"Oh this?" he waved his hand lightly through the air as the wire formed into his hands. "I don't summon it, I imagine it. You had a run in with an Imagination user. I can do wonders with my mind." he balled his hand up and reopened it. The string was now a dagger. "See that?"

Chris internally wished he had that power. It seemed really cool. He could summon anything he wanted at will really. It seemed to be the best type of magic, and so far, Ice wasn't doing much for him. He still couldn't aim his spells.

"See here's the thing I have my limitations. I have a vivid imagination, but if I can't think of anything I'm dead. So, I have to keep myself inspired."

"That's so cool..." Chris smiled. "Better than Ice."

"Depends on the user. All magic types are equal," he said, correcting Chris' notion. "Oh, and about Tori?"

"Yes...?" Chris admittedly wanted to avoid this subject.

"She really did think you and Penny are going to be fantastic partners," Miyato informed Chris. "I mean it. We were going to go out to eat one time and she took off to see you. Tori wanted to see how you were coming along in your combat skills."

"I... I didn't know that," Chris smiled.

"So, if you ever need help training or whatever let me know. She was a good friend of mine," his smile dropped a little. "It stings that she's gone, but if she says you're a big deal I trust her. I mean you're the only other person to get Penny so happy, apparently."

"Thanks, Miyato," Chris felt a little bit relieved to see that he wasn't going to pin her death on him. He was actually encouraging him.

Penny returned to Chris' side, took his hand and tugged, "We have what we need," she informed him.

"Well I guess see you later, I've got important things to do!" Miyato told them.

"He's guarding the city," Morgan said simply as she passed by Miyato and returned to the table. She seemed a little bit off to Chris, maybe even spooked.

Penny pulled Chris out of the room and back the way they came. On the way she told him about what Morgan had shared with her. Hunter had not been back for some time, and during the attack he had told her he was going to check on something 'suspicious.' He never came back, and she went to look for him, but she assumed he was fine. After the attack he came back and told Morgan he was going to go apologize to Emily. He never came back after that.

Morgan had apparently insisted that Hunter was a good person. She had been partners with him and Jerard for a while, and never sensed anything wrong with Hunter. She had described him as 'misunderstood,' however if she needed to she would take the steps necessary to handle him.

"Chris?" Penny began. "I don't want you fighting Hunter alone if he really is the one who--"

"Why would I? I have you," he smiled.

"If they make me separate from you and stop being partners I-- I'll still have your back okay?" she walked a little faster. Chris caught her by her wrist and stopped walking. He looked her directly in her brown eyes and took her by her shoulders.

"I will fight for you tomorrow. I'm going to be there too and I won't let them hurt you. You're a good person and I *know* you're innocent," he assured her. Penny nodded.

The early warning siren began to blare loudly. A few planes flew overhead from the airfield. Everyone in the city began to scatter to safety. Soldiers and Wizards came running out of the military building along with the Mages.

"It's an airstrike..." Penny murmured. "We need to get off the street. The city defenses will shoot them down, but they're going to pick at them."

"Then where do we go?" Chris questioned.

"To the airfield...We'll see if they need help. It's only an air attack from what I can tell. It's an Imperial tactic to do this before--" there was a large explosion that shook the ground and sent a large gust of wind.

One of the Alliance planes was plummeting to the ground. Miyato ran past them, created a web of string and caught the plane. He began to make his way up to the plane that was now ensnared between two buildings to retrieve the pilot.

"They'll need help," Penny insisted as she took Chris' hand and began to hurry toward the airfield. The explosions began to ignite the clouds. Missiles and rapid-fire weapons could be heard above them and in the distance. Anti-air guns were sprouting from the tops of buildings to open fire. Chris's heart sank as he ran.

1 5

AVIATOR

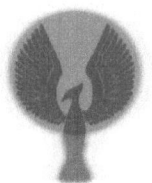

W hen they arrived at the airfield they noticed that a few planes had not yet taken off. There were a considerable number of pilots boarding their planes. Some planes were different colors from the rest, and must have been recently added by the reinforcements. Some of the aircrafts were being wheeled out to the strip.

"Move! Don't slow down! Get our people in the air!" Chris heard a man barking. "Get that one fueled up and in the air!"

"Yes sir!" one said.

"Right away!" another replied as he ran off, almost tripping over nothing to get to the fuel line. Chris assumed this man must have been one of the mechanics, because he had oil all over his blue coveralls.

"We need more pilots! Tell the city to send some Wizards who already got their training! We need them in the air!" a mechanic instructed as he pointed at a soldier.

"I'll relay the message right away," he assured as he got on his radio.

"We need a plane," Penny whispered to Chris. "They won't let us take one because we don't have the proper hours...but I can fly it."

"Okay, I trust you," Chris concurred. He ran over to one of the side hangars near the main building. Nothing. He continued to the second on and there was a plane, but it was falling apart from the last attack.

Penny followed closely behind Chris. She was keeping watch whilst they searched. There was a plane in the next hanger from them. It appeared to be a fighter plane. It had a dual cockpit. Two seats in the front, slightly spaced out. It was orange with a black interior. It had the appearance of a jet, but something more. Chris had never really seen a plane like this.

Penny wasted no time to scale the plane, pop the hatch, and enter. Chris followed suit. She sat on the left side while Chris sat on the right. Penny had controls on her side, and so did Chris, but it would not control the plane's aerial movement.

"I'm nervous, I've never been in a plane...A dogfight..." he began.

"Trust me," Penny pleaded. "I've been learning to fly a plane since I was eight and I was in multiple dogfights."

Chris took a deep breath as Penny strapped in. Chris quickly did the same upon seeing her do this. Penny took the headset that was resting nearby and placed it on her head. Chris did the same with the pair near him. She gave him a moment to slow his breathing. Admittedly he was nervous that they would get in trouble, but the city needed all of the help it could get.

Penny hit the red start button and the plane came to life. The engine roared outside of the plane. The many mechanisms of the fighter began to illuminate before them. *Radar, altitude, missile warning, missile capacity, ammo capacity*, and more. They began to slowly roll forward as Penny guided them out of the hangar and onto the runway.

"Hey!" Chris heard a mechanic cry as he came running toward them. He was coming up on Penny's side and screaming after them. "Stop! Stop!"

"Sorry, can't hear you," Penny replied without a care.

"Stop you're not authorized! That is a prototype plane!" he pleaded, panting as he went.

"It's okay I've been doing this a while. We'll clear the sky and come right back," Penny replied simply as she began to close the hatch.

"We're Wizards so it's okay! It's part of the job!" Chris laughed enthusiastically as they began to reach the point where they could take off. The hatch closed completely, the man threw his hands forward as if to say, *whatever*.

The plane began to gain altitude and leave the ground. Penny pulled up gently on the controls with both hands. This plane did not have a throttle like the majority of other planes. It had something of a steering wheel with two handles that could be pulled up, down, left, and right. There were also buttons to fire missiles and machine gun rounds.

"Chris can you check the radar?" Penny asked.

"Uh--" Chris began to look around for it.

"On your right," she said pointing with her right hand and then replacing it on the controls.

Chris leaned in and examined it. There were multiple dots on the radar. Some were red and some were blue. The red ones must have been Imperials.

"We've got two planes on our right and left," he informed her, glancing up for a moment to try to see.

"Wh-what?" Penny sounded confused. "Okay no. I need you to like tell me if they're friendly or not," she was still focused on flying.

It was getting harder to see in the clouds, but she didn't seem worried.

"Friendly. They're both pulling ahead--" he explained. "A yellow plane and a black plane came into view in front of them."

Chris thought he heard the sound of a person yawning for a moment. The screen in between Chris and Penny began to turn on. Soundwaves appeared on screen as a robotic voice spoke, "What's going on? Who's piloting me? Is this a test flight?"

"Nope it's the real deal," Chris replied. "Who even are you?"

A sad face appeared on screen as the AI replied, "Oh no! No no no! Not combat! Land!"

"We can't land. We need to help," Penny said simply as she rolled them slightly and turned left with the other planes.

"We'll be destroyed! The Spark is still a prototype!"

"The Spark?" Chris questioned.

"I-- Wait," a nervous face appeared on screen. "You're not even authorized! You didn't even know the name!"

"Look, calm down," Penny muttered. "We're busy."

There were a few flashes of yellow as Penny quickly performed a barrel roll to dodge a missile. She began to increase their speed as the ai began to scream frantically. Chris checked the radar again. Both allied planes had gone in separate directions to shake off two Imperial planes.

"Penny we're alone," Chris warned her.

"That's fine," she assured. "You should have a way of controlling the rear gun and a few of the forward guns over there..."

"I see them," he answered.

"I need you to use them now, I see two of them," Penny began to fire the machine guns.

There were also shots coming back at them, none of them hit, but they came close. Penny pulled up to avoid a collision with another plane. Chris did not get a good look to see which faction that plane belonged to, but it didn't matter once it took a missile to the rear, caught fire, and exploded violently. Some of the rubble flew up and went past the cockpit.

"Oh god. Penny are you sure you know what you're doing?" he asked.

"Do you trust me?" she answered with a question.

"Yes, but I'm scared," he said honestly.

"Hold on okay? There's one behind us. I'm going to position us I need you to shoot him," she told him. "We're going to get kind of close to the ground."

"What?"

"I know what I'm doing, I'm relying on you to get a good hit."

Penny pressed a few buttons and for a moment nothing happened, but then they began to fall backwards. Chris flinched as the enemy plane flew beside his side of the cockpit and then turned hard to go after them again. He took the controls and began attempting to shoot the enemy plane down. He used the screen on his side to see them. The plane was highlighted in red near the nose of the plane. Chris fired at the closest part of their aircraft. The left wing of their jet broke off as they began to spiral out of control and spin wildly toward the ground.

"Woohoo!" Chris cried as he pumped his fist into the air.

"Hold tight," Penny warned.

"Okay," Chris shouted over the explosions.

Penny reactivated the engines as they left the clouds and flew quickly toward the enemy planes. Alliance planes were actually just behind them. Penny seemed to have a really good sense of where she was. She locked on and upon hearing a 'beep' she fired three missiles. Two of the missiles hit and eradicated their targets.

"Shoot! Shoot!" Penny told him.

Chris began to fire at the fighters directly in their path. That plane began to spit smoke before losing altitude. Penny made the plane go straight down and flew slightly lower before coming back up and firing into the belly of another jet. They exploded. One of the blue alliance planes crashed into some of the debris from the destroyed Imperial plane and began to go toward the ground. They appeared to be trying to land.

"Alpha-47 pull up," a deep voice on the radio ordered.

"No can-do sir, multiple systems down losing control." a young male voice answered back. There was a bit of static but the plane was still intact. It landed in the grassy green plains below.

"Are you still with us, son?" the deep voice asked again. "If you're still alive let us know."

"I'm alive. I'm shaken, but alive. Go wreck their expensive planes," he replied back. "Going off coms-- need to get out of this tin can."

"Whoever is flying the Spark right now knows how to fight," a mature female voice cheered. "That's some fancy flying!"

"Clear radio of unnecessary chatter," a voice commanded. Chris recognized it as Violet. "I don't know who is flying it, but I have some guesses. Delta is that you?"

"Affirmative," Penny replied. "Thought we'd lend a hand."

"If you break that plane..." Violet began. Penny rolled her eyes and went back to scanning the sky.

"Penny is really good. I think she's got this," Chris was feeling very positive by now. He felt a little nauseous, but he was okay.

More Imperial planes appeared on the horizon. They were in a clustered formation, and there was a large ship in the middle of them. There were also a few large bombers and attack bombers with them. Chris looked over at Penny who rolled to the right and changed direction. She then flew up for a moment so they flew upside down, and then rolled back to normal once she reached the height that she wanted.

"What are they guarding?" a grizzled male voice asked.

"That's a transport!" Ian's voice came onto the comms now.

"Then take it out," Violet instructed. "And clear those bombers before they drop their payload."

"I just scanned that plane. There is no substantial force on that transport. That's...weird," Megan's voice chimed in.

"What?" Violet questioned. "Why would they--"

"The traitor!" Chris interrupted them all. "It's here to pick them up!"

"Delta, Bravo, Alpha, Echo on those bombers! Foxtrot, get that transport. The rest of you on those fighters! We'll focus fire on the attack planes after they're down!" Violet commanded.

"Go!"

Every plane increased their speed and headed straight for their targets. Penny peeled off and began to fire at one of the bombers from above. The bomber fired back. A few bullets hit the Spark and caused a bit of damage to the armor and cockpit hatch. Penny fired a missile into the cockpit and flew past them as they began to lose control and veer off to the left.

Chris noticed a purple plane flying circles around the Imperial fighters. It destroyed the transport, and tore through multiple of their fighters. Chris was so focused on Violet's spectacular performance that he had not seen the plane on their tail. He only remembered when the plane shook violently upon taking a hit. Chris's head hit the controls in front of him; he began rubbing his head.

"Chris, come on I need you focused..." Penny urged as she turned as hard as she could to the left; reducing speed, and then increasing once again as soon as the turn finished to shake the fighter. It was coming back to attack them again. The black plane from earlier appeared behind the fighter chasing them. "If we keep taking hits like that we'll--"

"Stand by. We'll take them out," Megan assured them. "Lining up..." Their plane centered behind the enemy's. "Firing."

Their plane fired a shotgun like blast. One shot was all it took, the enemy fighter burst into flames as it fell through the clouds. The black plane caught up and flew beside them. Megan waved at them from the back seat, Ian was in the front seat flying. Penny glanced over and smiled a little bit, she looked relieved.

"Thanks, guys," Penny breathed.

"I know. I know. Good shot, right?" Ian sounded like he was congratulating himself.

"Ian please...modesty," Megan sighed. "Geez, it's like you have no filter."

Their conversation was cut short as cut short as Violet's voice came, "Change of plans. We're falling back to the airport and landing. One of our capital ships just arrived. We're letting them handle this."

"But Violet we can help them, right?" Megan asked.

"No. They can clean this up, we need to get back to the city and handle the stragglers," she told them.

Violet turned hard and pulled away, the others followed. Penny took out one last plane before performing a corkscrew maneuver and following right behind the others. Chris turned to see the Imperials attempting to retreat and being chased closely by friendly newcomers.

"Thanks, Fleur. We'll take it from here. You barely left us any..." a voice on the comms grumbled. "Quite efficient."

"Thank you, admiral," Violet replied briefly. "We'll go clean up the air above the city and then make our landing."

DOUBLE CROSSED

T he planes had begun to land back at the airfield. Chris and Penny began their descent. Penny reduced the aircraft's speed as they came to the ground. They stopped just behind Megan and Ian. Chris laid back in his seat and shut his eyes for a moment to relax himself. It was over. He felt a little sick, but also very glad they could help.

A few of the planes in front of them began to open their cockpits. A male voice on the comms began to speak, "I think-- Negative that's not everyone who went up in the sky. The only one missing is Alpha number forty-seven."

"Come in air traffic control, this is Violet. Alpha forty-seven had a system malfunction upon taking damage. Suspected engine failure. He and his plane will need pick up. Sending you coordinates. Over," Violet answered back almost immediately.

"Air traffic control to Violet, receiving now. Stand by..." a female voice responded to Violet this time. "Received. A crew will be dispatched shortly for Alpha four-seven along with an armed cleanup crew for the rest out there, over."

"Roger that command," Violet answered back. "Over and out." Chris watched as Violet leapt out of her fighter jet. She placed both hands on her helmet, removed it. She had her hair in a double French braid; both braids were tied together.

Penny looked over at Chris and gave him an amused look. He looked very nauseous and somewhat dizzy. Chris sunk back into his seat and turned his head toward her. Penny began to giggle a little.

"You did good," Penny smiled softly. "You're really accurate. Are you okay?"

"I feel sick, but yeah," he replied in a slight grumble. "Just trying to process that."

Penny stopped laughing and shook her head, "You did great. I'm very impressed."

"Violet didn't seem to think so though," Chris reminded her. "She seemed pretty unhappy about it."

"She's only impressed with herself," Penny commented, rolling her eyes and unbuckling herself.

"But isn't she better than most of the pilots here?" he wondered aloud, turning back to the window to look at Violet again.

"Ha! She's good, but someone is always better. Eventually someone will be better than her," Penny assured. "It's just the way it works. She doesn't even try to get better."

"I think you're better," Chris complimented. "Seriously, you're a badass."

Penny's face flushed a bright pink. She seemed surprised, and Chris could tell she was caught off guard. She stared at him for a moment before smiling. She pressed the button to release the hatch and sat up in her seat. Penny seemed rather thankful for this comment, and he thought she appeared more confident.

One of the mechanics brought over a white ladder and rested it on the right side of the plane. Chris climbed down first. Penny crossed over to his side and climbed down next. She nudged him as if to say 'thanks.' They began to walk toward the crowd of pilots that had gathered together. They appeared to be celebrating already.

"I hate to say it, but Penny and her partner may have saved my ass. I didn't see that plane at all in the clouds. And then there was a second one on top of that," said one male pilot. He had blonde hair, green eyes, a small beard, and appeared to be 29. "Guys that prototype plane does wonders!"

"I'll say," Ian replied. He was wearing a black t-shirt, jeans, and black shoes. "They were all like zoom and bang! Bang! And Vwooooosh!" he exaggerated as he moved his hands along to the movements.

Megan began to laugh at her partner's theatrics. She was wearing a green long-sleeved shirt, skinny jeans, and white shoes. She shook her head and hit him in the arm to get him to stop.

A man wearing a black military uniform, a black beret with the Alliance bird symbol on it, and combat boots was approaching them. He had two holsters forming an X shape across his chest. He also had a lit cigarette in his hand. He looked to be in his late forties or early fifties. He cleared his throat to get everyone's attention. He took the cigarette up to his lips for a moment before exhaling a puff of smoke. Then he spoke.

"I want to thank every last one of you for your service just now. That was at a moment's notice," he started. "Pennelopie. Christopher. You weren't authorized, but I thank you as well. I'll be doing everything in my power to get you both under my command. That was the best flying I've ever seen. More kills than the average pilot. Pennelopie?"

"Y-yes sir?" Penny exclaimed.

"You flew for the Empire, didn't you?" he guessed. "Our spies told us you did. I didn't think much of it until now." Penny began to lower her head in shame. "I'm astounded. I want you to fly for us. Your partner too."

"S-Sir?" Penny questioned, perplexed.

"But sir she's a-" one pilot began; he stepped forward. He had greying hair, a small mustache, and a beard.

"Is she a good pilot?" the man cut him off. "It's not about what she is or where she came from. She just saved some of your hides. More than that she's done more for the Alliance than some people hope to."

"But still-- the higher ups would never agree," the pilot tried again.

"If those suits won't listen to their highest ranked General then they're foolish. I'll be attending that damn hearing," he replaced his cigarette between his lips and pushed it to the side as he spoke again. "And I'll have some words. This is ridiculous. Girl like this shouldn't lose her partner," he muttered. "Foolishness."

"But aren't you mad we stole a prototype?" Chris was very puzzled.

"Not one bit. You put it to good use so I'm making it yours. You damn well deserve it," he praised. "But the mechanic who works on this plane might have your head over the damages."

"Thank you, sir," Penny beamed.

"Don't get the wrong idea. You'll both have to work hard. That doesn't shy you away does it?" he extended his hand to both of them.

"Not one bit," Penny said as she took his hand and shook it. Chris shook his hand next. The general had a very strong grip. Chris was always told that having a strong grip during a handshake was good, but he didn't understand why. All he knew was that this general was a big deal and extremely high ranked. As he let go of the general's hand he began to wonder just how much action he had seen.

Ian came over and threw his arms around Chris and Penny. He brought them both in close. All three of them began to laugh; Megan shook her head, but Chris could see she was smiling. He figured

Megan just liked to seem intelligent, and she probably was, but she could still have fun like the rest of them.

"Tomorrow we're going to make sure you and Chris stay partners! You guys are *awesome*," Ian chucked.

"Yes, we will," Megan agreed. "I'm not sure if we'll be allowed to go, but we'll be supporting you regardless."

"You don't think you can go?" Chris was curious if they could be there.

"I'm not sure, but regardless, you have many people supporting you," Megan said encouragingly.

Chris smiled. Penny had people that cared about her, and that was enough for him. She actually seemed really happy; of course, Megan and Ian knew Penny already, but it was nice to know other people would be there for her. She seemed much different than when they had first met. He wasn't sure what caused it, but he liked to think he had a part in it.

By now some of the pilots had come up to talk to Penny. They were shaking her hand or congratulating her. Even the one that had objected earlier. He didn't seem as pleased as the others, but he had some matter of respect for Penny now. Not only was Penny an exceptional fighter and pilot, but she had the general back her up.

Chris's smile dropped for a moment. He saw Hunter in the distance carrying something. He seemed to be in a hurry and was heading for the city. He appeared to be wearing a red shirt, a black jacket, and black leather combat boots. Chris couldn't tell what he had in both of his arms, but it was obviously important. He was in a hurry.

Chris tugged on Ian's arm as best he could. "I just saw Hunter," he tried. Ian seemed too preoccupied to notice. Penny was deep in a conversation and Megan was inspecting her plane. Chris was in a hurry and so, he wasn't really sure what he should do. He wasn't sure if he would get the chance to catch Hunter again.

"Megan," Chris called out to her as he ran over to her and attempted to pull her from the plane. Megan fought back a little and looked thoroughly confused.

"What are you doing?" she asked, looking completely lost.

"I just saw Hunter!" Chris tried frantically.

"What about him?" she questioned.

"I think he's the traitor! Penny and I were supposed to keep an eye out for him!" he continued on.

Megan looked behind Chris and shook her head, "Chris he's not there." Chris turned back to see she was right. He was indeed gone. "But he was--"

"Chris listen, I really need to make sure our plane didn't sustain any meaningful damage," and with that Megan turned right back to what she was doing.

Forget it, Chris said internally as he ran off in the direction in which he had seen Hunter. Chris knew he was going toward the city, and that was all he needed. He would head in that direction until he saw him again. He wanted to find Emily and that was exactly what he would do even without help.

Chris kept running until the airfield was much farther away than when he started. He still had not seen any sign of Hunter. A few moments passed before he saw him. He was nearing the city by now. He seemed to have slowed to a walk. Chris could roughly make out that the person he was carrying was female. *Emily,* he concluded. He figured Hunter must have had Emily.

Chris caught up to them, and Hunter reacted before he did. He turned back to see Chris and seemed relieved. He stopped walking and waited. He appeared as if he was panting, and was obviously on edge. He was sweaty and looked tired.

"Chris..." Hunter managed. "Help me with Emily, she got hurt!" he was gasping for air.

"What happened?!" Chris demanded as he came over to check

on Emily. He pushed her hair out of her face to see her unconscious. He immediately directed his attention to Hunter, giving him a hateful glare.

"We were outside of the city making sure no more wolf attacks could happen. I convinced her to come with me and find out where they were coming from. Before we even got to the forest," he explained, stopping to catch his breath. "So, then we saw Imperial planes start attacking Alliance planes."

"What happened?" Chris repeated.

"Emily got hurt during all of the chaos and one of the planes even crashed down. I tried helping the pilot and he got pretty far, but he died not far from his plane. I think he was trying to get back to the city on his own."

"Alpha forty-seven is dead?" Chris seemed shocked.

"I guess that was his identification? I was going to ask him for help but when I rolled him over he had a huge wound across his face. I don't have time to explain; I'm getting Emily back to the city for some aid."

"Let me help," Chris offered.

"Fine just come on," Hunter said rather harshly as he jogged into the city.

They continued on for a few moments. Chris began to wonder if he had wrongly believed it was Hunter. He was a jerk, but he was a jerk that cared deeply about his sister. He didn't seem to care that Chris was with him, he was so desperate to get Emily back to the city that he was willing to take any help. Chris felt kind of sick; it was hard seeing Emily like this. She didn't have any visible injuries. Her wounds may have healed, but she looked vulnerable and that was something he was not used to. In fact, he could not recall the last time he ever saw her sleep, because she was always hard at work.

"We need to help her as fast as we can," Chris reminded Hunter.

"Thanks Chris, but I know what's best for her. Just hurry up," Hunter shot back.

"I'm trying to help," Chris argued.

"Is now the time?" Hunter asked angrily.

Hunter was still leading the way. Chris began to have even more doubts about Hunter being the traitor. He was trying to help Emily. He wasn't wasting a single second to help her. He almost felt bad for Hunter. He got so much heat from everyone, but he was only ever trying to help. Chris considered apologizing for a moment.

"Sorry Chris," he called back as he extended his hand and fired an extremely powerful blast of fire from his hand. The building beside Chris began to fall. Chris attempted to move, but the brown brick building was coming down too fast. He sprinted full speed forward after Hunter, but the building collapsed on top of him. He shielded himself as best he could.

Chris was now trapped under the destroyed building. He couldn't free any part of his body. He didn't hear anyone nearby but Hunter: meaning no one would be coming to help.

"Hunter!" Chris yelled out from under the rubble, slamming the back of his hand on the rubble above him angrily. He attempted to remove himself, but he was buried so deep that there was no way. On top of everything else, he felt a sharp pain in his gut. Something had impaled him when the building fell. Perhaps a part of the building had cut him, but he could feel himself bleeding badly. His body was healing slowly, but since he was also being crushed it couldn't work as well and was struggling to keep up.

Chris attempted to free himself again, but he could feel himself getting weaker over time. He managed to free his arms. He then tried to use them to lift the rubble off. No luck. *The watch*, he remembered Emily had given it to him not long ago. She had said to use it to call for help in the case of emergencies, but he didn't actually think he would need it. Chris lifted his right wrist up to where his eyes could see and began to fiddle with the device. In truth, he had not taken the time to learn how it worked yet, but he had to now.

The screen illuminated. An interface projected from the watch, and formed almost a holographic touch screen in front of him. He saw multiple names that Emily had entered into his contact list: *Emily S., Penny D., Ian, Megan F.,* and *Victoria D.* Chris wasn't sure who to call, he assumed they were all back at the airfield celebrating, or in Megan's case working. Someone must have noticed he was gone, but he couldn't take the chance. Chris wasn't sure who to call, they were all very busy. The only one who he was sure saw him leave was Megan. Would she stop her work just to answer? He was in such a panic, and he felt so weak that he just pressed the first button that his left finger touched.

"Hello? Chris?" Megan's voice answered loud and clear. "Where did you run off to? When I finished checking my plane, I turned to talk to you about it more but you were gone."

"Megan..." Chris managed, trying to keep his words from slurring.

"What's wrong? Where are you?" she sounded concerned now.

"Help..." he could hardly even hear his own plea.

"General Nick!" he heard Megan shout on the other end. "Penny! Your partner needs help!"

Megan must have hung up so Penny could call, because the call ended right as Penny's name appeared on the interface as the watch began to go off. Chris tried to reach up to press the answer button, but he felt faint for a moment and unable to move. He didn't pass out, but he couldn't move very well, and probably needed to save energy. The watch continued to ring for a moment before going silent and going into sleep mode. Chris laid there attempting to keep himself calm and hoped that they would arrive in time.

Chris felt as if he had been waiting there for hours. He wasn't sure how much time had passed but he had begun to lapse in and out.

He'd be fine one moment and then black out, and then wake up again. He began to hear people around him, but he didn't think it was his friends. He didn't recognize any voices. These people probably didn't even know he was under the building, and more than likely they figured it was from the air attack. Chris did his absolute best to stay calm, but he could feel himself panicking, he wasn't sure how much time he would really have.

"Are you sure he's here?" Ian sounded close.

"I know he is, I tracked his watch," Megan declared. "And Penny probably can sense him in danger."

"Yeah but where is he in all of this mess?" Penny sounded worked up. "Find him please. Help me."

"Chris? Can you hear us?" Megan called out. "Chris?"

"Chris!" Penny tried, "Ian if we find him we'll need you."

"I'll get my buddy out," Ian promised.

Chris relaxed a little, but it was hard to stay conscious. He continued to lapse in and out. Every time he came to he heard something different. He could hear them moving the bricks, but they weren't close. How was he going to get their attention though? He was buried, and Penny couldn't quite pinpoint where he was just yet with her magic.

He wasn't going to die. Not only because he wanted to protect Penny and stay with his friends, but because he had to make Hunter pay and save Emily. Chris began to push as hard as he could with his right hand. His hand began to slip through some of the wreckage. He could feel his hand being cut by the sharp pieces, but he had to get their attention. His fast healing was starting to fail and time was short. His hand was just barely being healed of the cuts and bruises.

Chris stopped for a moment to regain his strength as much as he could. He gave it one more good push. He had broken through and he could feel his hand in the fall breeze above. He winced, worn out. If he didn't have adrenaline pumping he wouldn't have been able to do that while injured.

"Over here!" he heard an unfamiliar male voice say. "Dig here!"

"Hurry Ian," Penny urged. "Please...Please..."

Ian began to throw rubble left and right. Chris couldn't see it, but he could hear it. He sounded like he was barely trying, and the others must have been helping him. Chris could see a little bit of light; however, it was still pretty far off. How long would it take? Hopefully not much longer. He felt faint.

Chris's heart began to beat faster. He could hear it in his own ears. He had never felt this before. He couldn't move and he could feel his breathing slowing against his will. He felt the weight on him disappearing as they continued to work. He wasn't sure what was happening to him. Chris felt dizzy and almost hazy.

The rubble cleared. Penny moved over Chris and held his face. She then began to check him. Penny must have noticed the dire wound and tried to keep him talking. Chris didn't hear most of what she said. She sounded so far away...

"Megan, heal him!" Penny pleaded.

"I can stabilize his wound, but he's lost way too much--" Megan explained to Penny.

Chris didn't hear the rest. It went almost inaudible. He was struggling to keep his eyes open, and by now he was panicking. There was nothing he could do. Ian was keeping the crowd back, but he could only see him from the corner of his eye. Megan was trying to heal his wound so he didn't bleed any further, his fast healing had finally failed.

"Don't die...Please...please don't die you're scaring me," Penny squeaked desperately. "You said you wouldn't. Please..."

"Get back a little," the unfamiliar male voice told Megan and Penny. They did. "Megan, is he stable?"

"Yes. Yes, I'm sure of it," she reassured everyone. Even Megan sounded nervous.

Ian rejoined them, "How is he?"

"I think he might--" the man started to examine Chris's wounds.

"No!" Penny cried. Chris didn't hear anymore. He relaxed, closing his eyes, and falling asleep completely.

DISEMBODIED

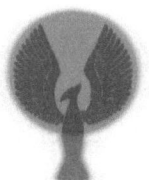

There was nothing but a quiet forest. Pure white snowflakes fell all around, the wind blew, animals scattered, desperately trying to find a spot to keep warm. The white sheets continued to pile up. There was a blizzard coming through. The only human for miles stood with their arms folded; trying to stay warm.

"Where am I?" Chris questioned. "Why am I here? This was just a dream...It's not real..." Chris lifted his hands and studied them as closely as he could. "Am I dead...? I couldn't have..."

Chris lifted his hand up in front of his face so he could see at least a little better. He began to make his way in the direction he was facing. There was nothing but trees and snow, it was dark and so he could barely see anything. He wasn't sure where he was, but he felt eyes on him somehow. Was someone watching him?

He began to get goosebumps; not only because it was cold, but he felt someone watching him. What was happening? Was this all a dream? Would he just wake up and realize he is back on Earth? He wanted to stay.

Chris stopped and attempted to calm his mind. He wasn't really sure what was going on, but none of this felt real. There must have been something he missed. He couldn't have been dead. Chris turned around to try the other direction and felt a chill go straight down his spine. There was a girl with red curly hair stood before him. She looked to be about his age, maybe a little older. She had no expression on her face. He eventually recognized it to be Autumn. She stared at him and he stared back. She had scared him half to death for some reason.

"Chris," she started. "You died."

"I couldn't have," he uttered in disbelief. He turned away for a moment and glanced around. He wondered if he could find a way to save himself. He figured if he followed his previous dream, he could get out.

"Wake up."

Chris turned back to speak to Autumn, but she was gone. In fact, he began to hear an owl for a moment. He glanced around left and right and couldn't find the source, until he looked up. The moment he found the snowy white owl it began to speak again, "Mr. Spell-crafter!" Chris approached it. It continued to call out to him, "Can you hear me?"

"I can hear you!" Chris called out. There was no reply. *How can I hear him, but he can't hear me?*

The snowy forest faded. Chris was now standing back on the street. He could see a crowd of people standing around the scene. There were guards telling them to keep back. The building that had fallen on him appeared to have been a convenience store. He couldn't quite tell, but it didn't seem like anyone had been in there-- at least he hoped that was true.

Megan, Ian, and Penny were all gathered around his body. There was a teacher with curly brown hair, a brown curly beard, brown pants, and a navy blue and red collared shirt attempting to revive him. He was rubbing his hands together and then touching it onto Chris's chest. His body would jump every time a jolt hit him.

Megan was rubbing Penny's back to try to calm her, Penny was crying, and Ian was pacing back and forth. All three of them were waiting anxiously to see if Chris would indeed be revived. There was no way to reach out to them, and all Chris could do was watch. It was strange for him to watch this all play out.

"Ian...you're not helping," Megan snapped. "Please stop."

"I'm nervous. Of course, I'm pacing," he replied. "I can't do anything..."

"Then we wait."

"Meg..."

"Ian just sit-" Megan cursed at him.

"It's fine...both of you please..." Penny pleaded softly as she shook her head. She was crying. She had almost no expression on her face, but he could tell she was freaking out. She was watching, her eyes following the teacher's hands every time they touched Chris' chest, then to his face to see if his condition changed, and then back to his hands. He wanted to hug her, but he knew he couldn't. He could hear her mumbling, "Please...not you too. You have to be okay--"

"Still nothing," the teacher said. "I'm going to try again. One of you go get the Life teacher. Someone else go get the headmaster. The paramedics should be here soon." The teacher gave Chris another good shock, this time as he pulled his hands away Chris felt a pull. He wasn't sure what it was, but it was like he was going back. "I got him back!" The teacher informed everyone.

18

LUCKY PENNY

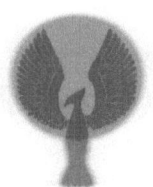

When Chris awoke, he felt absolutely horrible. It was as if he had been knocked around all over the place by an angry animal. He felt as if he was laying in the most comfortable bed imaginable. Warm sheets were covering him. The lights of the white room stung his eyes as he reopened them for the first time. It was so bright that he was starting to tear up and slightly close his eyes to see. He raised his left hand to shield them from their rays; upon doing so, he felt something in his arm. It felt like it was sticking him a little. Then, Chris brought his hand closer to his face, he felt it rub against something. He was wearing a mask that was pumping air into his nose. The tube was connecting to somewhere.

On his chest there were some sort of stickers with wires connected to them all over his bare chest. They felt strange and he didn't dare remove them. It felt as if every time his heartbeat he would hear mechanical feedback beside him. He concluded that he was in the hospital. There was a window to his left that was closed by blue curtains with golden yellow stars. Beside the window was a green vase with yellow roses and the name *Megan*, a black and red box of what appeared to be chocolate that said, *get well. I'm going to punch him for you, Ian.* To the right of those was a snow globe that had the name, *Norora.* There was a card that he couldn't read very well from this distance, but he could make out a few words, *it is not easy to evade death's pull, you are fortunate. I wish you quick recovery. A wonderful partner for a student of Death, such as Penny.*

He began to pan around the room slowly observing his surroundings. There was a sink on the farthest wall near the white door. There was a red chair sitting to the left of the door. To the far most right near the T.V was a brown door leading off somewhere (most likely the bathroom.) Next to him was a screen monitoring his blood pressure, heart rate, and a few other values that he wasn't sure of, an IV stand with the bag, and a keyboard embedded into the wall.

There was movement to his right. Chris shifted his gaze down to see what it was. Penny was sitting in a cushioned tan chair. She was laying her head on the bed. She was wearing a black long-sleeved shirt with yellow and blue star outlines, and dark blue skinny jeans. He saw her shoes sitting beside her, so she must have gotten comfortable. The shoes were popcorn knitted white and blue boots with fur and buttons. *I've never seen her wear anything like this before,* he thought.

Chris wondered how long she had been here for. Considering that she had been wearing different clothes than when he last saw her; it must have been at least a day. His right hand was interlocked with hers. She wasn't wearing her gloves anymore. Her hands were really soft and send tingles up his arm. They weren't exactly small, but they weren't quite as big as his hands. Was she comforting him?

Penny let out a gentle sigh and squeezed his hand. She showed no sign of waking up. He wondered when everyone else had come to visit, but the only one to stay was Penny. Was it because he was her partner or was it because she felt like staying with him? *Maybe she just fell asleep by accident and the doctors allowed her to stay,* Chris assumed. He would ask her later if she wanted to tell him.

Chris took a moment to reflect on what had happened. He had come so close to dying, and it had felt as if he was outside of himself. He had watched them trying to revive him. It wasn't pretty, and he really should be dead. Any normal person would have been dead, but his magic kept him sustained long enough to get help. He died, but they revived him rapidly.

The white door slid open with a light humming sound. A doctor wearing a red shirt, white coat, and grey pants entered. He had square glasses, brown eyes, and curly hair. He appeared to be about thirty. He crossed over to Chris's bed and removed a clipboard that had been hanging on the left side. His name tag read Anthony Italiano.

"So, how are you feeling?" Anthony asked. "You're finally awake. This is this first time I've seen you conscious," he began to write on the clipboard he picked up before replacing it.

"Weird. Nothing hurts...Can I take this mask off?" Chris asked.

"Yes. Your lungs have healed from the damage. Nothing to worry about," Anthony replied as he adjusted his glasses.

Chris pulled the strap from behind his ears and removed the mask by pulling it over his head. The doctor held out his hand. Chris gave it to him.

"You know they didn't think that you'd wake up so soon," he commented.

"What do you mean?" Chris asked.

"It's been a little over a week," he stated. "Today is Friday."

"Holy--" Chris was taken aback by this. "Penny's senate meeting..."

"Calm down and breathe. It was moved due to the attack and the headmaster wouldn't allow Penny to go without you," he told him.

"It's tomorrow whether you're better or not. They held a vote just to decide if they would give her more time and it failed."

"Am I good to go?" Chris asked hastily.

"For the most part, but you'll have to take it easy tomorrow. You'll be fine by Sunday."

"Thanks...But I lost a lot of blood, right?"

The doctor smiled and nodded. He crossed over to the sink and began to wash his hands. He then placed on a pair of replaceable blue gloves. He then returned to Chris and finally spoke, "You have o-negative blood. We had trouble finding a donor, and we were about to start calling for people to get checked." Chris nodded as the doctor gave his recount. Anthony continued on, "So Penny insisted that we check her blood. She flat out begged for us to prick her finger and check. We did and lo and behold she had an exact match. She's a generous donor. It only took a moment..."

"Really?" Chris turned and looked at Penny in disbelief. She was still sound asleep, holding his hand.

"Yeah, the other doctors were surprised that she gave blood. She gave more than what was recommended, and she was dizzy afterwards. We gave her fruit and water to help her make up for that. We gave you a few things too. She didn't even flinch at the needle like most people or cringe," he recounted. "So, we transferred her blood as fast as we could into you. You pretty much recovered on your own after that. We tried to tell her she could go home, but we couldn't get her to. She stayed in this room with you and only left to get something to eat or help one of her friends, and when she did, she made me keep an ear out for you."

"Really?" Chris began to blush.

"Oh yeah, man. She really cares about you. She seriously left here to get a change of clothes one time...She spent the nights just as she is right now, and when your friends came she was usually still by your side. Actually...she held your hand when giving blood too. I don't understand partners, seeing as I don't have magic, but I admire her bravery."

"Yeah," Chris smiled and began to pet her head with his free hand. "She's strange, but I like it."

"I didn't know she was a Sorcerer until someone told me! I don't get the big deal. She saved you," Anthony told him. "Leave whenever you'd like but let me know first. I'll be back soon. And you go nowhere without Penny," he began toward the door.

"Because it's dangerous?" Chris asked.

"Because she won't let you," he answered back.

"Doctor?"

"Yes?"

"Is it...at all possible to send letters to other planets?" Chris inquired.

"Everyone does," he replied as he turned back, raising his eyebrow.

"I want to send a letter to Earth," Chris told him. His mind was lingering on Jackie and Ty. In truth, he missed them, and he was wondering how they were doing. Not only that, but Jackie would flip out if she found out that he died for any amount of time. He figured they'd want to know.

The doctor made a sound with his throat, "That would be difficult. Earth doesn't like Terminus," he answered.

"Is it possible?" he persisted. "Please?"

"I don't know," he told Chris honestly, Chris's smile dropped a little at this response. "But I can try. Write one out and I'll try to get it to the right person," he agreed. "Just be prepared if it doesn't make it or if you don't get a reply."

Chris scribbled as fast as he could on a piece of paper the doctor had brought him. He wrote about two pages of his adventures and folded it neatly into a white envelope with golden edges. The doctor stamped it with a blue alliance bird to seal it. Chris made sure to properly add their names and that it was from him, and then handed it off to doctor Anthony who left with it.

Chris hoped that his friends would receive his message. They no doubt wanted to hear about what had been going on, and he knew Earth's officials wouldn't tell them much. He tried to leave out the more gruesome details about his near-death experience, but it wasn't easy. It still sounded pretty bad. *Maybe I should have said I was unconscious instead,* he thought.

Penny began to stir. She lifted her head and removed her hand from his. She opened her eyes and as soon as she did she immediately became happy. She threw her arms around him and squeezed tightly, he didn't mind one bit. He hugged her back just as tight.

"You're finally awake!" she said with a big smile on her face. Penny let go and stared at him for a moment before sitting back in her chair. "Thank goodness..."

"Did I scare you that much?" Chris asked.

"Of course!" Penny rebuked. "I was worried sick. Your friends were worried sick. The headmaster started a manhunt for Hunter and the general was really angry when he found out about him. I've never seen him so angry in front of a crowd."

"Yeah I must have missed a lot," he guessed as he shrugged his shoulders and laid his head against the soft pillow. "I can't imagine how much."

"Well...Morgan is trying to find Hunter and the whole city is locked down. No one can leave without reason and there are so many checks," she smiled. "Hunter has nowhere to go!"

"Well then let's get him as soon as possible. As soon as your hearing is over, we'll take him down!" Chris said enthusiastically. He sat up.

"No," Penny replied, shooting him down. "You're not fighting him again. At least not without me. That was beyond dangerous running off like that..."

"I had to...everyone was busy," he apologized. "Sorry..."

"Chris, I'm your partner," she said softly as she took his right hand in both of hers. "I don't care what I'm doing, you have my ear. You always do. Just please don't run off without me like that. I was having an anxiety attack the whole time they were trying to revive you. I still couldn't calm down when the doctors took you," Penny mumbled, staring at his hand.

Chris lowered his head for a moment. He felt guilty for all the trouble he had caused her. It was true that now everyone knew Hunter was the traitor, but he almost didn't make it. He almost ended up like Myra and Victoria. Penny was having a complete breakdown the whole time, and he could only assume she was for days after.

Doctor Anthony had come back after a while and removed everything else from Chris. Once he was fully unhooked from the equipment, he was free to go. Chris had to be placed in a wheelchair for the moment. He was able to walk a little bit, but the doctors wanted to stay on the safe side. They estimated that he would not need it tomorrow.

As Penny wheeled him out of the hospital, he was greeted with the blinding yellow horizon. They were in an unfamiliar part of town, but according to Penny they weren't far from the magic schools. It appeared to be nearing sunset.

"Hey Penny? I'm hungry, can we stop to get something?" he requested.

"Actually, we are going to Megan's place. She's cooking right now," she told him. "I called her while you were being put in the wheelchair and talking to the doctor...Ian will be there too."

"That's great, but the stairs on the way to our dorm and her house..." he began.

"Then we'll go the long way," she decided as she began to push him forward carefully. She didn't go too fast either, she stayed at a good pace, and was extremely careful with him.

They talked along the way, and Penny caught him up to speed. She told him about how furious the headmaster was about Hunter's betrayal and what he had done to Chris and Emily. He ordered all transportation on and off the planet to be suspended and for Hunter to show himself. The only ones allowed on and off the planet were checked and had to have clearance. The headmaster was apparently going to lock down Hunter's plane too, but it had gone missing. He had also placed a ship in orbit monitoring the passing ships and planes. Chris could tell he wasn't playing at all. After all, what chance did Hunter have now?

"I heard you gave blood for me," Chris smiled and looked back at Penny. They were currently passing through the market.

"I did," she admitted. "I didn't think they'd tell you."

"Penny, you saved my life."

"And I would do it again in a heartbeat...Err no pun intended," she laughed a little. "Seriously."

"I'm so lucky that you're my partner," Chris gushed. "Oh, I have a nickname for you now!"

"What?" she asked, completely curious now.

"My lucky Penny!" he said excitedly.

Penny tilted her head in complete bewilderment, "Your what?"

"Lucky Penny!" he repeated the same way. "On Earth we have money called pennies that are worth one cent. Some people say they are lucky. So, you're like my lucky Penny."

"I don't know about that name," she said honestly.

"How about Penn?" he tried, considering that she didn't like the last nickname.

"I'm fine with that one," she agreed with a slight smile.

They arrived at Megan's house. It was white and green. It wasn't too particularly big, but it was large enough for her and now Ian. It wasn't too particularly far from the dorm, but it also wasn't too close.

Penny took him up to the door and knocked. After a moment Megan answered.

Megan was wearing her white outfit from when he had first met her, and she had her hair in a ponytail. Ian could be seen behind her, asleep on the sofa. He must have fallen asleep on their way to Megan's house. He was wearing a white shirt, black jacket, jeans, and black shoes.

"He's asleep?" Penny asked, astounded. "Now?"

"Uh-huh," Megan muttered. "After I told him you were coming."

"What's he tired from?" Chris asked her, trying to look past her.

"He offered to help clean up the city, and immediately regretted it. They have nearly finished, but he's acting like he did all the work..." Megan sounded unimpressed.

"Ian is pretty strong, maybe it was hard after all," Chris said in defense of Ian. "Cut him some slack."

Megan stepped aside and let them enter. She closed the door behind them and locked it. Penny wheeled Chris over to the dining room table near Ian and headed into the kitchen with Megan.

"I'll be back," Penny told Chris. "I need to talk to Megan," and with that both Megan and Penny proceeded into the kitchen.

Megan's living room was quite nice. It had a brown rug with multiple shapes for design, a see-through coffee table, three windows that were facing each other, two ceramic lamps facing each other on either side of the room, and three sofas (Ian hogged one of them.) He wheeled himself closer to Ian and tried to wake him. Ian sat up and groaned. He glanced around the room before locking eyes with Chris.

"Oh my god! Chris!" Ian stopped mid-sentence. "You're in a chair..." he stared at Chris, looking him up and down. "Was it that bad?"

"No, I'm okay. It's just in case I need it," Chris assured.

"Can you stand?"

"With enough effort, it just feels weird," he replied, placing his hand on his forehead.

"On the bright side you get more time with Penny, right?" Ian burst into laughter, slapping his leg.

"So?" Chris began to blush and his voice went higher.

"It's obvious."

"It's not that obvious--"

"Megan and I were talking about it. Don't worry your secret's safe with me...For now."

"For now?" Chris echoed, raising his eyebrow.

"I'll keep it for now, but you need to talk to her or I will," Ian said, punching his arm. Chris winced and took in a deep breath. "Oh...right sorry."

"No... It's healed, you just hit hard," Chris answered.

"I can't help it, I'm pretty tough," Ian bragged as he flexed his arms. Megan walked past Ian and slapped him as hard as she could on the arm, leaving a red mark. "Ow!" he yelped.

"Dumbass," Megan said as she placed a plate of salad on the coffee table in front of Chris. She also placed one in front of Ian. She had a cup of tea that she was sipping slowly.

Ian began to complain about the salad. Megan didn't say anything, she sent him a disapproving glare. He explained that Megan almost never made him have salad, but she told him that he needed to. They began to go back and forth, and Chris merely listened as he began to eat slowly.

"But why salad?" Ian maintained, muttering under his breath.

"Because *you* complained about being tired when you came back," Megan began. "Then, you fell asleep when I said Chris was coming. So, here's the thing Ian," she continued on, casting him a mean glance. "If you had *that* much trouble, you need to eat healthy," she pointed a finger at Chris now. "Plus, it's not fair to Chris if only he has to have salad."

"I don't want salad, I need something more...It's just leaves," Ian persisted, pushing his plate away slightly. He silenced himself when Megan held up her hand as if to cast a spell at him, holding her tea with her free hand. He grudgingly began to eat.

Megan smiled, satisfied. She returned her attention to Chris as she placed her teacup on the table. Chris stopped eating for a moment, because he figured she wanted to say something, but she didn't. Megan raised her hand up to her chin and continued to stare for a moment. He wondered if she was looking into his mental state again.

"Meg, you're staring," Ian yawned, moving his arms behind his head. "You're freaking him out."

"No, it's just-- I was thinking about something," Megan said quietly. "Have either of you by any chance noticed how different Penny acts around Chris?" she spoke in a hushed tone, leaning forward to be sure they could both hear her.

"Yeah, but I figured she was just in a good mood all this time," Ian replied nonchalantly. "Mr. Chris here obviously is acting differently though.

"Ian, I know Chris likes her. I'm talking about Penny..."

"Well...She hasn't acted like she did when I first met her," Chris told her truthfully, leaning forward and meeting her gaze. "Where is Penny?" Chris asked.

"She's handling something for me," Megan answered. Almost immediately, Penny reentered the room and sat beside Megan. She handed Megan a pink book of some sort and nodded at her.

"I wrote what you told me to," Penny informed her.

"What is it?" Chris asked without thinking.

Penny jumped slightly, turned a shade of pink, and opened her mouth to speak. Megan answered for her, "Sorry girl stuff!"

"Ew," Ian muttered.

"Grow up," Megan hissed.

Chris asked Megan if school had started again. Ian answered for her, telling Chris that ever since the attack, the teachers have been busy helping with repairs. The schools didn't take much damage, but they still needed fixing, and they might actually expand the schools a little. Penny nodded to confirm the story. Megan eventually decided to change the subject to a more pressing matter...

"About the hearing..." Megan began. The room went silent upon mention of it. Penny tensed up, but Chris sat up in his seat.

"I'll make sure we stay partners," Chris promised.

"You'll need to have your points organized if you want to win," Megan warned, twisting her finger in her hair.

"She will, and I'll back her up."

"Chris they'll mostly want to hear from Penny," she reminded him, leaning back onto the sofa.

"I know what I'll say," Penny said, interrupting them. "Or...I think I do."

"Chris," Ian whispered. "Let's go talk in private," he took Chris's wheelchair and pushed him outside.

Chris folded his arms, wondering what Ian could've needed. He wasn't laughing or smiling like usual, he actually had a very serious expression. He closed the door behind them and took a moment before speaking.

"You know I'm a sorcerer, right?" Ian questioned. "Most people don't know, but it's true."

"You are?" Chris's eyes widened, speaking louder than he should have.

"Yes," Ian said, speaking quietly, raising his finger to quiet Chris. "It was easier to make sure people didn't know I was one, because unlike Penny I wasn't the big man's child."

"Does Megan know?" Chris asked, concern littering his voice.

"No..."

"You should tell her," Chris implored.

"I can't. That's a bad idea."

"She seems to get along fine with Penny," Chris tried. "I'm sure that--"

"Penny hasn't done some of the things I have. She would lose it, Chris."

"Oh..."

"Yeah-" guilt riddled Ian's face, he rubbed the back of his neck.

"If you don't tell her she may get more angry," Chris urged.

"Oh yeah, I'll just be like 'hey Megan? I helped destroy Japan! Sorry! Oh, but I didn't kill your parents,'" Ian seemed annoyed now.

"Sorry. You're right," Chris agreed, taking a moment to think. He rubbed his arm. "Maybe just tell her you're a sorcerer?"

"No... Look I just needed you to know. Penny knows because we worked together a few times. Meg probably knows I'm a Sorcerer, but if I tell her the rest she may do something dangerous..."

Chris agreed to keep Ian's secret. Ian actually made Chris swear not to tell Megan at all. He explained that he planned to tell Megan in time. Chris felt guilty, but he kept it deep down anyway. He couldn't explain any of this to anyone really. He could always confide in Penny and do his best to help Ian, but Chris felt like he was digging his own grave. However, he didn't have time to worry about it, he had to prepare for what was to come the next day.

19

THE WORLD OF AURRERA

The morning came, and with it came the day of the hearing. Penny wore a black dress, it didn't seem too formal or too casual. Her hair was pulled back in a braided ponytail. She had also decided to wear a bit of makeup. Chris tried telling her she didn't need it, but she applied it anyway. Penny wanted to look her best for this, and it made sense. This was extremely important and would decide both of their fates, so he didn't argue with her.

Chris did his best to match Penny, but he had slightly less options than her. He didn't really wear suits and he had never touched a tux. The only times he wore suits was when he went to church with his parents when he was very little, or to a school dance. He never really bothered much. He found a grey suit in the closet with a black tie. There were also some black dress shoes. He figured it was close enough to what Penny was wearing, and fit the occasion.

Penny had not stopped moving since they woke up. She was going over what she would say over and over. Practicing aloud, and begging Chris to listen to her. Of course, he would listen, but he was worried about her. His eyes followed her about the room. Once to the bathroom to speak in the mirror and to check herself, then back to him to experiment, and then back to the mirror once again. Repeat. It was tiring him out just watching. He could almost feel how nervous she was just by watching these movements.

When the headmaster came to their door, he was wearing what he usually did. Alleyne was with him. He wore a blue tweed suit, a blue vest, blue dress pants, and white dress shirt. His tie was black, he wore a tan flat cap with black dress shoes. He was leaning against his cane with both arms, smiling. Alleyne seemed the most calm out of all of them.

Chris wondered why Alleyne was with Headmaster Brood. He was a teacher and so he couldn't think of any reason why he would need to go. Then, it occurred to Chris that Alleyne had known a lot about Penny. More than the average person in Terminus did or even some of the other teachers. He had also defended Penny the first time they had met. Perhaps his presence alone would be a good thing, even if it only kept their nerves right.

The morning was cold and the sun had not yet fully risen to give them light. Colorful leaves littered the ground. Even more were floating in the pond by the dorm. Fall in Terminus was a little colder than on Earth. The sky was clear and slowly getting lighter, transitioning to a blue color. As the four of them walked, the ground crunched and crackled below them. Every step was another crunch.

Chris asked where Penny's trial would be held. Alleyne replied that it would be in the Alliance capital. They would need to take a ship to get there. It wasn't far, at least according to him. Alleyne made it sound like the planets were extremely close, but Chris knew that it would be millions of miles.

"This whole time I thought this was the capital," Chris admitted, rubbing his hands together to keep warm.

"Ah, but that would be impossible. We only have one city on this planet, and so that wouldn't work," Headmaster Brood corrected.

"This is the Wizard capital. It's the main magic school for the Alliance, many of our Wizards and mages are here. The capital is the big city. The senate is there, the house of representatives, and a lot of the government."

"The whole planet is a city, Brood," Alleyne chortled.

"Oh really? I'm amazed." the headmaster rolled his eyes. "You always did state the obvious."

"Only when you're around," Alleyne added with an amused look.

They were heading out to the airfield. When they arrived, there were two pilots waiting. Behind them was a silver plane, with blue wings. One pilot had climbed up into the plane and began checking things. What he was checking, Chris couldn't tell. The remaining pilot saluted them and then moved their hands behind their back, locking them together. They were wearing a black flight suit with yellow markings. The Alliance symbol resided on their left shoulder; with a yellow sun behind it. *That's new,* Chris thought as he noticed the symbol. *I guess that means they're from the capital,* He concluded.

"We are ready to get underway, sir!" the pilot said respectfully. The pilot voice was extremely young, and clearly female. "I ask you to board and prepare for takeoff."

"Has the general departed already then?" Brood asked the pilot.

"He wastes no time," Alleyne reminded him as he boarded the plane that was to transport them. "Cozy," Chris heard from inside. "I'm fine with this."

"He left some time ago, sir. Maybe an hour earlier. For security reasons we were told to transport you separately. There is an escort in orbit waiting now," the pilot answered.

"Very well. Come along you two," the Headmaster told them as he entered. They followed up. Going up the steps. The ship had a white interior with white and blue seats. There were also pillows in each seat and each seat was facing another. It looked like a private jet.

Chris and Penny sat beside each other. Brood and Alleyne sat on the other side of the plane.

When they finally took off, Chris could feel the ship vibrating lightly. It wasn't that bad, but it felt extremely weird. Penny was closest to the window, but he could still see that they were leaving the ground, going higher than the city, and into the sky. It took a few minutes for the sky to dim. It got darker and darker until finally they were finally among the stars. Chris asked Penny to scoot back and she did. He wanted to see it, he wanted to see what the astronauts had seen.

Chris saw the billions and billions of bright shining stars. It was like color on a blank canvas. He could see a few nearby planets, but they were fairly small from this distance. Terminus was behind them. It was almost completely green because of the land, but there were patches of blue. He could barely see the planet, seeing as he had to shift himself to even see a little, but the view was still breathtaking. He never got to see this when he came to Terminus from Earth, because Victoria had teleported them back to her marked location. He sat back in his seat, allowing Penny to relax again.

"You're not scared?" Penny questioned. "You were nervous about flying before."

"I am. But...that view is amazing," Chris explained, completely awed. "That window can't break right?"

"It's reinforced," Penny shrugged as she gently took her hand and tapped on the glass a few times.

"Don't do that!" Chris gasped, clasping his hand over his heart.

Penny smiled and turned toward him, crossing her leg, "You really haven't been in one of these. My hand can't break it, dingus," she began to laugh. "Oh my god, your face!"

Chris pushed her lightly, sat back in his seat, and began to relax. Penny smiled at him for a while before looking out the window. A few planes began to get into formation around them. At first Chris thought they were ships, but they were indeed planes. They must have had some sort of feature that allowed space travel, but considering their size, they probably couldn't fly too long. Chris had recognized one plane. It belonged to Violet.

The journey was not too long. A few hours must have passed by now. Chris wasn't sure when they would arrive. Penny had begun tapping her hand on her leg and tapping her right foot. She was staring out of the window with a blank expression. Penny had done this a few times in the past few minutes, but he didn't bother her. He was worried about her, and he had helped before, so he figured he could calm her right now. Chris placed his hand on her shoulder and gently shook her. Penny turned herself toward him.

"You were tapping again..." he said, expressing his concern.

Penny lifted her hand and placed it over his, lightly squeezing, "I'm okay. I'm just feeling a little worried. I know they'll be unfair about this."

"We'll win," he squeezed her hand back and gave her a look of determination.

"But Chris, you don't understand. I've done some messed up things in my past...whether it was by choice or not doesn't matter to them," she lowered her head. "And because I'm a Sorcerer...a pure blood Sorcerer they'll do everything they can to stop this. You may be at a disadvantage because of me."

"That won't happen," Chris declared, shaking his head. "If I have to fight a senator, I will," he added jokingly.

Penny giggled a little, "I don't know, Chris--"

"I wonder if a senator can fight..." Chris continued on in his attempts to relax her.

She began to laugh a bit harder at this comment, "You're crazy..." Penny laid her head on his shoulder and took a deep breath. "Well...Maybe it'll be okay..."

"It *will* be okay," he promised.

"Thank you..." she whispered. "It's weird how you didn't judge me when we first met."

"Nah, I thought you were nice. I didn't have much time to think on it though," he reminisced.

"Why?" she seemed confused, staring up at him.

"You put me to sleep," he chuckled. "I woke up in your lap."

"About that- I'm uh..." she began. Chris placed his hand over hers and held it. Penny seemed to instantly know that this was his way of saying 'it's okay.'

"Thanks for taking care of me," Penny said instead. She sounded drowsy.

She hadn't gotten much sleep the night before, and he kept hearing her get up, or shift around. Even when he had fallen asleep, he could now feel her emotions better than ever. He had never learned how to sense her emotions in class, and yet he could feel them. He knew they were hers, because sometimes when he felt one way, he felt something else in his heart. That night he felt her anxiety, and even though it wasn't very strong, it kept him awake most of the night. It stopped after she fell asleep, but he still felt exhausted even now. The only thing that was keeping him awake, was wanting to stay alert in case she needed him.

Chris was doing his absolute best to keep his eyes open. They felt heavy, and he felt a force on his body. He must have been more tired than he thought. Both he and Penny fell asleep, both of their heads laying together, Penny holding onto his arm. Alleyne pointed his thumb back at them. Headmaster Brood smiled to himself and removed his jacket, leaving only a yellow shirt. He made his way over to Chris and Penny and placed his jacket over them. He made sure that it covered both of them, and then made his way back to his seat and sat down.

"Always protecting the students," Alleyne supposed, going

through a bunch of papers, before setting them in the chair beside him. "I hope we get the schools up and running again soon."

"You know me too well, Alleyne," Headmaster Brood admitted. "I'll always protect my students. The schools will be better than ever. I'm also hoping to fill the vacant mage seat, but that is up to the remaining seven."

"Brood? How can you be so calm about another war?" Alleyne inquired.

"I need to keep a cool head and focus. My students need me, and as do the teachers and even the soldiers at times," he responded.

Alleyne crossed and leaned forward, placing his arm on his leg. "After this, let's get a drink."

"A drink sounds nice right now..." Brood heaved. "But again, not much. I can't. I need to stay vigilant."

"And, Brood? Did we ever find out what that second attack was about? That wasn't an invasion force. No ground forces. It was weird," he probed.

"They had bombers with them, so I assume they wanted to do some damage. However, in Violet's report she talked about a transport in the battle."

"A transport?" Alleyne repeated. "Why? If there were no troops then..."

"To retrieve their rather evasive ally. They're stuck in the city now, and have gone into hiding. We know it's Hunter, and he killed one of our pilots," he sounded angry, but he kept his voice down. "He'll pay for his actions."

"The pilot was new right?" Alleyne asked.

"Yes."

"I hate to ask...But which one?" he put forth hesitantly.

"Dominic E. Stern, or Alpha four-seven. He was found dead near his plane," Brood whispered even softer, doing his best to avoid speaking too loud in case Chris and Penny were awake. "Then, he convinced Christopher to help him. He had nowhere else to go but back into the city," he gestured in Chris's direction. "He's very lucky to be alive. If he hadn't called for help, he wouldn't have reached him in time."

"Hairston did a good job reviving him. He told me he wasn't sure if he could bring him back, and even when he did they had to rush him to the hospital. I don't know the rest,"

"I'll tell you later. For now," Brood lifted his finger up to his lips. "Stop talking." Alleyne raised his eyebrow as Brood lowered his head and closed his eyes.

"Only you can sleep after that conversation," Alleyne scoffed and starred.

"I just want to rest up, because I know I'm going to have to yell at these people. They'll split them up over my dead body. I'm tired of this."

"Ah- yeah true," he agreed, understanding now.

They were coming up on a large world. There were ships and planes going to and fro. Their escort broke off from around the plane and began to follow behind them. The pilots in the front had to transfer their identification codes, and once it was verified they were allowed to continue toward the great giant. The planet was very bright from orbit. The whole planet was one big city, there was no water, and no nature really.

The pilots took the ship in carefully. There wasn't any shaking as they entered the atmosphere and began their descent. The pilots answered the radio in the front as they passed through the thin layer of clouds. A bustling city was revealed as they broke through. The many tall buildings, and crowded streets. A pair of Wizards flying on brooms flew to either side of the cockpit. They began to do hand signals to direct the pilots. The co-pilot signaled back and informed the other that they were to land on pad one-hundred and fourteen.

They changed direction slightly, passing by a large skyscraper with a large neon sign that read 'Denim manufacturing.'

Penny shook Chris until he woke up again. Upon waking up, Chris was a bit dazed. He blinked a few times in an attempt to wake up more. He was laying on Penny's shoulder. Chris sat up and looked around for a moment to remember where he was, and then returned his attention to Penny.

"I didn't want to wake you up," she admitted.

"How long have you been up?" he yawned, raising his arms out above his head.

"Half an hour maybe. We're landing soon. You'll need to stay awake," she told him. "We have to go straight there."

"Are you scared?" Chris questioned. "Not as much because of you, but I am a little nervous."

"We'll still be partners at the end of this, I promise," he declared, confident and sure as ever.

The plane landed on a floating airport above the city. They touched down gently and after a moment they were allowed to disembark. The airport was very busy. People were boarding planes; bags in tow. This was the big city, and big was an understatement. The weather was cold and fall-like. Chris followed behind the other three as they headed across the area to a glass tube (or at least that's what Chris thought it was.) It was actually a tram that transported people around the city. They went all around the planet, and you could get anywhere. You could even get underground should you wish to.

"It's a train?" Chris wondered aloud.

"I wouldn't call it a train, because it doesn't go on rails. I guess," the Headmaster shrugged his shoulders. "To tell you the truth, I don't even know how they run, Christopher."

"Well don't look at me," Alleyne said as Chris turned to look at him. "I haven't a clue. It works."

Penny giggled a little, "You always want to know how things work," she smiled widely at him. "Dingus"

Chris began to turn a bright red, "I uh-"

The train arrived at the station quickly. It stopped in front of the large crowd that had gathered overtime to wait for it. The glass slid aside to form a large door, and the tram opened its doors as well. The tram was white with many windows. Chris figured it was a favorite of any tourists who came. They boarded the tram and for the most part they split up. Alleyne stood up and held onto a strap that dangled from the ceiling, Brood had made his way over to a seat, and as he approached, space was cleared so he could sit down. Chris was amazed about how fast they let him sit down with how crowded it was, and how so many people immediately engaged in conversation with him.

"My child goes to Terminus and at first I was nervous, but I heard he's doing well. Did the recent attacks do any damage? Tim sent me a video to let me know he was okay," he heard a woman say.

"Yes, but the repairs are practically over. No need to be nervous, he's in good hands. Tim works hard. You must be proud," Headmaster Brood indulged this conversation.

Chris moved through the tram in an attempt to find Penny, but she had actually not gone far. She was staring out of one of the largest windows. Chris moved to stand beside her, pushing past a girl wearing a red and black dress with black hair. The girl seemed to turn to look at him. There were many things below, and it was a long way down. Cars that hovered above the ground, people flying on brooms, a few planes, and more buildings than a person could count. One building stuck out the most though, and that was the senate building. It took up a large amount of space, it appeared to have multiple levels, and had red flags with a sun.

"I feel out of my element," Penny admitted, seeing that he had taken his place beside her. "Seriously, I feel like I stick out."

"You don't," he promised. "If you need to, you can hold my hand."

"I can wha-" she turned her head to look at him.

"Nothing," he said quickly.

"I want to know," she persisted.

"You can hold my hand if you need me," he answered awkwardly, trying to smile as best he could. His heart was attacking his chest now, and he could hear and feel it happening. His heart nearly leapt out of his chest when Penny's soft hand slipped into his. She laid her head on his shoulder and continued to watch as they were transported across the city. He gulped and gave her hand a little squeeze. "I uhm," he babbled. "Hope it helps."

"It does," Penny beamed.

My cheeks hurt. They were nearing the building. The tube seemed to stop right at the entrance. There was a large red and gold rug laid out leading up the stairs and into the grand building. Penny pulled him with her to the exit and readied herself. She seemed less nervous now, a confident look replacing her previously uncertain one.

The doors opened, no one moved forward in the lobby but their party. The rest stayed. A man in a white and black guard attire stepped forward with three more guards behind him. He demanded to know the purpose of their visit, proof of their identities, and then they were allowed to get off. The guards here were more formal. While the guards on Terminus were more loose; these did not deviate from their duties, flinch, or leave their position. They stood in a line on either side of the rug. They held futuristic white and black muskets with ornate designs and bayonets. They held these muskets in the palm of their right hand, allowing the gun to rest on their shoulder.

The interior housed a red rug, many vases and pieces of art. There were a considerable amount of people just in the lobby. The designs on the walls and ceiling were incredible to him, and chandeliers were magnificent. They had to wait to be called in. The senators were having trouble, because a few decided to simply not show up. They had refused to decide on if Penny should be Chris's partner, and so they chose not to attend. The house was massive and there were thousands of senators. Of course, only a few needed to attend. Just enough to reach quorum, but that number had not been reached. They were close, in fact only three were missing. They were instructed to wait in the hallway.

If they did not reach the minimum number needed to start, then Penny would be separated from Chris regardless. The senators who did not attend must have known this. It angered Chris even more that some of the senators were threatening to walk out if it had not started soon. Sure enough; however, more did come. More than they needed actually, dressed in their senatorial attire. Majestic capes followed them as they entered through a large pair of brown doors. When the doors came together again they formed a golden Alliance bird.

"Shall we begin?" he heard a female senator begin to speak in the next room. "Hurry. Hurry, bring them in. My time is valuable. My people need me, and we have a war going on."

"Yes ma'am!" There was the sound of footsteps coming to the brown door beside where they were waiting outside. The doors opened. The guard from earlier explained that they were to go in now.

"Mind your tone, speak when spoken to, and do not argue," he hissed at Penny. "You are allowed to be here, but that can change."

"She will," Chris shot back as he pulled her past him by her hand.

Penny walked ahead of all of them. The room was gigantic. There were about three or four levels. The walls were a deep red. The roof, a golden dome. The room was warm, so it was fairly relaxing to Chris. He scanned over the different senators; of which there were too many to count. There was a man who stood in the center of the room waiting for them. He wore a teal blue cape that draped down to his feet; it wrapped around him so that you could not see what else he was wearing. He had black combed hair that looked extremely healthy. Actually, this man looked rather young, he seemed to be no older than thirty.

"I see you've arrived," he said kindly. "We are about to begin. You two stand over there. Alleyne, Headmaster-- please stand over there," he said as he directed them.

"Who is he?" Chris asked.

"*He* is on your side," The man answered before anyone else. "Not to worry, I not only represent the capital, but now I represent you."

Chris asked himself who else could be on their side. The room appeared to be split in half, so it wasn't hard to tell that this was a very divided issue. There were more against them than there were supporting them. Most of the senators appeared to be older gentlemen. There were younger senators, those of which the majority appeared to be primarily female. Chris was not at all surprised that most of the younger senators sat on the right side, and most of the elderly senators sat on the left. Therefore, he deduced that the right side was for them, while the left stood against them.

General Nicholas came in sometime later. He apologized to the room for coming so late and delaying the process. Apparently, he had to handle a situation. A woman had been robbed, and since he and his escort witnessed it, he sprang into action. They had left the criminal with authorities. Chris didn't notice any damage on the general, and considering that he wasn't a magic user, this impressed Chris a great deal. The proceedings began shortly after. The general took his place beside Brood and Alleyne.

"Did I miss much?" The General asked them.

"No. Not at all," Alleyne clapped his hands together. "We almost started without you Nick."

The General made a disapproving noise with his throat, "Hmph. You have no idea how angry I would have been."

"You're always angry," Alleyne waved his hand dismissively.

"No, I'm not. It's about to start. Hush," he grumbled.

Brood crossed his leg and folded his arms. He watched and waited. The headmaster's face was extremely intent on this going well. Chris wondered if he was worried, but if anything, he seemed irritated about some of the senators. He was the only one not talking on their bench, and when the hearing began, he sat forward.

Chris and Penny stood together in the center of the room. The young senator standing just a few feet away from them. He brought out his papers and prepared to speak. The room went entirely silent. No one moved. The senator pulled at his collar and then spoke.

"One of the bedrock beliefs of Wizards is that if you allow Sorcerers to have a place in the Alliance, or even have a partner that everything will be thrown into disarray," he began to pace to his right before planting his feet again and looking specifically at the right of the room. "That one Sorcerer could throw things out of balance, and would destroy the very foundation that the Alliance was built on." some of the members on the right side began to nod in agreement. "The Sorcerers are not always a peaceful people, but this girl left her home with her sister to seek us out."

"Senator Quinn," an old senator addressed him in a rather harsh tone, his raspy voice echoing throughout the room. He stood up, adjusting his round glasses. "We continue to hear that Sorcerers should be allowed to be in the Alliance, and to have partners. We hear this over and over again, but didn't we try that experiment before? And it failed." the room began to break into mini conversations, some in agreement some in disagreement. "And the very person who this experiment was conducted on; being the same man that birthed this one." he pointed a shaky finger at Penny. "And didn't Chaos Dreadful leave our attempts at peace in shambles? Did we not give them the opportunity?"

There were nods of agreement and conversation on the left side, and harrumphs on the right side. The man tried to speak more, but Senator Quinn interrupted them. Moving closer to Chris and Penny, planning his next words. Once he had them figured out, his expression changed to one of extreme confidence.

"Could I take a little trip down memory lane with my friend, Jacob Brood who I had the great privilege of knowing a few years ago. Thirty twenty-three to be exact." Senator Quinn proposed. "He and I spoke on that matter, and I asked him what he thought. He told me that he would happily continue to try, because he felt that Sorcerers were people too. He was even friends with Chaos, am I wrong?" he questioned, turning himself to Brood who nodded in agreement. He almost cracked a smile. "I respect the hell out of him, and you should too. This headmaster had been through hell and back to build up and protect this Alliance-his students-"

"Let me just say-" the older senator tried.

"Now just hold on a second and let me finish," Quinn raised his hand to the man to show he was not done yet. "We were negotiating with the Empire, leaving them supplies and trading, and the tension was going away. And guess what? We had one of the strongest, most talented, aspiring Sorcerers on Terminus. Training to be one of us," he raised his voice a little. "And we drove him away; because--"

"Can I just-" the older gentlemen tried again. Quinn interrupted him again, the older senator smiled, nodded, and reluctantly allowed him to keep the floor.

"*Because*, we wouldn't help his people, and his wife was dying. We forced him there, and if he was willing to be one of us, why not? But we did not help them, and we wanted them to stay peaceful without meeting them in the middle. They didn't owe us!"

"Senator Quinn, that is where I have to stop you," a middle-aged gentleman stood up, determined to speak. He was closer to the upper level, and so he needed a small microphone to speak. "According to the Universal Treaty, the Empire is to abide by any laws set by the

Alliance. They are not to build a military larger than what is needed for defense, and furthermore they were not to engage in any warmongering activities near or on any planet in the Light Realm." Chris could see Quinn was biting his tongue as the man continued his point. "So, they not only came into the Light Realm without permission and attacked Earth, leveling the country of Japan, but they also amassed a military larger than the treaty allowed. We are at war with the Empire. Therefore; I suggest that Penny Dreadful be locked away until this war is over," there were many harrumphs as he continued on. "Not in prison, but somewhere, where she is unable to pry."

"Senator, she has been here a year and has done better than many of our senior military officials and the most seasoned Wizards. This year she's done even more, and if you can believe it, even more with Christopher Spellcrafter by her side," Quinn rebuked.

"The previous headmaster administration was not acceptable and led to the deaths of multiple students and teachers. Because we allowed Chaos to be among the Wizards. He became a menace and left Brood, Atalanta, and the other students to die," he sat, pleased with himself and his argument. "Let's not have a repeat of that. It was an embarrassment."

"He did what he felt he-\-" Quinn began to tense up slightly, obviously feeling some irritation or discomfort.

"He jettisoned them into space!" one cried. "An attempt on their lives! Are you so dense that you can't see what is occurring around you? Or have you blinded yourself to what they're capable of? You're an idiot, Quinn."

Penny took a deep breath and took Chris's hand into her own. She was mustering up the courage to speak. She closed her eyes, let out a soft staggered breath, and then spoke up for herself. The room silenced itself. Quinn also stopped talking, unsurprised by her wanting to speak on this.

"That has nothing to do with this," Penny managed. "I... just want to make up for what I had done. I know what I did, but back then I didn't know. I was confused and the only person I had was my father. I had no mother to turn to, and I had my sister, but at the time I thought she was crazy."

"Your sister, Victoria?" Quinn turned his head to her, attempting to both confirm and help her.

"Yes," Penny looked down for a moment. "I wish I had listened to her sooner, but regardless I am here."

"Is your sister in league with you? She came here with you," a senator in the front had also begun to grill Penny.

"What? No..."

"Why is she not here to support you then?" he pressed on.

"My sister is *dead!*" Penny cried out hysterically. The room silenced, the senator sat down, feeling small. "She died fighting for your Alliance in a war against our people, and friends and father just to do what was right. We didn't *have* to do any of this," she spat, looking directly at the man who spoke out. "And I won't stand by as you shit all over her memories and what she meant to *me.*"

Chris squeezed her hand to relax her. "Breathe," he whispered. Penny nodded in agreement and lowered her head, hiding behind her hair. She was trying to calm down, but they were pushing her buttons. He didn't need to feel it. He could tell just by how she was squeezing his hand.

Quinn pressed on with this. "You see? It's not fair to Penny. It's not fair to Victoria's memory. It's not fair to Christopher, that their--" he stuttered a moment to formulate what he would say before going on. He wiped his forehead with the back of his hand. "Their *flawed* philosophical views about the future of the Alliance are not going to allow us to get the sixty percent majority votes we need; to allow them to stay partners and do some *good.* It would not only allow us to get another partner team out there in the fight, but Sorcerers will see one of their own fighting and ask themselves, *why did she go over there?* So, I think it was not only wrong, but I think it's not *fair* to them that this is stunting their partnership."

"*Stunting?* We're protecting this boy from a threat. A threat to all of us!"

"Your narrow-minded view is going to get us all killed," Quinn threw his hand up in frustration and walked back to Chris and Penny. He appeared to be calming his nerves so he would not say anything rash. He had to be calm and work this through without being too aggressive. They needed these votes.

Before Quinn had begun to speak again many of the present members began to argue; some even yelling at each other at the top of their lungs. Quinn was the senator selected to lead this debate, and he could no longer get control of them. They did not care what he had to say, and they only stuck to their own views. Penny lowered her head and let out a heavy sigh as she watched.

"We must allow her to be his partner. What is done is done. She has done well so far," one on the right argued.

"I will not have our soldiers or our generals fighting alongside that filthy woman!" another on the left sneered. "She has *corrupted* the mind of that boy!"

"You are absurd."

"Her even being allowed to run through the partner competition was absurd!" the voices in the room were starting to grow louder.

Chris bit his tongue and balled up his hand. He would give anything to start yelling back now. They continued to insult her on the left. He could not stand what they were saying about her. Penny was an extraordinary person to him and to many other people. It was nearly impossible to not start yelling.

Chris was debating what to do, but it seemed that he would not need to. The headmaster whispered something to Alleyne, who merely took his fingers and plugged his ears with them. Headmaster Brood stood, his face showing clear displeasure. Chris figured he was about to do something big, and so Chris decided to cover Penny's ears with his own hands. She looked back at him confused.

"*Enough!*" The Headmaster's voice boomed. The entire building shook, lights flickered and items fell over. Many of the senators leapt to their feet in terror. There was a certain aura he gave off as he said this; it was even enough to terrify Chris a little, even if he was helping them. The lights went out completely for a few seconds before coming back on. "This foolishness has gone on long enough! I've sat through this entire session and you haven't given either of them a chance to talk, and you have entirely disrespected Quinn, despite the fact that he presides over all of you." Brood began to scan the room slowly, his red eyes moving slowly from person to person, "Now you deal with me."

"A-and what do you think Brood," the previous senator had replaced himself in his chair and readjusted his eyewear with a shaky hand.

"I think they should be partners, of course. Do you object then?"

"Well...Sir, the trivial matter is that there is still a traitor on the loose and we can't just--"

"We're looking for Hunter. Calm yourself," he held his hand up. "You may have more power than me in a government setting, but I know what I am talking about. Pennelopie is not the traitor, nor would she ever do such a thing."

"He's right," Chris put in. "I know you can trust her. She wants to get Hunter for what he did to me, and it's an honor working with her. And well...she honestly does make me happy, she even taught me to fight for the most part."

"Brood? What is this boy's skill level?" he questioned.

"When he first came here he could not defeat Hunter. Upon receiving her help, he learned faster than the other students. I should also add in the fact that they had the fastest time so far in the partner competition. They beat my time."

"I'd say we bring it to a vote," Quinn offered. "Unless you would all like to hear more from Christopher and Pennelopie."

"Before we vote," a young woman with a turquoise dress had soon up to speak. "I'd like to know who they would serve under?"

"Well, there are many generals," Quinn assured. "And not many would be willing to have Pennelopie under their command. Which is exactly why--"

"I've seen them fight. I've seen them fly. I want 'em," General Nick interjected. "I won't take no for an answer if this gets passed."

"Her serving under our top general would allow you to monitor her closely, while also keeping her and her partner in a place where they can do more good than most," Quinn quickly jumped on this opportunity and rode it. He had regained his footing in this debate and was ready to drive the point home. "So, let's take a vote."

Every senator in the room reached forward and picked up a tablet like device. As they entered in their votes; Penny became rather nervous. She took Chris's hand again and squeezed it for comfort, he squeezed hers back. No matter what happened, he would remain her partner. He was determined to stay by her side. Penny would always be Chris's partner.

"Are all of the votes in?" Senator Quinn looked around the room. He gave it a few more moments before staring at the results on his own tablet in disbelief. He made a face before quickly taking it over to the Headmaster. He took it into his hands, read over the results and made his way toward Chris and Penny. His expression was very well hidden, and so Chris did not know what to expect. He could sense Penny's uneasiness.

"Well you two," he started. "Here you go." Brood gave Penny the results and patted Chris's shoulder.

Penny reluctantly brought it up with a trembling hand. Her eyes began to sparkle, and a smile formed rapidly on her face. She began to bounce up and down with joy and clap her hands. Chris held out his hand. Penny immediately gave him the results and continued to bounce up and down. The results were six-hundred for them and four-hundred against them. There was also a list of senators, and who they voted for, and as he scrolled through it he saw that they had indeed convinced the majority. Quite a few of the senators who were previously against it had voted for them.

Penny leapt at him and threw her arms around his neck, hugging him as tight as she could. Chris instinctively hugged her back. She let him go and smiled at him. Her eyes were vibrant and he could tell how happy she was. Penny just could not stop smiling and all he could sense from her was complete and utter joy.

Chris could see senator Quinn behind Penny. He was sitting in a chair and dabbing his forehead while drinking water. Quinn looked exhausted. General Nick had gone over to check on him and talk, and Alleyne was just laughing at how burnt out he was. Chris was going to thank him whenever he got the chance. Quinn noticed Chris looking in his direction and gave him a thumbs up. Chris began to laugh at him as Quinn hunched over again.

"What?" Penny smiled and began to laugh as well.

"Look at Quinn," Chris pointed at him, still laughing.

"*Everyone* is laughing at me," Quinn threw up his arms as he threw his head back and released an exhausted and chuckle. "I expected better from the two kids I helped."

"Thank you," Penny smiled and made her way over to him. Joy was extremely apparent in her voice. "I want to thank all of you."

"Well it was wrong, so I had your back. Brood is an old friend, so when he told me about you I was on it."

"You did awesome," Chris clapped to encourage him. He merely groaned in reply.

"My throat is going to be scratched up," Quinn chuckled. "I better get the conversation out of me now. You two are going to do the Alliance proud. I just know it."

20

A SPARK

The sound of wheels rolling on asphalt broke the silence. The vehicle was creeping along the airfield. Slowly but surely. The sound of grunts and groans could also be heard. The plane stopped for a moment before beginning to move yet again. It could only move at a snail's pace.

"We should be celebrating that you won," Ian's voice sounded strained as he pushed. "Instead, we're being punished."

"Stop whining and push," Megan grumbled. "You're taking oxygen away from your muscles. That's why we're moving so slow..."

"I forgot we were going to get punished for taking the plane," Chris began to let up a little, exhausted.

"Keep pushing before I hit you," Ian grunted, wiping the sweat with his right arm before replacing it on the metal.

"I am, I am," Chris continued to push with them, speaking through gritted teeth.

"It could be worse," Penny panted between words.

"We're going to have to fix the plane and then go and help at the village. We have to help there for a week," Megan huffed. "Can't get much worse."

"Wait a minute," Ian stopped pushing for a moment and thought. "Wait! Wait a minute! Why are we being punished for something they did?"

"If you don't get over here and push..." Megan began through gritted teeth. Ian rushed over and continued to push.

"This mechanic is mean..." Chris whined.

"I'm sorry, guys," Penny apologized quietly.

"We don't mind," Chris smiled at her. Penny smiled back.

"*We?*" Ian looked at Chris. "I mind a lot!" he pushed harder. "I thought we were closer! It didn't take this long to walk over to the plane!"

"We weren't pushing the plane before," Megan reminded him. "Just push. You're the main one moving it."

"He wouldn't even notice if we--" Chris began.

"Don't even think about it!" Ian protested. "I'm not pushing this alone. You're suffering with me!"

"Are the wheel brakes on?" Penny stopped pushing and leaned against the plane with her arm. "Chris, are you *absolutely* sure you took them off..."

"I think so?" Chris hesitated as he said this. "Give me a boost."

Ian cupped his hands and allowed Chris to fit his foot in. Once Chris was ready he tossed Chris upwards. Chris landed on the left wing and pulled his feet up the rest of the way. He then popped the hatch and crawled into the plane to check.

"It was on," Chris reported, popping his head over the side. They were all sitting down beside the plane looking up at him and groaning.

"Sorry," he rubbed the back of his neck. "Oops--"

"*Chris!*" they all cried in unison.

"Get down here so I can kill you," Ian waved his fist in the air and forced himself back to his feet.

Chris hopped down and took up his side again, "Let's try pushing again."

"Alright," Penny agreed.

"Yup," Megan replied. The plane moved at the exact same pace. Perhaps it was moving faster, but it was not noticeable to them. It seemed as if the brakes made little to no difference; either that or they were just tired.

By now their muscles were aching and they were longing for water. Beads of sweat littered their faces. Megan was worried they would get sick if they continued to sweat in the cool weather, but she knew as well as everyone else that they had to continue on. It was taking an extremely long time to reach their destination.

One of the pilots felt bad for them and so he brought them all water bottles and towels. They thanked him and continued to push the plane through the airfield to the last garage in the far back. This was the building that Chris and Penny had snuck into and taken the fighter plane. There was no one inside and the only light was a holo-gram schematic of the aircraft. Once they had stopped pushing, Chris moved over to it so he could inspect it. Below the holographic image, there was text that read: 'The Spark.'

Ian made his way over to the right side of the garage and flicked the switch; the lights flicked on row by row to reveal multiple tools and parts. There were wrenches, hammers, and other tools littered about the room. A machine that appeared to lift heavy objects was in the center of the room. There were schematics of different planes and designs tapped to the right wall.

The mechanic had also had a workbench beside the table where Chris had found the hologram. Above the workbench was a note board with multiple pinned reminders and deadlines. In the center of the board, Chris noticed a lone picture. It was of a young man kneeling down with a small boy sitting on his knee. The young man had a small beard and dark green eyes. The boy seemed completely disinterested in the picture and was more focused on the cookie he held to his chest, and so it was hard to tell his facial features. They were both wearing button up shirts and it appeared to be a picture shot professionally.

"What's that?" Penny came over to his side and examined the picture.

"Probably his son," Chris raised his shoulders. "That's just a guess. I just couldn't help but notice it."

"Hmm," Penny walked back over to the Spark and stared at the plane. She ran her hand over its armor and felt the bullet holes. *She loves to fly, doesn't she?* Chris smiled to himself. Penny turned back to him suddenly and spoke. "Do you think we can fix it?"

"We have to, but I think we can," he nodded his head. "It's just going to be hard, because I don't know how."

"I don't either," she admitted. "But I really want to fix it. I want to fly it again. It felt right."

"I'm sure we can repair it quickly," Megan fanned herself. "If only the mechanic wasn't late."

"He probably got tired of waiting. I would too," Ian leaned against the plane. "This plane is pretty messed up."

"We'll get it fixed," Penny retorted. "I want to."

The garage doors opened abruptly as a pair of legs were revealed. An old man in black mechanic boots and a navy-blue mechanic outfit. He had a straight face that only dropped as he saw the four friends. He had a stubble beard and completely grey combed hair.

"Right..." the old man sighed as he walked passed them without a word. He took a swig of his coffee before placing it on the table beside his workbench and beginning to write some things down. Megan tried to speak, but the old man hushed her by holding up a finger. He finished writing and put the paper aside, then he moved over to a green file cabinet and pulled out a schematic of some sort.

"Coffee in the afternoon?" Megan questioned politely.

"Well young lady," he said, addressing her without so much as turning. "This is going to take me a while now, ain' it?"

"Yes sir, sorry sir," Megan apologized instantly. "I wasn't thinking."

"No, you were not," he agreed as he unfolded the schematics and spread it across the workbench. "Let's see the damage..."

"Well," Chris stepped toward the man. He was shorter than Chris was expecting, but not much shorter. "From what I can tell it's just damage to the armor and to the uh..."

"Wrong."

"What?"

"It's worse," the mechanic pulled out a small flashlight and shined it into the exhaust.

"Worse, how?" Chris asked as he looked inside. There were bullet holes everywhere inside one of the tubes. It looked as if one bullet ricocheted over and over inside, but the holes above and below the tube suggested that they had been shot from above and the shots cut through.

"That ain't good," the man cursed under his breath. "And if that is damaged- I'm glad I got a spare engine."

"By the way, what is your-" Chris started.

"Hourev," he told Chris.

"Well I'm-"

"Christopher Spellcrafter."

"You know my name?" Chris raised his eyebrow. The man ignored this question.

"Hand me that big wrench," the man pointed at a collection of wrenches back on his workbench. There were two wrenches that appeared to be the largest, so Chris grabbed both just in case. He did not need to anger this man anymore. He had an extremely bad temper already. Why would he risk doing anything to push him further? The man turned his head back and shook his head, "I said the big one," he took both. "But I do need that one too."

"You really think it can be fixed?" Chris asked.

"Hah," he cackled as he began to disassemble part of the plane. "Boy, I could fix it on my own. But not only is this your punishment, but you'd be better off knowing how the Spark works."

"I don't fly it-"

"Don't matter!" he stopped what he was doing and turned suddenly. "It's important that you do so this doesn't happen again. It'll serve you better and you can take care of it."

"I don't think-"

"Pft," Hourev turned back to the plane and ignored what Chris had to say.

A few hours went by as they helped Hourev disassemble their plane. He briefly explained all of the different components to them as he worked. He mostly directed these explanations to Chris, and had him assist more than the rest. He worked Chris the hardest and made sure he knew, and before he could replace a part Hourev would ask him what its purpose was. If he did not know, he could not put it there until he could answer. *I can't remember all of this.*

Ian carried in the heavy engine and the old man set to work on installing it. This engine was entirely new and just ordered, and it was the newest model. It seemed fitting for the Spark. He added in his own modifications to the engine that he had been working on as well. He never stopped working or even took a moment to think about his next action.

Eventually, they once again had the Spark in all its glory. Megan repainted the armor with Ian, and Chris and Penny went behind them to make sure they did not miss any spots. The plane was red with yellow symbols on the wings that would represent their call sign,

'Delta.' The interior was black with a completely new and updated functionality. cockpit glass that could display images, help track targets, and allow easier communication.

"Is this the color you're going with?" the old man questioned. Chris and Penny agreed. Hourev clapped his hands together and passed out water. "Alright...now we just need to do a few more things."

"There's more?" Ian held his face in his hand and made an annoyed sound.

"Just need to add the bullet resistant coating, heat shield, and update your A.I."

"He sure can complain," Ian thought aloud.

"You mean Cornelius?" the old man laughed under his breath. "Well he's one of a kind, but he's good. He's just got a temper. This next update will allow him to autopilot more efficiently and engage in combat when unmanned. He can even extract these two from the most dangerous situations."

"No, I was talking about--"

Megan elbowed Ian in the lungs and smiled. Chris smiled back at her and shook his head. He always found their bickering to be funny, but he couldn't help but wonder what their partnership was like. Each partnership appeared to be very different, even if only a little. He wondered about this as he continued his work on the Spark, and he would sneak glances at Penny while working. He was so distracted that he almost messed up while painting; much to the old mechanic's displeasure.

"Alright. You're done," Hourev clapped his hands together.

"Don't we need to check if it runs?" Penny asked.

"Hop in and try," he paused. "Do. Not. Take. Off."

Penny placed a ladder against the plane and climbed up. Chris followed behind her. The cockpit was completely outfitted. Comfortable black seats, new controls, light blue screens, and more weaponry on Chris's side. He would now have control of a guided missile, secondary guns, target highlighting, and a few more features. The screens illuminated as the plane came to life. Penny smiled to herself and looked at Chris. "Well, we did it."

"Yeah," he smiled.

The AI Cornelius appeared on the center screen between them just below the engine readings. A smiley face appeared with the text 'updating' over it. The text faded and Cornelius began to speak. "I've gotten an update! Splendid!"

"I almost forgot about him, honestly," Penny shrugged.

"Uh-huh," Chris agreed.

"Not you two again!" Cornelius whined as a crying face appeared on screen. "Don't do this to me, Hourev!" he begged.

"They're your pilots. You're to take care of them," he declared.

"No! God why?!" he sobbed as his screen shut off abruptly.

"He'll get used to you," Hourev waved his hand, disregarding its pleas.

When the plane was finished, they were allowed to go. The four of them still had another punishment, but it would have to be the next day. It was late and they were all tired. Their second punishment was to go down to the village a few miles from the city. The headmaster's instructions were *very* clear. They were to assist the villagers with whatever they needed for a whole two weeks. It was a long walk, and so they needed to rest up.

21

FOUR THEY ARE

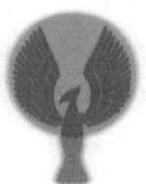

F or the next two weeks Chris, Penny, Megan, and Ian were to go down to the village and help out. It didn't matter what they did, but they had to assist in some form or fashion. The walk was rather long. The path to the village led to a long covered wooden bridge. The bridge was brown and red and was the only way to get across the lake quickly. On the other side of the bridge was a dirt path and a small hut that appeared to be meant for resting. It was kept in good condition, but they never really used it. The village was not far from that point, and so they continued on. The only time they stopped was the first time they came down. They had all been tired from working on the plane and wanted to take a short nap before continuing on.

The village wasn't too much to marvel at. They had supplied most of the food that went to the city along with water. There were no magic users. Everyone in the village was powerless. They had some fighters, but no firearms. Most of the villagers were farmers and builders, and there was a fairly large number of children (much to Megan's delight.) So naturally Megan tended to the children by playing with them and babysitting while the parents worked. At times she helped the farmers. At times Penny would help her, but she had her own job.

Chris and Ian would help the builders by moving heavy things like barrels of water and food. They would also help to thin the local wolf population. Penny accompanied them from time to time, but Chris would try to impress her by insisting he didn't need help. They were much easier to deal with now and he was glad. However, they were moving out farther. The headmaster wanted them to clear out nearby wolf dens in the forest. It was a little cruel, but it had to be done so more people did not get hurt.

"On your left!" Ian called out to Chris. Chris quickly spun around and fired an ice shard into an airborne wolf and dodged under it as it crashed into the ground. Ian smashed his broadsword into three wolves and punched another in the face before cutting clean through it with one great swing.

"They keep coming," Chris swung his sword once to clean it. "Where is that den?"

"We need to find it soon," Ian groaned. "We've been at this for God knows how long..."

A wolf on Chris's right began to howl and paw the ground. Suddenly, its fur caught fire as its eyes turned ruby red. It snarled and began to circle them. All of the other wolves did the same. "What the--?!" Chris pressed his back to Ian's. Both of them readied their weapons once again and tensed up. Chris was ready for any attack to come his way at this point. He could not relax or let his guard down. Who knew when they would attack. He could not chance trying to attack just yet. There were too many. They would have to defend each other.

"Is this what happens when you enhance an animal with magic?"

"I wouldn't know. I've never seen this crap before."

Penny came down from the sky, landing on top of one of the

many hostiles. She flipped forward and landed beside Chris. The wind blew hard as their fur was extinguished. Megan was flying toward them on the head of a giant sunflower. The yellow petals were spinning rapidly, allowing her to move rapidly through the sky. Her hand outstretched again as the wind intensified around them, blowing away the wolves to give them breathing room.

"We thought you needed help," Penny smiled at Chris.

"Nah," Chris said, trying to play it cool. "We had this under control."

"He's not a very good liar," Megan noted as she flew overhead, firing life energy down at the wolves. A few were killed by it instantly, but some shook it off.

"I'm a great liar!" Chris said he swung his sword at a wolf. It jumped back in response to avoid the hit.

"Then I can't be friends with you," Megan stopped flying around and hovered just above them. "I've got you covered."

"Aww. You do care about me," Ian replied as he countered a wolf by catching it by the maw and throwing it back.

He did not care that it bit his hand, and he did not appear to feel it. It healed almost instantly anyway. Since he was a tank, Chris figured this was normal for most.

"I don't," she rolled her eyes. "Chris, your left."

Chris attempted to block, but he was a little too late. The creature bit into his arm and burned him as it caught fire once again. He screamed out in pain, and almost instantly caught Penny's attention. Penny ignored all other wolves as she ran over and sliced clean through Chris's attacker. She spared no time to spin back around and follow up the first attack with a second. It fell to the ground in the form of ash. Penny had seemed very intent on making it pay for that.

Megan held out her hand as a green beam of energy shot from her hand onto Chris's arm and healed the wound and the burns. She then used yet another spell to increase his stamina slightly. Chris sprinted forward and cut down five wolves rapidly; darting from one to the other in seconds. It wore him out a little, but it went away quickly as Megan used yet another spell. *She's really good at that.*

The last wolf fell with a loud thud. They all lowered their weapons and scanned for more, but it was finally clear. Megan deduced that this must have been their den due to the sheer quantity alone. It took them minutes for the four of them to finish them all off.

"Thanks for that, Penny," Chris held up his hand.

"You don't have to thank me," Penny high-fived him. "You're my partner."

"Still, thank you. That hurt..."

"Does it still hurt?" Megan asked as she leapt off of the sunflower, which turned into pollen as soon as she did. She descended slowly and landed gracefully near them.

"No, thanks."

"Good. I thought I made a mistake there."

"Perfectionist..." Ian shook his head. "Now you see why she drives me crazy."

Megan walked over and pressed her finger hard into his chest, "At least I'm organized and get things done efficiently! I think it's best to be a perfectionist than to be a bumbling--"

"Guys," Chris said simply.

"They argue like this all the time," Penny assured. "You get used to it."

"Still."

They made their way back to the village and reported their successful subjugation. The wolves had been given magical abilities, but it was an extremely painful process. They could not control what was happening to them, and it was not their fault. According to the villagers, the wolves used to not pay them much attention, and some would come to the village for food until recently. Now they were only interested in harm. The way they acted when they fought, Chris would tell they were in a great deal of pain. At the very least, they were put out of their misery. They could not perceive what was going on with them.

When they returned back to the city, they were exhausted, but they couldn't relax just yet. The headmaster had called them to his office. After cleaning up, they headed straight there. Megan was not with them, because she had gone on ahead without them.

Chris changed into a white shirt, a black and blue jacket, jeans, and white shoes. Penny wore the outfit that she wore when he had first met her. Ian simply wore his usual attire with his hood drawn back. Once all three of them met up they headed to the administration building. Megan was waiting there for them on the steps playing with a daisy. She was twirling it around in her fingertips slowly, admiring it.

Megan had her hair in a French braid. She wore a green shirt with a thick black line going down the center, a green and black jacket, green gloves, and a green skirt. Black stockings, and green boots with a slight incline in the back. The undersides of these shoes were black. Megan also wore a green wizard hat.

Ian gawked at her for a moment before coming back to his senses. This was merely her outfit from when Chris first met her-- or at least it appeared to be. It was a different color and more accurately represented her school of magic. Chris wondered why she only just now decided to wear her school colors. It seemed like the thing all students did, and yet she had not previously done this.

"You're staring, Ian," Megan continued to admire her flower. She glanced up at all three of them. "You're all staring actually. What?"

"I've just never seen you wear this color," Chris told her.

"Eh." Ian shrugged.

"You do look nice though," Penny complimented.

"Well thank you, Penny," she said kindly. "And Chris, it's a long story. It had to do with me training under the headmaster. I didn't have the best past."

"Uh-huh?" Chris nodded, trying to understand.

"It represented purity. I did some...messed up things at one point," she admitted with a sigh. "I'll tell you what, since you're another earthling I'll tell you later. But you have to tell me about how you got here!"

"Deal," Chris extended his hand and helped her to her feet. "I'm looking forward to it."

They entered the headmaster's office and waited for him to finish speaking to Autumn. After Autumn left he began to address them.

"I would like to make you four into a squad," he told them. "I think it's about time. Considering that you will be serving under General Nicholas soon, I do believe I should. It's a bit earlier than most, but even so it is necessary."

"Yes sir," Megan nodded. "I remember you telling me about this."

"You knew?" Ian questioned. "And didn't tell us?"

"I knew, but couldn't tell you," she corrected. "Why else would he have us help them with their plane? Helping them with the village...He wanted us to get used to each other."

"She's right," he extended his hand toward them before intertwining his fingers and staring at them intently. "She was the only one of you to know. I was looking for a squad to place her."

"Then why didn't I know?" Ian seemed really confused.

"You two are still learning to get along," he sighed slightly. "I just know it would have been a mess someway-somehow if I told you both," he continued on. "I wanted to find another partner group that synchronized with yours. In truth, not many people can keep up with you Ian, but it makes sense."

The headmaster sat forward in his chair, "An extremely strong, active and self-confident partner pairs well with an intelligent, planning, insecure partner. Strength and wisdom don't always agree, but they make a fine team."

"What about us?" Penny stepped forward, taking Chris's hand and bringing him with her.

The headmaster turned toward them and smiled his warm smile, "An extremely protective and heroic partner who is good at everything, but excels at nothing. Positivity, but uncertainty." *Me?* Chris thought. *That does sound like me.*

Now he addressed Penny, "A veteran who would love more than to protect others as she learns who she is. So many questions about simple things, and yet a knowledge of all others," he glanced at Chris for a moment. "And it seems complete trust for her new partner. And something more between them that is developing."

They both looked at each other. They were extremely confused and unsure of what he could mean. Chris obviously had feelings for Penny, but he did not believe she returned them at all. In fact, she seemed utterly clueless about his feelings or romance. Even so, knowing that she trusted him was enough for now. She was definitely his closest friend here. Penny was his *best* friend. Perhaps that is what he meant.

"Harmony," he raised his right hand toward Chris and Penny. "And discord," he now raised his left hand to Megan and Ian. Headmaster Brood then brought his hands together. "A perfect team. Despite what you may think, it still makes a balance. But even so, there must be a leader."

All four looked at each other for a moment. Who would be the leader? Chris wasn't really sure, but he figured Megan would be most qualified. She seemed extremely smart and the most knowledgeable. On the other hand, Penny knew so much about the Empire. She was even a Sorcerer from the Shadow Realm, and in most cases, she is calm and collective. It would make sense for it to be one of those two.

"I don't know if I can do it," Megan said humbly.

"I agree Megan. You are very intelligent and skilled, but you are not a leader. You are the backbone of this team."

"Yes sir, I understand," she nodded.

"What about me?" Ian asked confidently as he placed his hand on his chest.

"Ian, with all due respect, you are unwilling to adapt to a situation, and you tend to act before you think. You are the strength of this team."

Ian grumped and dropped his hand back to his side. Megan laughed quietly, but Chris could hear it. These two really did like to bicker. Yet, when they worked together they accomplished so much. It was extremely unusual to him. That was the best way he could describe their partnership, but the same could be said of his.

"Penny, I want you to know it is not because you are a Sorcerer. I think you are a wonderful student, an amazing fighter, and an extraordinary pilot. You can be impulsive at times, but I do think with practice you could be a great leader--"

"I don't want to be a leader," she interrupted abruptly. "I never have and never will. I just don't like making decisions like that. Tori was a leader, but I guess I didn't pick up on that." Penny didn't seem to mind as much as the other two. *I kind of want to be a leader*, Chris thought to himself. *But I'd find a way to mess it up. I usually stayed quiet in group activities at school. Ty usually was the group leader.*

Penny spoke suddenly and clearly, interrupting his thoughts, "Chris wants to be leader."

"What?" Chris was now staring at her, completely stunned.

"I heard you," Penny explained confidently. "You said you wanted to. I heard it clearly."

The headmaster raised his head as she said this. Chris was awed by the fact that she had known this. She had said what he was thinking. Penny had read his thoughts in an *instant*. He wondered how she did that.

"*I just focused on you. I can't explain it*", Penny's voice was now in his thoughts.

I can hear you now, Chris replied mentally. Penny smiled at him and nodded, he in turn smiled back.

"Christopher, you have leadership skills, but you need practice. You tend to think you have to do everything alone, and you are afraid of the worst outcome occurring. Even so you stay positive for the sake of those around you," the headmaster studied Chris carefully. "It makes sense as you are Emily's brother. She always has been calm and collective in a dangerous situation, but you're more active. I think you'll make a fine leader."

"The healer, the knight, the shield, and the leader," Ian thought aloud. He placed his arms behind his head and yawned. "Best team composition I've ever seen. I can't help but feel like most teams aren't this balanced."

"You're treating this like a game," the headmaster sounded amused. "Do any of you object?"

"I don't," Ian shrugged.

"I don't disagree, but I do hope you realize the responsibility," Megan placed her hand on her hip and looked at Chris. "I need one mature guy in this group." Ian made a face behind her. "I trust you."

"No problem, but--" Chris began.

"I know you can do it," Penny said sweetly. "I know it's big, but I believe you can." Chris's heart skipped a beat.

The headmaster began to make a note of the team on an official document. Chris wanted to say something, but his chest was tight. He couldn't. He couldn't, because everyone believed in him and he didn't want to let them down. Chris wanted Megan or Penny to be leader. Of course, he thought he wanted to be a leader, but now that it was happening he was having second thoughts.

"You can all leave, dismissed," he said cheerfully. "Have a good night."

The others began to leave the office at once. Chris was the only one to stay. Only Penny turned to see what he was doing.

"Sir," he found himself saying suddenly. "Can I speak to you?"

"Of course," he nodded his head and gestured his head at Penny who was standing by the door. "Would you like her here?"

"Well, she can," he agreed. Penny left anyway, respecting his privacy. "*I'll be outside*", she communicated as the door shut. It was just them.

Chris and this man who ran the entire school. Would he seem pathetic if he told him honestly that he did not want to be leader? He had high expectations for him due to Emily Chris didn't even know most of the things Emily did. She was simply the headmaster's right hand to him.

"With all due respect...why did you pick me as leader? I'm the weakest and I'm still fairly new at this. I know what you said about the others, but I had flaws too."

"Flaws make you human, Christopher," the headmaster stood up from his comfy chair and came over to Chris's side of the desk. "A person I should say. Not all of my students are human."

"Why...I can't."

"You can," he said as he took Chris's shoulders. "You're strong and you don't even know it. You keep shifting from overconfident to fearful. Find a balance. They need you. Those three out there are counting on you."

"What if I let them down?" Chris lowered his head. He did not want to make eye contact after this comment. It was a pathetic thing to say and would typically get someone teased or scolded. The headmaster softened his grip on Chris's shoulders and knelt down.

"You want the honest answer?"

"Yes..."

"You learn. You try again. They may not always understand, but they'll look to you. Even other leaders may. If you need advice go to Emily. You can even come to me," he smiled again.

"You're one of the best students I've seen. You grew fast, and you still have a long way to go, but you'll be there in no time."

"What's the reason you picked me?" Chris tried again. "The real reason?"

Headmaster Brood stood and placed his hand on Chris's back and guided him to the door. He opened it and let Chris out. He gave him one simple answer that Chris was not expecting. Even though it was simple; it was clear and made sense. "Because you wanted to be one, Christopher."

CONFRONTATION

C hris couldn't believe he was the leader of the squad. Not only that, but the other three agreed. From the moment that he came to Terminus he thought he would just die. He didn't know anything, and Penny was basically the only thing keeping him from doing something stupid or dying. Chris learned to fight and use magic in a relatively short time, but he still had much to learn. Once the schools were done; he could do even more.

Right now, Chris's focus was on finding Emily. With everything going on, he did not have much time to look. Now he did, but it was getting late. The sun setting low and practically disappearing behind the many buildings. The lights were starting to come on in the city, and in the distance village fires could be seen burning. More people were out tonight and it was a fairly cool night.

Ian claimed that he was tired and so he headed back to Megan's house. Megan decided to go along with him to relax. After everything she just wanted a small nap. Chris didn't object to this at all and neither did Penny. Penny told Chris she was going to pick up something to eat and bring it back to the dorm, so Chris decided to head back to their dorm and wait for her.

The dorm wasn't very far, but he was tired of walking after going down to the village, fighting, and then walking all the way back to see the headmaster. Chris had done a lot of walking, but he would soon be off of his feet enjoying a meal with Penny. It sounded nice after everything, but he couldn't help but worry about his sister. She was still in the city, and Hunter had no way to escape besides his plane, but he would simply be blown out of the sky if he tried. He stopped walking to think, *He'd be blown out of the sky...with Emily onboard. I can't risk that. I have to find Hunter.*

Chris stopped walking and took a deep breath to calm himself down, he could feel himself getting anxious. The sky began to pour down heavy rain as the sun finally disappeared completely. The rain felt painful as it splashed onto his skin. The rain stung slightly, it was not a storm, but it could become one. Chris pushed himself forward and began to try to solve the mystery of where Hunter could be. He was in the city, and yet no one had found him. How? Surely, he could not just walk on the open streets, he would be discovered immediately.

He took cover under buildings as he went, but he wanted to keep going so he could reach the dorm. However, he could not shake the feeling of eyes on him. Was someone watching him? He turned back to look and the street was mostly empty. Only a mother and her daughter were present. The mother had curly brown hair and orange eyes, she wore a yellow dress and carried a yellow umbrella. The little girl also had brown curly hair, but she wore a green dress.

"Sunale, stop," the mother spoke in a disapproving tone. Her daughter ran ahead and began jumping into one puddle after another. Splash. Splash. "Sunale, come back!"

"I'll come back in a minute, mommy!" Sunale continued to run forward and hop into any puddle of water she could find in the street. The mother was unable to catch her.

"No, come back here now! I'm worried about you!" the mother demanded.

Chris smiled to himself, but internally frowned. Unwanted memories pushed through the cracks of his mind to the surface. The little girl began to look like him from when he was five, and the mother began to look like Emily. How could such an old memory still feel so fresh?

"Chris, stop," Emily chased after him. "Chris, come back here!"

"I'll come back in a minute, Emily!" Chris laughed as he ran faster.

She couldn't catch him. He loved the park and the freedom it gave him. Being with Emily was nice, but she was always so sad. Why was she always so sad? Mom and dad had just disappeared for a while, but they would be back eventually. Chris was *convinced* that they would. Emily probably just missed them. Emily sighed and gave up her chase. Chris stopped in his tracks and spun, smiling.

"What's wrong, big sis?" he stepped toward her slowly.

"Nothing, lil bro," she knelt down to his level. "Just a lot on my mind."

"Like what?" he questioned, poking her cheek.

"Like you staying close and not running off," she answered with a straight face, holding his finger momentarily to stop him.

"Sis...I didn't go far."

"I know."

"And it was just over that way," he pointed.

"I know. Just please don't go far."

"Why?"

"Because," she reached out and placed her hand on his head. "I can't lose you. I have to protect you. You're my only brother. My only family. It scares me."

"...What could happen to me? You're protecting me, aren't you?"

"I..." she ran her fingers through his hair, tangling it between her fingers. "I will, but I need you to realize there are bad people out there. Mom and dad--"

"They'll be back like you said right?"

"I said we'll see them again one day," she corrected.

"When?" he questioned.

"...Let's go get some ice cream," she stood and took his little hand and guided him to a white ice cream cart with a red and white umbrella. He took her hand and stared up at her with wonder, his sister knew so much and she protected him. What more could he ask for? If Chris's parents were here it would have been perfect. They never really did get to be a family very long, but they would reunite.

"Chris?" Emily's voice interrupted his thoughts. "No matter what, remember one way or another I'll be looking out for you." He stared up at her, listening and grasping onto every word. "I love you. Please realize that--mom and dad are-- you know what? Nothing, okay? Let's get you that yummy ice cream!" she smiled, but he knew something was wrong. That wasn't her smile.

Chris recalled her crying that night when they got home after she put him to bed. He snuck out of bed to check on her and sat outside of her room door only to hear her crying.

He chose to wait until she fell asleep to make his move. He pushed the door aside and crawled stealthily to her. Emily was asleep and half dangling off of her bed. He didn't recall what she was wearing at all; he just wanted to help her, he was worried. Chris climbed into the bed with her, pushed her arm slightly and slipped under it and lay with her. When he couldn't sleep he had a teddy bear, so he would be hers. When she woke up, she would most certainly wonder what he was doing in her bed, and to that he would answer as he always did: I had a nightmare. It was a lie. It all felt so fresh and vivid to him, like it was just yesterday and now she was missing - again. He would find her one way or another.

Chris came to his senses as another splash echoed along the walls of the buildings. The little girl was coming in his direction. He could only imagine how much that mother worried about her safety, and so he decided to do something. Chris stepped in front of the girl just as she was about to pass and caught her. He knelt down to her level. "Hey...she said to come back," he said this as calm and soft as he could.

"But she's always worrying! I know the way home and every-thing!" the girl groaned. "I've got it."

"You need to go back," he persisted, glancing behind the girl to see the mother.

"Why?" the familiar question finally came. *Why?*

"Because she cares and worries for you. She doesn't want anything to happen to you," Chris looked her in the eyes. "I know how you feel, but you need to listen to her."

"What makes you say that? She's always bossy and--"

"I know because of my sister. It took me a while though. I want you to apologize and walk with her this time," he turned her back so she could see her mother. The mother seemed to be rather confused about what was going on.

The little girl nodded and returned to her mother with a lowered head. Chris walked with her until she reached her waiting mother. There was silence for a moment before the child apologized and looked back at Chris. He smiled a little and gave her a nod of approval.

"Please don't run off again, Sunale," the mother instructed.

"'Kay..."

"Spellcrafter? Thank you," the mother hugged her child to her side, as if to make sure not to lose her again. "She always does this..."

"You know my name?" Chris returned his attention to the mother now.

"Yes, your sister is Emily. She helped me find my daughter when she ran off and got lost during a parade one time," she explained. "I was about to panic when I saw her walking with Sunale."

"Really? How did she find her?"

"She had heard me call for her. Your sister walked off without any words to me or even a simple 'I'm going to go look for her,' she simply went and found her for me in a crowd of-- there were a lot of people."

I guess...I'm not so different from her, Chris smiled to himself and nodded his head. "Anytime, but I don't think she'll do it again."

"I don't know. My little Sunale always does this. You had better get out of the rain before you catch a cold."

Chris waved them off as they left down the street, turning to head toward north Terminus. He lowered his hand and held it in front of his face. He stared at it and relaxed a little, continuing in the direction he was going before.

Chris was about to pass by an alleyway, but as he was passing he was grabbed and pulled in. Someone had their hand over his mouth so he could not scream for help. His back was pushed against the brick wall as a pistol was pressed against his stomach. He could not see the person very well, but they were female. There was just enough light for him to tell what they were wearing: a long black and red dress that was cut in such a way that it would reveal the right-side leg, a black serpent design wrapped around the other leg. The chest of the dress was slightly revealing with black and red laces. Her hair appeared to fall a little past her shoulders. The figure stepped into light. Her eyes seemed unfamiliar to him; not the brown that he had come to know, but a spine-tingling purple. A small grin formed on her mouth, but not one that he expected. It was not like the one Gatchi had made when he had encountered her. It was shadow Victoria.

"I knew I'd catch you," she seemed to be applauding herself haughty.

"I thought you left the city," Chris felt uneasy now. Who knew what she wanted? "You got what you wanted."

"Looks can be deceiving. I was at the hearing too," she walked over to his left and leaned against his shoulder, pointing her gun at his head. *She was there? Where? How?* "For example, I look like Victoria, and sound like her-"

"You aren't," he spat instantaneously.

"My, my aren't we angry? I didn't kill her, Vedi did."

"I don't care. You aren't her."

She rolled her eyes. "Misdirected anger isn't good for you, Christopher."

"You still aren't her."

"I *will* tell you this though," she lowered her gun for a moment. "I think you and I can...help each other." Victoria paused to let her words sink in for a moment. She waited for some form of reaction or reply.

"Why would I ever help you?" he turned his head toward her.

"You wouldn't help me out of the kindness of your heart?" she sighed sarcastically as she placed one of her hands to her chest, acting hurt and offended. "I guess it's a good thing that I have something you want." She got on her toes and whispered into his right ear as clear as she could, "Because I know where Hunter is."

"What?" Chris was taken aback. "Where?" he demanded.

Victoria had a telling smirk on her face. Chris could tell he had made a mistake in showing such interest in the subject. At first, she said nothing, then she turned and waved her gun toward the clock tower looming in the distance of the clouded night sky, "He's been moving constantly to different buildings, but right now he's in there," she lowered her gun and turned back toward him. "I've been helping him relocate every night."

"Wait, you work with Hunter? I thought you were a part of the Empire."

"I work for myself," she turned her back to him, still aiming her gun over her shoulder. "The Empire can go to hell."

"But your sister-" Chris furrowed his eyebrows. "Isn't your version of Penny with the Empire?"

"Yes. Okay...And?" she shrugged her shoulders.

"And she's your sister."

Victoria began to laugh. Apparently, something was funny, she turned toward him shaking her head, "Just because your Penny got along with her sister, doesn't mean I want to," she shook her head. "No, I'm going to kill her."

"Kill her? What-"

"Bang," she said as she pointed her pistol at her head. "A shot to the noggin."

"That's horrible," Chris shook his head. "How can you say that?"

"I just did. Enough about me. Watch this," Victoria reached down into her boot and removed a small golden computer chip. She took it and inserted it into his watch before he could ask. A holographic video jumped out from the watch. Hunter was rummaging through a backpack. He was indeed in the clock tower. Emily was behind him, conscious now, but her hands and feet were tied up. Chris figured that if she hadn't been tied up, that he would have been dealt with by now. Her hair was messy, but she seemed mostly okay. He had not hurt her as far as he could tell.

Hunter was wearing the same thing that he had worn previously: a red shirt, a black jacket, and black leather combat boots. He was talking on some sort of device that he had set up. It was not very large and it was simply sitting on the wooden clock tower floor.

"I can't seem to get a very good signal," he heard him say, throwing his arms up.

"Maybe that's because your friends left you," Emily was trying to free herself, but Hunter had clearly not caught on. She was having very little luck, but alas she kept trying. "The Alliance reinforcements are pushing them further from Terminus as we speak. "

"Be quiet..." he muttered. "I don't need your--"

"Hunter, this is wrong and you know it!" she seemed to be trying to get through to him.

"You don't know right from wrong. You're just lucky I care about you more than anyone else here," he muttered, casting her a mean glance. "I could have killed you. You're here because of me."

"You were setting the wolves on the town! You were helping to attack and sabotage the city!" Emily screamed. "You tried to kill my brother too." she lowered her head. "If I wasn't tied up..."

"I wasn't trying to kill him. Although he did die briefly from what I heard. Lucky for him he's got that girl that drags him around."

"How can you say that so easily?" Emily's face showed that she was in shock, her mouth slightly agape. "This-- isn't even-- what's wrong with you!?"

Hunter ignored her and went back to trying to fix his device. He turned toward the holographic image, "Victoria, hand me that screwdriver."

"Of course," Victoria came into frame and handed it to him. "They won't be sending anyone to come get us anyway."

"Maybe they are. Maybe they're not. And if not, we can run that blockade. It just wouldn't be pretty," Hunter began to fix the device as best he could, but his efforts were fruitless.

The device began to power up and glow red, before sparking violently and powering down. It was clear that it would no longer work.

Victoria stepped away from where Hunter was and headed toward the device capturing it all. Her hand covered it briefly. Once her hand had moved, Chris could see everything again. But what he saw next astounded him. Victoria pulled her gun on Hunter. She had done this without a moment's hesitation.

"Victoria?!" Hunter stood up quickly.

"Na-uh. Don't move," she said as she began to back away. "I'm leaving, okay?"

"Is that my watch?!"

"It would seem so."

"What's wrong?" Emily rolled her eyes as she focused her efforts on escaping her bindings. "Don't like when you get double-crossed?"

"Shut up!" Hunter shot at Emily. Hunter turned to Victoria, he pointed a finger at her, shaking with rage. "Victoria...I am giving you-- one-- warning."

"Oh Hunter," she smiled and placed her hand on her chest. "You talk far too much," Victoria stepped forward, tempting fate. "You want to kill me so bad right now, don't you?"

Hunter said nothing, he took deep breaths, he seemed to be debating his next move. She had him in a bad position and there was almost nothing he could really do. Perhaps he had underestimated how dangerous she was. He did seem legitimately surprised by this betrayal. He didn't seem as cool or level headed as when Chris had seen him last.

"Are you afraid to make a move?" Victoria took another step forward in one smooth motion, daring him to strike. "Don't tell me you're surprised. You're too pathetic and-"

Hunter swung. Victoria's lip curled immediately. There was a sudden movement upwards so Chris couldn't see what was happening. A ruby red orb flew by quickly, blocking something with a loud *crash*. Powerful gunshots could be heard soon after; it sounded like two pistols firing one after another. The camera moved back down, cartridges and bullet holes littered the floor in front of Hunter. His sword had been knocked out of his hand and landed on the other side of the room. He had tried closing the distance, but she promptly disarmed him, shot eight rounds at his feet, and was now giving him a smug look. Victoria laughed as she waved goodbye at the now defeated Hunter. The recording ended soon after.

Chris looked up from his watch to see Victoria dangling a brown and red watch from her fingertips. At this point, Chris figured that this version of Victoria had no allegiance, did not care about morals, and was good at deception. What he had seen was entirely true, and he figured Hunter was preparing to leave at this very moment.

"Now that I showed you all of this," she took her finger and pressed it against his chest. "You owe me."

"Owe you?" Chris echoed, in complete and utter disbelief. "Yeah, no." Chris turned to leave.

"You owe me and I know exactly what I'll use you for," Victoria grabbed his wrist. "I'm keeping Hunter's watch so you can contact me when we work together."

"Won't you need to contact me?" he raised his eyebrow as Victoria stepped in front of him once again.

"No, I can find you," a sly smile appeared on her face. "I'll know where you are, Christopher. Once you do me this certain favor, you won't owe me again."

"I--" he paused, mulling this all over. *I really don't have a choice at all...*" Fine," he heaved.

"Good boy," Victoria seemed pleased. "Call your little friends."

Chris turned his back to Victoria and began to access his watch. He tried to call Megan and Ian, but they did not answer. Where were they? Neither of them were answering their watch, and no matter how many times he called, it was the same result. He tried calling Penny next and this time he actually got an answer pretty immediately. Penny's voice began to speak.

"Hey, are you okay?" Penny sounded rather relaxed. "I was heading back to the dorm. I'll have to get the food later, they had to close shop because--"

"Not now!" Chris found himself saying this louder than he meant to. "I know where Hunter is, but he's leaving soon! I'm about to head there now."

"Where?" Penny sounded concerned. "Are you heading there now?"

"No. I'm--" Chris looked back at Victoria and stopped himself from finishing that statement. Could he tell her about Shadow Victoria? It might just hurt her to find out about her being in the city, and she had only just recently gotten happy again. "I found out from someone working with Hunter," he said finally, slurring his words slightly. "I... I'm very sure I know where."

"Where?"

"The clocktower," he said as he lifted his wrist to his mouth to talk better, looking up at the ghostly structure. The clock appeared to have a ghostly yellow glow in the rain and the fog. "I'm heading there now."

"*No.* Not without me!" Penny disagreed immediately.

"He'll get away," Chris argued. "I have to."

"Chris, I need you to wait," Penny begged. "I'm worried. Last time--"

"I can do it," Chris assured. "I can't let him get away, especially with Emily."

"I'll be there soon..." Penny hung up her watch, but before she did Chris could have sworn he had heard her begin to run.

Chris turned back to Victoria who was obviously listening in on his conversation. She spoke first and made each word very clear, "If you wait like that girl wants you to, you'll lose Hunter and your sister. Hunter won't wait."

"I see that," Chris looked back at the big clock ticking away in the night. "I don't think I can take him alone, though. Can you help?"

"I have things to do," Victoria purred. "But, I suppose I can tell your two friends about your whereabouts."

"Megan and Ian?"

"Who else?" she replied harshly, casting him a glance. "I mean really...now run along."

"How will you get around the city without--"

"They haven't caught me. They never will, I'll be taking my leave after this," Victoria stepped backwards and faded into the darkness of the alley. Her eyes seemed to glow red in the shadows and it was rather terrifying to Chris. She stood there, waiting for him to leave.

Chris walked out from the alley and looked left and then right. *What's the fastest way?* Chris had never been near the clocktower in all of his time here; how was he supposed to find the fastest way there? *There's no time.* He ran forward toward a stack of boxes and climbed up as fast as he could. He then turned and leapt toward the building in between him and the way forward, slipping slightly due to the heavy amounts of rain. Chris managed to get his leg up first, and then his elbow, and then he was able to pull the rest of himself up.

He leapt from building to building, and once the buildings became too far apart he dropped down and continued on. It was not far now. The clock tower's grey bricks were soaked in rainwater that slid down to the stone streets below. Its door was a dark brown wood with two large marble handles on each side.

Hunter was in this clocktower. He was planning his escape right this second, there was no time to waste. Chris took a deep breath and pressed his hands against the doors and slowly pushed them apart. Light began to escape the interior, Chris pushed the doors more so he could get a better look.

Chris could see Emily tied up in that same corner with her head down. Hunter was nowhere to be seen in the room. Chris was nervous about where he could have gone, but there was no time for that. He quickly moved across the wooden floor and began to untie her. She needed him, Hunter could come last. Emily began to stir, her voice put him at ease slightly.

"Oh...little- bro..." she lifted her head to look him in the eyes. "How did you get here?"

"Can I use my sword on this?"

"You can try," she moaned. "I don't know, he kept a good eye on me."

Chris hastily untied her feet, "Where is he?" Chris looked left and right to try to locate his adversary.

"He? Oh...Hunter...?" Emily sounded very dazed. "I don't know...my head hurts so much."

"That's fine," Chris finished untying her feet, now he moved on to her hands that were behind her back. "Don't move."

"*Chris!*" Emily screamed. Chris quickly spun and summoned his sword all in one motion, placing his hand on the other end of his blade to block the death blow. He winced slightly as the edge cut his finger and palm. He threw the assailant off.

Hunter stood before him, pointing his sword at him. Chris leapt to his feet and pointed his sword back. There was nothing to say at all. Chris had no intention of speaking one word to this scum. He probably had a few seconds to plan his attack and he was not going to waste one second.

Hunter took a step forward and jabbed his sword, Chris stepped to the right to dodge and swung his sword upward to the left to knock it away with both hands. Hunter swung downward, Chris blocked up and elbowed him as hard as he could in the gut, pushing him back against the wall. Chris slashed down, Hunter slid along the wall to dodge. He then tackled Chris to the ground. Both swords went flying away.

Chris crawled quickly toward his weapon, getting to his feet and rearmed himself. Hunter had done the same, but by the time Chris turned back to continue the fight, Hunter was about to finish him off.

Hunter fired a massive ball of fire was coming toward him. He had no chance of dodging in time. Emily made a move to get involved, but she did not have the strength to move at this time, and so she collapsed. Chris raised his hand in an attempt to protect himself and flinched.

Someone flew in front of Chris, stepping in and blocking the devastating flames. It was Penny. Her shield was raised, protecting him entirely from the magic. She called over the roar of the fire, "Are you hurt?"

"Nothing serious!" he replied.

"Good. Go. Now!"

Penny stepped aside. Chris took her place and fired a blast of Ice magic. Hunter's fire was blown back toward him, stopping in between them. Hunter broke the engagement and dodged what was left of Chris magic, running up the wooden stairs to the next floor.

"*After him!*" Penny's voice came into his mind once again loud and clear. She took off up the stairs and he followed behind her, only stopping to look back at Emily.

"Chris." Emily managed weakly.

"Stay there!" Chris urged. "Megan and Ian should be coming soon. He's got nowhere to go." he ran after Penny. Hunter had ascended the many floors to the top. The ticking of the clock and turning of the gears could be heard.

Hunter paused and closed his eyes, taking a slow breath and releasing it. He turned back toward them, his expression showing nothing but irritation and discontent. He grasped his sword tightly in his hand and looked at the pair in front of him.

Chris and Penny pointed their swords at him at the same time. Hunter readied himself. He obviously wasn't going to surrender. Chris figured that he couldn't take them both together, especially without his partner. No one said a word; the only sound was that of the mechanisms around them.

Chris moved forward and stuck out with a long slash, Hunter parried. Hunter countered with two quick sword swings. Penny moved forward in an instant and blocked both, spinning and smacking him in the face with her shield. Hunter stepped back and covered his now bloodied cheek. Penny moved in again and swung her small sword, Hunter caught her wrist and squeezed hard, but Penny did not let it go. Chris moved in as he attempted to cut Penny down. He managed to block Hunter's first blow, but the second cut his shoulder. He returned the favor by lashing out at Hunter who was forced to retreat backwards.

Chris stepped back and held his arm that now had blood trickling down. It was healing, but it was very much open

"Come on," Hunter readied himself for another assault. "I thought you were a team."

"*Heal. I got him*", Penny told him. She moved in and began to engage him once again. Chris knelt down on the floor, catching his breath. Once his arm had fully healed, he returned to the fight. He hoped Megan and Ian would arrive soon and free Emily, preferably with help.

Chris charged in and collided swords with Hunter. They stayed that way until Penny made a move to cut him across his face. Hunter pushed Chris back and shot Fire magic at Penny, she raised her shield to block the blast. Chris came in one again, this time focusing on disabling Hunter. He held his sword in a horizontal manner and charged directly at him. This caught him off guard, but Hunter prepared in the short time he had to think.

Hunter stepped aside and threw Chris into the wall; his sword became stuck in the wall. Hunter grabbed the back of Chris's head and slammed it hard into the butt of the sword. Chris fell, disoriented. Everything was spinning and he could hear a ringing. All he could make out was Penny still engaged with Hunter. He was healing once again, but it was taking time. Chris needed to get back on his feet and help.

He placed both hands in front of him and lifted himself up shakily. He could barely see, but he needed to keep moving. He turned back toward his blade, placed his foot against the wall and attempted to pry it out. It inched out, but it was barely moving. Penny was still engaged with Hunter behind him, but she seemed to be doing just fine. How long could she continue without him? She was mostly on the defensive, but she was also striking out.

Hunter caught Penny's blade as she attempted a desperate attack and threw it over to where Chris was trying to retrieve his sword. Chris glanced down at it, realizing Penny was in trouble, turning back to see what was happening. Penny was struggling now, Hunter was pressing his advantage, she was backing away and blocking what she could with her shield, but he was overwhelming her. Finally, Hunter punched Penny causing her to turn away and slashed her across the spine. Penny's eyes went wide as she fell to the ground. Chris tried harder to free his weapon.

Chris turned back, "Penny!" No reply at all. Her eyes were closed and she was not moving or making any sounds. *Is... she...* Chris felt his eyes sting, but he was not going to cry. Could Penny actually be dead? He was alone again...against Hunter. Chris was not afraid, he wanted nothing more than to kill him now. Hunter wouldn't escape.

Hunter ran up behind Chris and attempted to strike, Chris ripped the sword violently from the wall with great effort and collided swords with him. Sparks flew as they both drew backwards. Chris reached down after knocking Hunter back and took Penny's small sword. He held Penny's sword in his right hand facing forward and his own sword in his left, reverse grip.

"If you want to get in my way," Hunter readied his sword, panting heavily. "I'm going to make sure you join her."

Chris charged forward and began relentless strikes with both hands. Hunter blocked as much as he could, but with every strike more blood was drawn. Hunter fired a blast of fire once again; this time Chris rolled under it and began to attack low. The blast of fire had made contact with the wooden parts of the structure, starting a fire that was now spreading along the walls.

Chris dodged left and then right, dancing around Hunter's attacks. "Hold--" Hunter gritted his teeth and collided swords with Chris's left sword. "Still!" Chris brought Penny's sword forward and plunged Penny's sword into Hunter's hip. Hunter cried out in pain as Chris ripped the sword out of his body and attempted to stab another location.

Hunter fired as much magic as he could to make Chris back off. Chris blocked every shot with his swords and dashed forward once again. Movement could be heard from downstairs. Voices. Hunter was running out of time, but Chris wasn't trying to stall. He was going to end this. Chris collided swords with Hunter once again, then he used his left hand to slash Hunter across the face from his right cheek to his nose, barely missing his eye.

The flames were getting worse now, engulfing most of the room except for where they were fighting and where Penny lay motionless. Smoke filled the air as the fight continued, both combatants were struggling to breathe by now. Chris was covered in sweat and blood, but he didn't care. He quickly used his sleeve to wipe off the liquids that were blocking his vision.

He charged, ignoring Hunter's blows and allowing them to land. He wrapped his arms around Hunter's torso and took him to the floor with a loud *thud*. Hunter slashed Penny's sword out of Chris's hand. Chris took his sword in both hands, sat on top of Hunter and began violently striking downward. Hunter blocked as best as he could. Chris collided swords with him one final time, this time he pushed the sword down with as much force as he could muster. Hunter's own sword was inching toward his neck, he struggled, but Chris was overpowering him. Hunter attempted to lean his head back to protect his neck, but it was inches from his skin.

The cold steel was beginning to make a cut on his neck. Hunter was like a cornered animal as he swiped his sword left, cutting the side of his neck slightly to smash the butt of his sword into Chris's face. Chris drew back just enough for Hunter to bring the sword back to the right and slash him across the stomach. He pushed Chris off hard so he rolled off and laid on his back, defeated and coughing up a little blood. Chris sat up as best he could and fired a shard of ice into Hunter's leg. Hunter yelped and knelt down, pulling it out.

"Why-?" Chris managed. "Why would you do this?"

Hunter limped his way over to one of the clock tower's faces and turned back toward Chris, holding his hip. He shook his head, "You still think people need a reason."

"You hurt my sister, betrayed the Alliance, got Tori killed, and Penny-" Chris choked and laid his head back on the floor, feeling the intense heat all around him.

"I'm not Imperial," Hunter said simply as loud shots fired and the clocktower face exploded. Glass and splinters of wood flew in all directions. "I did what I had to do."

Behind him was a dark purple fighter plane. He limped over to it as best he could, pulled himself up into the cockpit, closed the glass. Chris gave him one last hateful glare as he flew away at full speed toward the sky.

Chris heard movement not too far from him, he turned his head to see. Penny was now conscious once again. Her spine had healed up and she was now crawling toward him. She placed her hand in his and stared down at him, panting heavily along with him. She squeezed, he squeezed back in return.

"Hey," he coughed.

"Hey," she shook her head. "No way out..."

"Yeah," Chris tried to sit up and so Penny helped him. He looked all around the room, but everywhere was engulfed in flames. "Are you still bleeding?"

"Yeah. He got something important," Penny answered as she moved her hand to show him that her side was bleeding profusely. "That's not the only place either...You?"

Chris moved his hand from his stomach to show his wound along with his many other injuries, "I can't stop it. I don't think it's healing right now," he admitted.

"You got hit too much," she sat down with him and laid her back against his and he did the same.

"Are you scared?"

"Of what?"

"Dying?"

"No," Penny removed her glove and reached back, taking his hand in her own and holding it tightly.

"Are you?"

"Kinda, yeah. But I'm alright with this," Chris coughed up a little more blood and laid his head back against hers.

"Why?"

"Because," he looked back. "I'm with you and we saved my sister."

"What do you mean by that?" Penny held her other hand over her wound once again. "You've been acting so strange. I want to know why, if this is it."

Chris felt uneasy, but he wanted to tell her. If this was really it, he had to tell her. Penny wanted to know and he wasn't afraid to say it. He squeezed her hand and opened his mouth, closing it for a moment to think of the best way to say the words. Finally, he decided to just say it: "I love you," Chris declared confidently.

"You...love me?" Penny repeated.

"Yes...I do," he nodded. "That's why."

"I don't understand..."

"That's okay," Chris chuckled, no longer able to move his body, going limp against her back. "I just needed you to know."

"I've only ever heard that from family," Penny breathed. "It's strange--" she glanced back to see Chris unconscious. "Unconscious again...god what am I going to do with you?"

The roof began to collapse around them and the fire continued to spread, embers filled the air. Penny began to cough uncontrollably. She saw someone moving through the smoke just before she closed her eyes.

23

REUNION

The flames had now fully enveloped the room. Chris and Penny were only moments away from being burned. Penny lifted her head with much effort, and studied the figure making their way toward her, squinting her eyes. The green outfit and pink hair were a dead giveaway: it was Megan. Penny attempted to speak but it appeared as if she could not. She looked back, as if to make sure her partner was okay and then returned her eyes to Megan.

Megan outstretched her hand, firing a burst of wind that momentarily cleared the way just long enough for her to move toward them. She stood next to Penny and held her hands up, a large green barrier surrounded them, it appeared to be made of wind. The fire had finally surrounded the floor, the only thing that was stopping it from killing them was Megan.

"Get Chris," Megan was very focused on keeping this barrier going. Chris started to come to, he was very confused about what was going on.

"Just walk slowly," Penny pulled his arm around her and placed her hand on his chest and began to walk slowly. "Megan, which way? The stairs are on fire!"

"Is there a way out?"

"There's a hole over there," Penny said, referencing the exit Hunter had created.

"We're jumping," Megan followed closely behind them, fending away the angry flames. "We need to get out of here. The tower is definitely coming down."

"But what about Chris?"

"Don't worry," Megan was struggling to hold the barrier up, almost as if it was getting heavier and crushing her. "You let me worry about that. Do *exactly* what I say."

They made their way over to the window, carefully avoiding the debris left behind by Hunter's plane. Chris tripped only to be caught by Penny, he could barely make out what was going on, only that they were going toward what was left of the clock tower face. Once they had made it to the edge Megan was shaking, struggling to keep the barrier up. It looked like she was being crushed.

"Jump!" Megan turned her back to them and held her hands toward the flames. "Hurry, I can't keep this up!"

Chris looked over the edge, seeing the ground and the entire city below them. It all looked very small from up here and it made him nervous along with everything else, but they didn't have many options. Even so, they had to be at least three hundred feet in the air. They took a step forward, Chris closed his eyes. The howl of the wind blared in his ear as they fell faster and faster. Penny squeezed Chris's hand almost as if to tell him it would be alright. Both of their bodies were in an X formation.

Megan took a step back, dropping the magic barrier, and falling right behind them. She spun herself around in the air and held out her hand, focusing straightforward. The giant sunflower appeared once again just below them. They landed on top of it sinking into the center, causing yellow pollen to fly up into the air. The petals were spinning rapidly, causing them to hover. Megan landed soon after them, catching herself with her hands.

The clocktower was collapsing behind them in a giant ball of fire. Megan caused them to fly forward as fast as possible, dodging the falling debris and continuing toward the ground. Chris could see the Headmaster, Alleyne, and Autumn preparing to prevent anyone from getting hurt. The three of them were using Imagination magic to create a giant net. The net caught every single piece of the clock tower that was falling before they lowered it to the ground. Autumn used both hands to extinguish the fires using water.

They landed right next to the action. Penny immediately helped Chris off and gently laid him on the ground. Megan knelt down across from her and went to work on his wounds; she also healed Penny's wounds, but according to Megan, she had healed for the most part on her own. Chris was the one who really needed attention due to his duel with Hunter. Autumn walked over to check on them.

"Is he okay?" Autumn questioned, pausing for a moment as she noticed the blood on Penny's side. "You too, are you okay?"

"I'm fine," Penny said quickly, turning back to focus on Chris. "Help Megan." Autumn seemed slightly astounded, but she helped anyway, understanding her position. Chris blacked out at some time during this process, but this time he felt relaxed-- safe.

After some time, Chris was awake again. Embers and ash were still floating in the air and things appeared to have calmed down. He no longer felt as if he was in pain, but he couldn't help but remember the sensation. Emily and Ian were now over him as well. He started to sit up and so they all sat back to give him space. Chris stared at Emily for a moment before lunging at her and hugging her. Emily's eyes went wide, stared at the others, fully baffled before embracing her brother once again.

"Are you okay?" Emily pulled away from him and held his shoulders. "That was dangerous. How did you know where I was?"

"It's a long story..." Chris admitted, looking over at Megan and Ian.

"Victoria-" Ian spoke out suddenly. Chris made a face, he did not know if Penny or Emily would be okay with hearing the news. However, Ian continued on. "We heard someone knocking on the door of our house and when we answered Victoria was there- told us where Chris and Penny would be and that Hunter would be there."

"*Shadow* Victoria," Chris corrected. "I- had to make a deal with her to find Hunter. She promised to tell you guys."

"Before we came to you, we told Autumn and one of the guards," Megan recalled. "Ian got Emily. I got you."

"Chris," Emily started. "What kind of deal..."

"I don't know. She said she'll tell me later. I doubt it's anything good."

"...I see..."

"I'll be careful," he assured. "It was the only way to find you."

"You need to be careful when dealing with her."

"I will, I promise."

"Well," Ian clapped his hands together, raising his voice. "I don't know about you guys, but I'm tired of the somber atmosphere! It's time to relax! Yeah?" he looked around to see who agreed. "Yeah guys?"

"Yeah," Chris smiled and shook his head.

"Yeah," Emily nodded and ruffled Chris's hair.

"Yeah," Penny smiled and sat beside Chris on the ground, nodding at Ian.

"I agree," Megan removed her hat and held it in both hands.

"Stiff," Ian commented.

Megan hit him with her hat immediately, "Idiot."

24

AFTERMATH

The cool winter breeze blew trees left and right, forward and back. The remainder of the fall leaves tumbled in the breeze, surrendering themselves to fly to somewhere new. Civilians moved to and fro, hurrying to prepare for the holidays. Christmas trees were being moved, lights being collected, and hot cocoa was on sale in the market district. Even the guards had joined in on the festivities, hanging up decorations in the streets and on the buildings. The soldiers that remained on the planet helped in any way they could, enjoying this moment of peace. The Headmaster's building was decorated with brilliant colors of red and green.

The Empire had reportedly been driven away from Terminus for the moment. There was nothing to worry about, at least for now. Despite the recent events, it was a time to regain themselves, to relax, and to heal. The war continued on, and once Christmas had passed the Wizards would be deployed with their respective leaders into the fight. It would not be joyous or wonderous, but there was much merriment to be had now.

"Package for Christopher Spellcrafter," Anthony Italiano stood in front of the dorm waiting for an answer. Chris opened the door, he was wearing a red jacket, blue jeans, and red shoes. He took the package into his hands and during the exchange Anthony said, "It wasn't easy, but I pulled some strings. I got your letter to the right people and after a few months, I got a package back addressed to you."

"Really?" Chris blinked, staring down at the brown package in his hands, taking note of its weight.

"I don't think I can do that again, but I'm glad I could help you speak to them again. Just try not to end up in the hospital again," Anthony made a gesture with his hands as if to say 'open it.'

Chris tore off the tape and opened the big box, setting it down on the ground for his convenience. There was a wrapped gift inside, but what was in it? Chris drew closer, tearing back the wrappings and the obvious red bow. Inside, there was a picture with a golden frame. The picture was of himself making a silly face, Ty who was wearing a purple shirt and smiling directly at the camera, and Jackie who was hugging them both in either arm, pulling them close for the picture. This picture was taken just a few months before Chris had left Earth, and before he had even spoken a word to Victoria. Chris started to put it down, but then he noticed a white letter wedged in between the glass and the golden frame.

Chris pulled out the letter, opened it, and read:

Dear Chris, we hope you're okay! Jackie has been flipping out since she heard the news, I hope you got the guy who did that to you. I can't help but wonder what it's like using magic, but I guess you can't tell me for a while, because of our government...ugh. We left you a little present and both of us chipped in. Jackie should have a letter in there too! Merry Christmas, good luck! Also, I can't believe you're already crushing on someone there. You've been there like...one year.

-Sincerely Ty.

Chris then reached in and pulled out a white envelope. This was Jackie's, it read:

CHRIS? ARE YOU OKAY?! Sorry but I heard what happened! Did you beat them up? Are they drinking through a straw? Ty made me rewrite my last few letters, because he said writing in all capital letters was a bit much. BUT YOU ALMOST DIED!! Anyway, Merry CHRISTMAS!!

- Jackie

Chris shook his head and started laughing. He thanked Doctor Anthony and shook his hand before he left. Chris collected his gift and the box and hung the picture above his bed. A wonderful reminder about his friends on Earth. He hoped he would see them again, but he was fairly sure he would one day. Perhaps in the future there would not be such harsh restrictions on travel, trade, and communication.

Later, Chris had to report to the Headmaster's office and explain what had occurred, Penny met him there. He told the Headmaster about Shadow Victoria and Hunter working together, how he had found Emily, and how he and Penny fought Hunter. Chris did not like recalling the feeling of the blood all over him, but he felt it was important to show just how dangerous Hunter was.

"Whoa," Autumn stared at Chris in awe. "You almost took Hunter by yourself?"

"...I thought he had killed Penny," Chris felt a little of the anger come back from the moment. "He hurt her so bad and she wasn't moving. I just went after him."

"You got reckless, but you almost beat him. If you let your anger blind you, you'll make mistakes."

"She's right," the Headmaster nodded his head. "Chris, be careful with your emotions. I am glad you are both alright. However, Hunter did escape. He ran the blockade...barely. His plane was on fire." *Good*, Chris smiled to himself. "We'll track him down in time. For now, our attention must be on the war."

"Yes sir," Chris nodded.

"I assume Shadow Victoria used a marker to teleport herself somewhere safe. Unfortunate, but she doesn't seem like she will do much hiding. I'm just glad that you are both alive."

"Chris?" Autumn turned her attention to Penny now. "How did you survive an injury like that? Even for a Wizard, that should have been death."

"Thank Megan," Penny answered for him. "She saved us both. I only healed enough to be able to walk. I couldn't have saved us both. Chris was bleeding really badly..." Penny balled her hand up.

"Emily would not want to hear you were sitting in a pool of blood," Headmaster Brood chimed in. "Tell her if you wish, but I'd let her enjoy the holidays. You should too."

"I will just after I-" Chris began.

"Christopher."

"Sir?"

The headmaster fished in his coat pocket for a moment before pulling out three orbs of energy, all three were gold. Penny's eyes widened as he did. He handed it over to Chris and stood up from his chair. His lips curved until they formed a great smile.

"Go have fun," he chuckled. "Seriously. That's enough to do *anything* in town. I need you to rest."

Penny took Chris's hand and pulled him outside immediately without even looking back. Chris called over his shoulder to say thank you as they left. Autumn erupted into laughter as Penny took off full speed, dragging Chris along. Chris could see the headmaster smiling to himself as they left.

"Wait, Penny. I was going to go talk to Emily," Chris told her, halting her advance.

"Okay...well I'll meet you at the overlook."

"Where is that?"

"Ask Emily, I have to go talk to Megan about something anyway."

"But I-" Chris didn't get to finish his sentence before Penny took off once again and vanished into the crowd.

25

JUST THE BEGINNING

Chris knocked lightly on Emily's door and waited for a response. Would this be awkward? They had just made up recently and he had saved her from being taken away by Hunter. What was he supposed to say? *Hello, it's your brother. You know, the one that saved you. Got a minute?*

As the door opened Chris saw Emily once again. She was wearing a black dress with laces. Her hair was now in a bob cut with a black ribbon in it. Chris had no time to react as she took him in her arms and ruffled his hair, he struggled, but he did quite enjoy her doing that again.

"You're messing up my hair!"

"Aw come on," Emily seemed very chipper. "I'm so happy to see you."

"Because I'm your favorite brother?"

"*That* and I got you a gift," Emily flicked her hand to the side and summoned a blue sword with a clean white blade. It looked as if it was made new, no marks or damage. "I'll also take your other sword," she held out her hand. Chris summoned his sword and gave it to her and in turn, she gave him the new one. "I'll get your old one fixed up," she continued.

"Why?"

"Well lil' bro," Emily smirked. "You did beat Hunter while dual wielding."

"How did you--"

"Penny."

"When?"

"When you were unconscious I talked to her in private. She told me all of it," Emily shook her head. "I figured I would teach you how to fight with two weapons after Christmas."

"Dual wielding?"

"Yup. I can see what you know. I'm not letting you onto any battlefield until you know what to do."

Chris examined the new sword, it had the same material as the previous sword and the same feel, but something was different about it. It seemed to have a sort of aura around it that he had never felt before. What was with this sword? It was so different and it seemed to connect with him, unlike his other weapon.

"Try to swing while using magic," Emily took a step back. As Chris readied himself. "Not near my house...oh and try reverse-grip."

Chris turned the sword so that he held it in reverse grip, taking his preferred combat stance. He gave the sword one good swing while also focusing on casting an ice spell. The sword reacted with these actions together as the blade began to emit Ice magic, slightly shooting out from the shape of the blade. It went away as he lowered the sword. He tried again, but swung harder. This time making the sword travel in an arc, the Ice magic did as well as if a wave of energy flew from it.

"You can use your Ice magic more aggressively now," Emily walked over and ruffled his hair. "Since you want to do damage so bad."

"Emily? This is sweet and all but I--" Chris began to turn a shade a red.

"What?"

"I'm gonna be hanging out with Penny," he shifted his glance away from her.

Emily had a moment of realization and before Chris had the chance to stop her she cried out, "You're going on a date!"

"It's not a date," he went wide-eyed at this accusation.

"Bull," Emily pinched his cheek hard and held it, Chris whined.

"Emily!"

"Aww you're so shy!"

"Emily," he tried again.

"Admit it," she mused.

"Okay okay...maybe a little. I mean I guess..." he sounded very small and shy now, his shoulders were raised slightly and he continued trying to dodge her eyes. "It's not a date unless she agrees to it."

"True, true. What will you be doing?"

"I have no clue, but she said to ask you where the overlook is."

"I'll take you," Emily wrapped her arm around Chris and guided him in the right direction. "I'll take your gift to your dorm."

Chris had finally begun to put his mind at ease. He had nothing to worry about, at least for the moment. Emily seemed to be slightly distracted though.

Without thinking he spoke, "Emily? What do you think Shadow Victoria wants with me?"

"I don't know. But I intend to find out. You'll tell me when she tries something, right?" Emily sounded very stern now, her smile dropping to a thin line.

"I will," Chris paused. "But can you handle her?"

"I could win in a fight," Emily turned her attention to Chris as they walked, pulling him closer.

"No, I mean...you and Victoria..."

"She's not *my* Tori. She sounds cruel and manipulative," Emily bit her tongue to stop herself from saying anymore in front of her brother. *It's a good thing I didn't tell her she had a gun pointed at me.*

"Well...maybe she'll be a help? She did help me find you..."

"For her own personal gain," Emily reminded him as they ascended a flight of stairs, pushing past someone. "Excuse me, sorry."

"You're probably right."

"She is *not* an ally. She is a threat," her expression changed as she said this. "A threat I intend to handle."

Emily had never been so intense in front of him before. Perhaps the death of Victoria had affected her, but Chris figured that couldn't have been it. Was she worried about his safety? Or was it something else entirely?

"Sis? You know I can take care of myself, right?"

"A little, but you're not ready for the real threats."

"Like?"

"Chaos and Vedi for starters. Vic-- Shadow Victoria is also too strong for you."

"I guess you're right..." Chris lowered his head, feeling his confidence plummet.

"Hey." Emily pulled him closer to her and rubbed his shoulder, her expression returned to normal. "But you did good for someone who hasn't been here long. You're picking up on your sister's spunk."

"What the...heck does that even mean?" Chris tilted his head in confusion. Emily shook her head and smiled.

The sky had begun to darken once again and the temperature was dropping at a rapid rate. According to his sister they were almost to the overlook. The overlook was located near the edge of town. From there you could see a good portion of the town, the village, the forests, and even Las Estrellas. There were glass panels lining the edge with golden railings.

Penny was there waiting for him. She was wearing a black V-neck style shirt with a subtle baby blue outline, a black undershirt, a black skirt that dropped just to her knees, black leggings, and black ankle boots. Penny was leaning on the railing waiting for him, staring off into the distance. He could tell that she was wondering where he was.

Chris started toward Penny but Emily pulled him back. She turned him to face her and gave him a soft look, "Before I let you go, promise me you'll stay out of trouble tonight."

"I will," he said quickly, determined to get to Penny as fast as possible.

"Back in your dorm by--"

"Emily..."

"You're just growing up on me..." she apologized. "Seems like just a while ago I was changing your diapers and--"

"*Emily*," Chris flushed to a slightly red color. Penny turned for a moment, saw it was them and smiled, waiting for him right where she was. Chris made a gesture with his head to remind Emily about Penny who was within earshot. "...Right. Right. Wouldn't want to embarrass you in front of your soon to be."

"We aren't seeing each other!" he hissed, his cheeks were starting to hurt now.

"Yeah, well you want it to happen," she teased, "Now go on," Emily kissed her brother's forehead and ruffled his hair one last time before turning him back and letting him go. She watched him walk for a moment before smiling and heading back the way she came, occasionally glancing back.

Chris made his way over to Penny and stood by her side, staring off into the distance. They stayed there in silence for a moment, and he really wasn't sure what to say. He felt his chest tighten and his cheeks began to burn just by being near her. Chris did his best to suppress his thoughts because he knew Penny would hear them.

"Hey," Penny smiled.

"Hey," Chris replied, sounding more shy than he had intended, clearing his throat to try to cover it up.

"I was starting to think you weren't coming..."

"I uh-- Emily..."

"I'm joking," she nudged him with her elbow. Penny paused and stared out into the distance. "I love this view...especially with the lights..."

"Yeah...it's cute--" *What did I just say?!* "I mean pretty!"

Penny giggled and smiled wider than ever. Once again, he had managed to amuse her, "You can't hide anything from me."

"Darn, I thought I was improving," he chortled.

"Gotta try harder." Penny rolled her eyes and returned back to the view, the same gleeful smile on her face.

"Hey Penn?" Chris paused, hesitating.

"Yes, Chris?"

Chris avoided eye contact, focusing only toward the distance. He was afraid to speak, but he did so anyway in a manner that made him seem confident, "I know you didn't ask for a partner like me and you're probably sick of me." Penny stared at him with her big brown eyes, her smile vanished. He continued on. "When I tried to help you a while back, you said that you didn't want a partner in the first place. And ever since then I felt like I got in your way," Penny started to turn toward him, but Chris kept talking. "I did my best to make myself useful, but I just kind of got in your way."

"Chris--"

"So, I'm sorry. I understand if you want a new partner," he smiled a little. "But I had fun working with you. You really are awesome."

Penny stared at Chris for a moment in disbelief. Chris attempted to speak again, but Penny covered up his mouth before he had the chance to say anything more.

She smiled and shook her head, "I didn't mean it. I was upset. I'm sorry..." Penny removed her hand from his mouth. "I wasn't used to you yet and after what happened to my sister...I just honestly didn't know what to do anymore."

"And now you do?"

"Yup. Win this war, keep you safe, and maybe...there can be more sorcerers like me here one day," she shrugged. "But mostly the second one."

"But...I got in your way."

"I was so used to fighting alone," Penny disregarded his previous comment, because she was about to address it, staring into the horizon where the sun had finally sunken into the sea of trees. "Then, I come across some crazy guy who wants to ask for my help, I punch him unconscious and then I'm fighting by his side..." she tilted her head up to look at the sky. "It felt good...having you by my side I mean..."

"Same," Chris felt warm inside knowing she felt the same in this regard. Snowflakes began to descend from the sky. Penny lowered her head and moved closer for warmth. *Oh, please let it keep snowing.*

"I heard that," Penny smirked as she hugged his arm closer to herself. "Stop moving, you're warm."

"Let's get going then. I hope wherever you want to go is inside," he chuckled.

"It is, but first," Penny let go of his arm. "I've been thinking about what you said in the clocktower." Chris's heart sank immediately. Penny resumed this thought, "You know...it was sweet. I've never had anyone but family tell me that and actually mean it, but I'll be honest... I don't fully know what love is outside of family."

"Really?"

"So," Penny dodged the question to continue her thought, she stepped closer and poked his nose. "I might just return your feelings."

"What do you mean?" Chris blushed hard, wanting more details on this. Penny had begun to walk off without him. Chris followed behind her. "What did you mean by that?"

"Chris?" Penny giggled.

"Yes?"

"Shhh," she burst into laughter as he walked at a brisk pace to keep up with her. "Patience."

"Patience...right."

"Right," Penny repeated, reassuring him that she would let him know.

They walked together through the snowy night. Chris wasn't sure what they were going to go do but he didn't really care, he was doing it with her. Even if they just walked around in the cold, he would be fine with it. Although the future would be rough for him, Chris had no problem cherishing this moment. This moment that he was lucky enough to share with Penny.

www.ingramcontent.com/pod-product-compliance
Lightning Source LLC
Chambersburg PA
CBHW032155190626
46808CB00020B/18